I0556259

A Destiny Found

Born of Destiny, Volume 3

H. M. Gooden

Published by H. M. Gooden, 2021.

This is a work of fiction. Similarities to real people, places, or events are entirely coincidental.

A DESTINY FOUND

First edition. January 18, 2021.

Written by H. M. Gooden.

To the book that introduced me to time travel-
there may not be any wardrobes found in this book,
but nothing transports me away from a bad day
more effectively than a book, even after all this time.

Thank you to those who opened my eyes to the
magic around me.

CHAPTER 1
Robin

Brrr!
Even though it was April and the sun was out, spring felt late this year, which did nothing to help my troubled spirits. The Montreal snow made everything slushy, but flowers sprang up anyway, as if playing peekaboo with the winter.

By the time I arrived at our second-floor apartment in an old house just off Sherbrooke, my cheeks were numb. I paused to look at them in the mirror in the foyer to make sure I didn't have any tell-tale white patches of frostbite and was happy to see they were still rosy.

After taking my gloves off, I placed the backs of my hands against them in an attempt to warm myself as I continued into the house, dropping my bag on the floor next to the door and latching it before walking into the kitchen to hit the kettle.

I was in my last year of Music and finals were looming, but I could hardly focus due to other concerns, specifically for my dad. He'd gone on what was supposed to be a routine business trip to France a few days ago and hadn't replied since a short text on landing. I generally gave him a day to get back to me, as he was the stereotypical absentminded professor, but it wasn't like him not to respond to any of my texts or emails.

I was in full-on, quiet panic mode now. This was beyond simple forgetting.

We were supposed to meet in two days in Paris, and I wasn't sure what to do. I hated not knowing the most. I had slowly assumed the role of his reminder as I'd grown, going as far as checking his schedule daily. We both spent most of our time at McGill University, which made it easier to keep track of things, even though I was a student in the Music department and he was a professor in the English department.

When I'd bagged my first European audition in time for finals and he'd gotten the job in Paris, it seemed like fate had stepped in to give us a nice trip together. But now that I couldn't contact him, I was more anxious something had happened to him than about the audition itself, something I hadn't thought possible.

I stood in the kitchen for a minute, tapping my fingers against my leg and tried to think. Maybe I was overreacting. It had only been a couple of days, after all. But still, it wasn't like him. Even though he was absentminded, he'd never been out of touch for this long, no matter how wrapped up in a book he was.

Which was good, seeing as how we'd only had each other since my mother died when I was little. Once I understood she wasn't coming home, I'd taken it upon myself to help around the house. To this day, I wasn't entirely sure who'd raised whom.

I chuckled, wondering how much extra work I'd caused him due to my early disastrous efforts, but despite my "help," somehow by the end of that first year, we'd been an unbeatable team. I'd always made sure he ate when he became absorbed in his work, and he'd opened my eyes to the world of wonder that existed in books and in music. And, when I finished high school, he'd supported me in my crazy plans to be an opera singer, never once doubting I could succeed if I wanted to and worked hard enough.

When the kettle clicked off, I poured boiling water over the lonely teabag I'd scrounged up from inside the cupboard. I hadn't gone shopping in a while, knowing we'd both be gone for a few weeks and having more important things on my check list. Now, I mentally added fresh tea to my grocery list as I let it steep. When it was ready, I carried it to my dad's study.

Although hardly grand by library standards, it was a cozy den off the living room where he'd made a nest of sorts and was my favorite room in the house. The glass French doors were kept open most of the time, framing the entrance and adding a certain ambience. There was a large bookshelf taking up most of the back wall, and in the center of the room was an old wooden roll top desk he used to do his paperwork. Tiffany lamp shades were in each corner on side tables, adding extra light for a reader next to plush armchairs my father had found at an antique store.

He liked everything old, not just books.

I headed to the desk, knowing it was the most likely place to find answers. I usually left it alone, knowing full well touching his papers would disrupt his "system," whatever that was. Looking at them now, it would be a stretch to say his system was anything another human would recognize.

Stacks of paper were piled haphazardly on top of each other. I spotted what appeared to be the crust of the sandwich peeking out from the middle. I wrinkled my nose and gingerly pulled it out. Yup, old sandwich. I was lucky there were no mice in here. At that horrifying thought, I paused, scanning the room while listening for any ominous rustling or squeaking noises.

When nothing stirred, I exhaled and began to sort through the stack, steeling myself for other gross food findings as a precaution. Next, I removed a mishmash of bills from student term papers. Thankfully, I'd set up automated payments for most things, so I knew the bills were statements and not past due notices. Then I pulled out the student papers he'd printed out, noting some were graded and others weren't.

I squinted, wincing when I saw one poor student's name next to a date in January. Hopefully they didn't need this mark to graduate. It took time, but slowly I made my way through the mess, sorting the items into broad categories I hoped wouldn't get me in trouble on his return. Bills, junk, term papers, essays, and finally what I was hoping to find—my dad's notes.

That was when things got weird.

I reached out for a folded piece of paper and noticed my hand was shaking. Why was it shaking? Even as I inspected the quivering appendage though, a sickening sense of premonition settled in my gut.

Dammit.

It wasn't something I liked to admit, even to myself, that whenever I got that particular feeling something momentous was about to happen. I didn't have a name for the eerie premonitions—maybe they would have been easier to deal with if I did. Perhaps it was a form of untapped intuition, but it thankfully didn't happen often. When it did though, I always listened.

It usually presented as a sudden, intense, and overwhelming anxiety. It was so powerful I was able to distinguish it instantly from my own emotions; almost like I was picking up on the universe's energy and getting a glimpse through a window into something I shouldn't. When I'd moved the paper, the sensation practically punched me, and that anxiety became firmly fixed upon the item in my hand.

Exhaling a deep, shuddering breath that seemed to echo in the quiet room, I opened the innocent, cream-colored rectangle. It was a letter addressed to me in my dad's handwriting.

Frowning, I looked at the paper then at the stack I'd retrieved it from. Was he that forgetful he'd tucked it into the middle? Or had he been hiding it? And hiding it from whom?

Looking around the room with narrowed eyes, I searched for signs anyone had been here. It hadn't crossed my mind before now, and I couldn't think of any reason someone would want to search the office. Nothing appeared to have been moved since my dad had flown to Paris, and the desk was undisturbed from this morning when I'd left for school.

Trying to shake off the weird paranoia gripping me, more because I didn't want to believe I was alone with someone in the house than for any other reason, I turned back to examine the paper. It was only a few paragraphs long, but more difficult to read than usual due to his handwriting, which looked as if he'd written in a rush.

Recognizing the date on top as the day he'd caught his flight, I wrinkled my nose. Strange. He hadn't mentioned leaving a letter for me. It wasn't something he usually did.

Dear Robin,

If you've found this letter, it means you're worried and something has happened to make me not reply to your other avenues of contact. For that, I'm deeply sorry. As far as I could predict, this was another routine book acquisition trip; although I debated whether to accept the commission due to the increased level of risk.

You see, the trip I am on right now isn't for the university, but a private buyer, Mr. Lavallee. Normally, I would've turned him down, given who he is and the way people who work for him seem to end up worse for the wear in his employ, but the book he wanted me to find was so intriguing I couldn't say no.

He has information which leads me to believe I would find the book in question located in rural France. Everything about the trip otherwise, I expect to be the usual, other than the prize I am hoping to find at the end is a book I have been searching for since you were a child. I am hoping it will be just another adventure for me to purchase a treasure from a willing seller before experiencing the highlight of my life; watching my little songbird achieve her goal of singing onstage at the Paris Opera.

But, if you are reading this letter now, it means things have not turned out the way I'd hoped, and the niggling concerns I had were well-founded.

The book I am searching for is known by many names. Most scholars don't believe it even exists. Of course, you know I couldn't resist the chance to see who's right. If it does exist and you haven't heard from me, please don't come looking. I could bear almost anything except knowing my little girl was injured, or worse, noticed by the man who hired me.

The letter drifted to the floor as my mind went blank. Mr. Lavallee? It couldn't be. There were many Lavallee's in Montreal. After all, it was Québec. It was as common a name as Smith or Jones in an English-speaking area. But the cryptic note made the anxiety inside me tighten and grow larger, causing it to move from my stomach to encase my heart in an icy shell of panic.

Could my dad have accepted a commission from *Guy* Lavallee? The same Guy Lavallee who headed the most notorious chapter of bikers in Montreal?

I looked around the empty study, swallowing hard. Had my father unwittingly put himself in the middle of something gang-related? Why would he be so reckless? It wasn't like him. But even as I tried to convince myself it was just my imagination, something else he'd mentioned percolated through my fear.

The book he was searching for.

He hadn't mentioned its name, but the way he'd described it made me wonder if other forces were at work. I'd interrupted him several times in the month prior to his trip. He'd been researching something which had absorbed all his attention. He'd commented more than once it was 'the secret to finally decoding the Voynich manuscript,' but had been secretive with other details.

I didn't know nearly as much as he did about rare books, but if he'd found a book with a translation for the Voynich manuscript, he'd have more to worry about than just a biker gang. People had been searching for the key to that puzzle for decades. Some thought it was a book on how to use magic, an instruction manual for medicine, and some particularly crazy bibliophiles even thought it was an alien tome dropped on Earth by some long-lost visitors when Stonehenge or the pyramids were built.

Decoding the Voynich manuscript was as important to historians as finding a spell that would turn lead to gold had been for alchemists. Come to think of it, some people thought that was one of the secrets it held, adding treasure hunters into the mix of people looking to translate the manuscript.

The tingle of anxiety loosened slightly. As I'd learned to do over the years, I allowed myself to listen with my inner ear. The logic felt right, even if the idea was completely ludicrous. If my dad had been on his way to find a translation text for the Voynich manuscript, I knew the starting point, what he'd been after, and who was backing his trip. But none of that explained where he was now, or why he wasn't responding to my calls.

I looked at my watch, finding it was almost seven, and sent another text. I didn't expect an answer and put my phone away without waiting for one. I hoped he would be able to see my message where ever he was, and know I understood the danger.

I'm coming Dad.
Love you,

xoxo

R

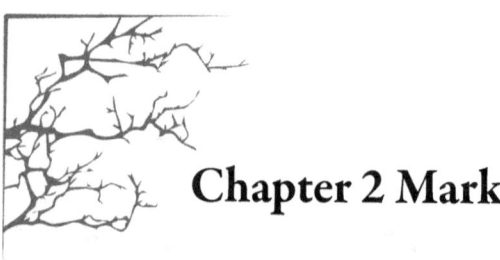

Chapter 2 Mark

I t was hard remaining still for so long.

The long periods of immobility were part of the reason I kept up such a rigorous physical training program. I had been working with CSIS for almost a year, but what I did was hardly worth writing home about.

Sure, there had been a few shining moments of excitement, but mostly my day-to-day activities involved acting like a regular Joe and hanging out in a variety of locations. Unfortunately, that *was* the exciting part. The less exciting portion involved hours and hours of paperwork, checking off the appropriate boxes, and trying to stay awake.

Being an agent wasn't what I'd envisioned when I'd signed up for it, but it was rewarding in its own way. When I wasn't cranky from sitting in a car for eight hours watching a house, I liked it a lot. At least this time, my subject was easy on the eyes.

I couldn't help wondering how she'd ended up being tailed by me. The briefing I'd been given on her was nothing extraordinary. She was a student in her last year of Music at McGill University, and far as I could tell, everything in her life revolved around that. Her father taught there and she had a few close friends who went there. She wasn't into drugs, alcohol, or smoking, or extracurricular activities apart from music stuff. From everything I could see, she was a typical, low-key girl.

Then again, I'd only gotten a two-page bio, which hardly did more than outline basic demographics. The sparse details, in combination with Professor Locksley, her father, leaving to go abroad led me to believe the reason I was watching her was for her own protection more than for any other reason. Not only did nothing in her dossier suggest she was up to anything illegal; I'd been tailing her for two weeks and hadn't seen a single break in her routine.

She left her house at approximately seven a.m. and walked to the McGill University Schulich School of Music building. Most days she used a practice room for about an hour then headed to the main campus for lectures. Her schedule varied, depending on the day of the week, but she was always on campus until at least five. Three evenings a week she sang at various locations in the evening, and after the concerts were over, she took the Metro home or accepted a ride from another singer.

In short, she appeared to be a nice girl. So why was I feeling the same tingle I got when something was about to happen? She was pretty, but that wasn't it. At least, not all of it. No, this was the feeling I had right before I was called to find something.

Was my premonition somehow related to her? It had to be. She was the only person I'd been following this week. I watched her move around inside her house, thinking back to the first time I'd heard her sing. I'd been impressed such a large voice could come from such a small-framed person. For some reason, I'd always thought opera singers were supposed to be huge, like the old Bugs Bunny cartoons with the Valkyrie wearing the horned hat on her head.

But this honey-blonde, sweet-faced woman made me interested in opera for the first time in my life and gave me the feeling I'd met her somewhere before. Shaking my head, I tried to put the thought behind me.

I needed to stay alert. Without knowing what was coming, I couldn't take anything for granted. Almost as soon as I had that thought, my phone vibrated. I checked the number then answered crisply.

"Agent Notting."

"Notting. We're going to be sending around another agent to keep an eye on the house tonight. I need you to pack."

"What? What do you mean?" I looked at the window, which was backlit enough to allow me to see Robin moving around on the second floor. An unexpected pang of loss hit me at the idea of being reassigned. For the first time ever, I didn't want to see a job end.

"We have a plane ticket and passport waiting for you in your drop box. Pack light."

I held back a comment, knowing my boss was really telling me not to lose my target. It was one of the first things they'd taught me. Only pack what you can bring in a carry-on. Everything else could be bought or would be provided.

Checking luggage while working was a hard no.

"Where am I going? Who's the mark?"

"You're going to Paris. You need to follow Ms. Locksley on her trip. We have reason to believe her father has gone missing. Someone may try to contact her to get to him and the item he was looking for. We think he was on the trail of something important."

I slowly nodded, even though he couldn't see me. I'd known about the trip, but assumed my duties were limited to watching her within the city. It wasn't a huge leap though, as I was supposed to be keeping her safe. Whether in Canada or France, apparently.

Another tingle came, stronger this time. Paying attention to the warning, I fished for more. "What happened to the agent following the professor?"

The man paused, and when he finally replied, his tone was gruff. "They haven't checked in."

I winced. That wasn't good. "Is there anything else I need to know?"

"Get a good night's sleep. Your plane departs at eight a.m. Another agent will watch her tonight and make sure she gets to the airport. The next time you'll get a visual will be after you pass through security. You may make contact once on the plane to place the tracking device."

"Copy. Then what?"

"Don't get drunk on the free booze. You'll be emailed an encrypted file with everything you need to know, which you can review on the plane. When you land in Paris, keep her in sight at all times. You're the only agent assigned to her unless you need help, in which case call the emergency line. If you can find a way to introduce yourself without raising suspicion, you are allowed to make direct contact."

I blinked. Until now, I'd either been part of a team or had instructions to watch from afar. I'd never been asked to engage a subject before.

"I'm sorry, sir. Did you say you want me to make friends with her?"

A dry chuckle came from the other end. "Sure, friends. Whatever it takes. She's a secondary target, which boils down to you being the only agent we can spare to keep track of her. Once you place the tracking device, it should be easier to monitor her whereabouts, but our information is sketchy. I don't like it. If you can find something that points us to what the professor was searching for, it may help find him. You can help her if she's willing. We need to know what Lavallee is after. Understand?"

"Roger that."

My superior hung up and a rush of anticipation filled me. They wanted me to help her find the professor? And with her knowledge, not just from a distance? Now, this was more like it! Images of James Bond flashed through my head, but I quickly reined in my expectations, knowing full well nothing turned out the way it did in the movies.

I waited for what felt like hours for the other agent to show up, but the clock in my car said it had only been thirty minutes. Finally, Agent Elise Derny, a middle-aged woman with a perm-a-scowl, arrived to relieve me. To the untrained observer, she looked an angry soccer mom, assuming the soccer mom in question had seven kids who screamed all the time.

Elise wasn't quite as bad as she looked though. I'd met her before, and she'd always been pleasant, even if her sense of humor was virtually non-existent. I glanced at the clock on the dashboard again. She was probably tired from all the night shifts she was called for, and I was responsible for yet another one.

"Any concerns?" She leaned down beside the car, pretending to tie her running shoe.

"Nothing. So far, routine has been, well, routine. I've been asked to pack."

Agent Derny stood, nodding. "I'll take over from here. I hear there's some travel in your future? Have fun."

The ghost of a smile surprised me. She seemed to really mean it.

"Um, thanks. Have a good night."

She gave me another tight smile and headed back to the company car she'd parked a few cars back, still in sight of the house. Once she was in position, I looked at the window I'd last seen Robin in. The light clicked off as I pulled away.

This time when I drove home, I couldn't help my excitement. It was a mission like I'd always dreamed of getting. Jetting off to an exotic European destination to help a beautiful woman find her father and a mysterious artifact shadowy people were after. Only one thing made me pause, and I wasn't sure why I hadn't thought of it before.

Was it my finding ability, or something else warning me not everything was as it appeared? The entire time I'd been following Robin, I hadn't known the professor was missing, only that he'd gone overseas. Why hadn't they told me earlier?

The tingle of awareness stayed with me as I packed, telling me to be on my guard. Things were about to change. I just didn't know how yet.

I wanted to call someone to let them know where I was going, but I couldn't. So, I made do with texting my mom to ask how things were going. When she didn't reply right away, I let her know I'd be tied up for a week or so, and would try to check in when I could.

The hardest thing about my job was not being able to tell the people I cared about what I was doing. As far as everyone but my parents knew, I was a lowly administrator in a government job somewhere in Ottawa. It was technically the truth; I did work for the government. And most of my days really were spent doing paperwork, even if my actual job title was a little cooler than admin or paper-pusher.

But once family obligations were taken care of, my thoughts quickly turned from regret to anticipation. I'd never been to France before, and my previous travel experience consisted entirely of one brief road-trip with a friend after graduation. My best friend, Paul, had been recovering from a horrible act of random violence and his doctors didn't want him flying because of recent brain surgery. It had been a great trip, but not exactly something which qualified me as a world traveler.

Now I was going to Paris, the first long-distance trip I'd been on since beginning with the agency and since that long-ago summer trip with Paul. I was excited and full of trepidation, even more so after I opened the encrypted email my supervisor had sent.

I scrolled quickly, scanning pages of information before going back to the start to read it more carefully. My cover story was simple—carefree backpacker—and most of the information involved maps and cultural highlights, but the details about Robin's father were what I was most interested in.

I already knew where Robin would be sitting, but reviewed the flight again. The trip across the pond was just over eight hours, and would land in Charles de Gaulle airport. Robin had a room rented at a hotel with her father, which was where she was expected to head once she arrived. Because her trip had been planned well over a month ago, we had several points of information. Tomorrow morning, at eleven a.m. Paris time, she'd audition at the Paris Opera House.

Once that was done, she had a voice lesson with Natalie Dessay, a world-renowned opera singer, after which point her itinerary was wide open except for staying at the hotel. From what I was able to glean, she planned to do some sightseeing with her dad before leaving Paris on day five. It was a short trip, but adequate to see the tourist areas in Paris.

It also meant she had a deadline to find her dad, unless she changed her flight home. I knew she had exams the following week, so I didn't think she'd have that opportunity. Shaking my head, I considered what a tough spot she was in. I knew how important exams were. Everything depended on them, especially if you planned on doing postgraduate work.

The timing of the professor's disappearance totally sucked. Even if she hadn't been a decent person, I'd have felt bad for her. Hopefully between the two of us we'd be able to find him, along with whatever it was the department was so interested in getting their hands on.

Chapter 3 Robin

I checked on my flight status for the tenth time that morning and promptly berated myself for looking. I knew nothing had changed, but my nerves were on edge. My plane was on time to leave at eight, my bags were packed, and I had all the required documents. Everything was fine, even if it had taken me most of the previous evening to pack.

I was traveling lighter than usual because with my dad missing, I didn't want to waste time waiting for luggage, or worse, lose my important items and have to file a claim with the airport. I'd heard horror stories of people having only the clothes on their backs and waiting up to a week before their bags arrived. I didn't have that kind of time or mental bandwidth left to deal with airport luggage disasters.

As a result, it had taken most of the night before I was able to choose my audition outfit and which accessories to pack along with it. I hadn't slept well thinking about all that could go wrong. In the end, I'd settled on an elegant amethyst sheath I'd found on sale in one of the shops along Saint Catherine's. It was one of my favorites, because although it wasn't expensive, the material draped in a figure-flattering way. And best of all, the stretchy fabric didn't need to be steamed or ironed and could be worn right out of the bag without worrying about wrinkles.

I packed comfortable silver flats to wear with it instead of the heels I'd normally wear. That way they could double for walking during the day if the weather was warm. Along with a few changes of underwear, a couple of wrinkle-resistant shirts, one bathing suit and nightgown, I packed a pair of stretchy yoga pants with a toiletry bag, then dressed in jeans, a button-down shirt with a tank top, and spring jacket. The final touch was a pair of ankle-boots warm enough for the Montreal spring, yet comfortable enough to walk in all day.

In my purse, I had my passport, wallet, and laptop. The extra weight caused me to debate the need, but in the end my laptop was a necessary appendage I wanted with me. I still had a few papers to finish and it might come in handy searching for my dad. I was still hoping he'd merely lost his phone and was waiting at the hotel, having forgotten my number, but that hope was growing fainter every day.

After taking one last look around the house to make sure I'd locked up and turned everything off, I gave my friend, Melissa, a text to let her know where the spare key was. I was finally off. I took the Metro to the airport without being more than peripherally aware of my surroundings, passing through the line at security in much the same way.

My internal dialogue consisted of the negative Nellie part of my brain arguing with the Pollyanna positive side. The swift back and forth between doom and gloom and the hope he'd lost his phone consumed all my concentration, and when I looked up, I was surprised to see I was already nearly through the line for security.

I felt a strange, prickling sensation on the back of my neck and turned around, but no one was paying any attention to me except the young security officer who'd pulled me over for the airport's 'special test' on my computer. He became excited when I mentioned I was bringing the computer because I was a student at McGill and had papers to finish.

"That's great! I went to McGill too. Hey, maybe when you get back we can go for a coffee, and trade stories of our time in the trenches of education."

I looked down, fiddling with the strap on my bag before giving him a bright stage-smile. I toned it down when his eyes widened with hope. Crap, overdid it. "I'm sorry, but I'll be in Paris for a while."

I waved as I took my computer back, smiling again in a more muted fashion as I walked away. I was hoping he wouldn't realize until after I left that I hadn't given him my number. I strode away quickly, searching for my gate. With the memory of the sensation of being watched, I kept a closer eye on my surroundings.

I scolded myself for being recklessly absorbed. I could have been mugged on my way to the airport, but I'd been so lost in thought I hadn't even considered anyone might be following me until security, when I'd felt eyes on me.

Now I scanned the area, wondering if someone actually was watching me or if I was becoming paranoid. This early in the morning there were the usual travelers one would expect to see in the Montréal airport. Families with loud children, retirees, and a few people with backpacks and eager faces.

I saw a guy around my age sitting off a little way by himself and found myself staring at him, even though he didn't look dangerous. He didn't seem like the kind of guy who would be in the Hells Angels. That was the nice thing about that gang—generally, if they were following you, you knew it.

This man didn't look like a biker or a metal-head. He was sitting off to the side of the waiting area reading a newspaper—who did that anymore— and was keeping to himself. He hadn't noticed me staring, hadn't even glanced up, for which I was grateful. He was attractive, but in a boy-next door way, so I wasn't sure why I was having such hard time looking away.

I narrowed my eyes, trying to get a better look at his face. Did I know him from somewhere? Something about him was familiar. Without being able to figure it out, I chose an open seat far away from him. Sitting near the desk in view of the gate attendant, I waited for boarding with my guard up and tried not to think about my dad.

On the plane, I gratefully sank into my business class seat. With all the travel my dad did, I'd been able to upgrade for free. Transatlantic flights were long and the extra legroom was appreciated. Not to mention the free food and alcohol.

I did up my seatbelt, gasping in pain a moment later as someone slammed a bag into my leg.

"Oh God! I'm so sorry!"

I rubbed my shin with a scowl, before composing my face into a polite smile at the sincerity in the voice, and told myself it had been an accident. I preferred the aisle seat for the easy access to the bathroom, but being injured by a fellow passenger or the food cart was the inevitable trade-off when one was cursed with long legs.

My smile faltered when I looked up and saw who had hit me. It was the same man who'd captured my attention earlier. Up close, I could see he was about my age. He looked contrite, and as he moved his bag out of the way, a shock of chestnut brown fell into something resembling a Superman curl, covering his forehead. As if noticing my attention, he brushed it back immediately.

I flushed, embarrassed at the prickle of heat in my cheeks. I hadn't figured out how to control blushes yet, especially around attractive men.

"It's fine. No harm done."

I kept rubbing my shin though, as it really did hurt.

He looked at my hand, then back up at my face with pleading, puppy-dog brown eyes. "Can I make it up to you? Buy you a drink?"

I shook my head, laughing even as a twinge of regret we hadn't met at another time somewhere else stabbed me. "Thanks, but alcohol is free on transatlantic flights. Really. No permanent damage done. I should have moved my leg out of the way. Have a good flight."

He nodded before smiling again, this time in an attractive, self-deprecating way. "Maybe some of that legendary Parisian grace will rub off on me. I'm sure my parents would be happy if I came back a little less like a bull-in-a-china-shop."

I chuckled, feeling better, and he waved as he continued to his seat a few rows back. My leg had almost stopped hurting and I was surprised how disappointed I was he wasn't sitting closer.

But, before long, thoughts of the looming audition and missing dad returned. I opened my bag with a sigh. Maybe if I reviewed everything I knew before landing, it would keep my mind busy. Pulling out my computer, I hoped I had better luck contacting my dad when I landed than I'd experienced in Montreal.

Chapter 4 Mark

I took one last look around my apartment as I slung my bag over my shoulder, then turned the lights off and locked the door. Since another agent would be watching Robin until we met up at the airport, I headed over earlier than the recommended three hours.

I wanted to make sure I was through security long before she arrived.

So, when I spotted her at the gate, I was already seated, reading a French newspaper with the vague hope it would help with my conversational French. She appeared casual, but beautiful, as she glanced around. If I didn't know better, I would have said she was looking for someone and I felt an unexpected tingle in my chest.

Ruthlessly, I shoved it aside. No matter what my boss said about making contact, I knew he wouldn't be happy if I became emotionally involved. If Robin was being tailed by someone dangerous, I needed to keep my eyes off her and on her surroundings.

If I couldn't stay objective, our life expectancies would potentially be at risk.

I was relieved when the plane boarded on time. It had been a challenge to keep myself occupied and look like I wasn't watching her, especially when I'd felt her eyes land on me. They had lingered on me for an uncomfortably long period of time, and I thought she'd caught me until she finally settled a few rows over.

That scare caused me to wait longer than normal to get in line, counting to ten after she stood to board, then casually stretching and meandering into a spot several people behind her. By the time I reached the aisle near her seat, she was already settled with her bag stowed. Taking a deep breath, I silently begged forgiveness for what I was about to do. Then I swung my bag toward her and deliberately hit her left shin.

I bent as if grabbing my bag, simultaneously obscuring my actions with my head. That allowed me to place a tiny tracker the size of a button battery into the tongue of her left ankle-boot. It slid into position between the leather.

I stood up and pretended to fumble with my bag. "Oh my God! I'm so sorry!"

Even though I was satisfied I'd achieved my goal of placing the tracker on her boot, I was sorry that I'd caused her pain. At least her on-stage performances involved singing and not dancing. I still needed to get a tracker on her phone, as it was improbable she'd always be wearing the boots, but overall, I was happy my first attempt at placing a tracker had gone well.

She rubbed her leg vigorously where I'd slammed my bag into her shin bone, breathing deeply as she worked to compose herself. When she finally looked up with a polite smile and flushed cheeks, I knew she was a better person than I was.

If someone had hit me like that, I'd have given them a piece of my mind, along with words that might make an old lady blush. I brushed my hair off my face and stood up, not even having to pretend I was remorseful.

"It's fine. No harm done."

She kept rubbing her shin though, and I felt worse than I'd expected. Hopefully I hadn't given her a bruise.

"Can I make it up to you? Buy you a drink?"

She laughed and sat up, shaking her head with an enigmatic look in her eyes. She was beautiful up close, and I found myself staring, hardly even registering her reply at first.

"Thanks, but alcohol is free on transatlantic flights. Really. No permanent damage done. I should have moved my leg out of the way. Have a good flight."

I recognized my cue to leave, but in case I hadn't, it was reinforced by an older man waiting in the aisle behind me clearing his throat in an exaggerated fashion. I smiled at her once more and loved the way her face lit up with a reciprocal smile. I mumbled something, gave what I hoped was a casual wave, and headed to my seat. Overall, I was pleased how my first contact had gone. Her reaction to my offer of a drink had gone over decently, even if she had been distracted by pain. I couldn't blame her for that, seeing as I was the one who'd caused it.

From that point on the flight was easy. Not only were we confined to a limited space, but it was a day flight, which meant I didn't have to force myself to stay awake. I got up a few times to use the washroom, making it look accidental when I caught her eye. I even surprised a smile once, enjoying how it made her cheeks bloom a rosy shade of pink. The word adorable sprang to mind, but I returned to my chair instead of talking to her the way I wanted.

I needed to keep my focus and was already worried I would screw up. I certainly would if I kept staring at her face instead of the people around her.

After attempting to reprimand myself and not sure how well I'd done, I succeeded in turning my attention to the others on the plane. I'd been trained to know what to watch out for, and once I was back in my chair, I went into the passenger manifest I'd been given. My contacts had already cross-matched the names on the flight, and now I looked at seat numbers. Only one name had lit up, but it was remote connection— a second cousin, thrice removed, of Lavallee's, but the man in question looked more like an accountant than a threat. With zero visible tattoos, there was no indication he was in a biker gang or watching Robin, but I settled in to monitor the situation anyway.

It felt like being on deck to bat in the finals for the World Series as I listened to my audiobook in French, and I was itching to get in the game.

I couldn't wait to land.

Chapter 5 Robin

I exhaled as the captain announced our final approach.

I'd already double and triple checked I had all my items before we taxied to the gate. As we shuffled off the plane, I was thankful I'd chosen to travel light. Everyone else headed to the luggage carousel, but I continued through customs with just the bag on my back and smiled as the bored customs agent stamped my passport.

"Bienvenue à Paris."

"Merci beaucoup." I smiled briefly as I took my passport then followed the signs for ground transport to the taxi stand.

Paris had a great metro system, but I wanted to see the city from above ground today. When I glanced back, I was surprised to see the attractive shin-destroyer from the plane sauntering up behind me. Nervously, I smoothed down my hair, wondering if it was as big and rumpled as I suspected it was post-flight.

He didn't appear to notice and gave me a relaxed wave. Flashing a quick smile with even, white teeth, he stopped a few feet away in line. "Hey, how was the flight? Where are you heading? I'm heading to the eighth district, if you want to share a ride, and save a few bucks."

My eyebrows shot up, but as I examined his open and good-natured face, I couldn't see any threat. Forcing myself to chill, I asked, "Whereabouts are you going in the eighth district?"

He scratched his head as if trying to think before holding up a finger. "Just a minute. I only booked it a few days ago. You'd think I'd remember the name. Gosh. I'm sorry. You must think I'm crazy. First, I maim you on the plane, and now I can't even remember where I'm staying tonight?"

He shook his head as if amazed by himself, and his thick brown hair flopped over his eyes. He took out his phone, opened the screen and after a minute looked up triumphantly, brushing the unruly hair back automatically.

"Aha! Success! I'm staying at the Fraser Suites hotel on Champs-Élysées."

I blinked with surprise. "Really? So am I."

Instead of being alarmed, something thawed inside me. It was almost as if I was meant to share a ride with him. And, if I was being completely honest with myself, I was grateful to see a friendly face. Even if it *was* attached to a guy I hardly knew.

I was so far out of my element I needed every kindness I could get.

Did that make me weak?

"That's awesome! You know what? I just realized I don't know your name. I really should introduce myself. I mean, I've already injured you." He grinned, revealing the faintest hint of dimple. "I'm Mark. Mark Notting."

"Nice to meet you, Mark. My name's Robin Locksley. Are you from Montréal?"

He shrugged. "You could say that. I'm doing some work at McGill right now, but I'm originally from Toronto. What about yourself?"

I nodded. "Yeah, born and raised. I live close to McGill with my dad. He's on a business trip, and I'm supposed to be meeting up with him."

My face fell as I remembered the text I'd sent on arrival. Once again there had been no reply. I'd tried to call him from the airport after I'd gone through customs as well, but it had gone straight to a full mailbox and I'd been unable to leave a message.

"Are you okay? You look kind of, well, devastated."

I blinked away the unwelcome sting of tears and took a deep breath in and out before replying. "I'm fine. There's just a lot going on right now with school, and tomorrow's kind of a big day for me."

I didn't mention my dad, because the small, paranoid part of me who didn't trust strangers whispered it was better if he thought I was meeting my dad immediately at the hotel. Although there was no logical way this attractive stranger had anything to do with my dad's disappearance, I still didn't know him. No matter how cute he was, dating 101 logic applied. Never go somewhere secluded, and always have an escape route.

He gave me a sympathetic look. "I get that. I was a basket case during finals week my last year. If it hadn't been for my mom bringing care packages every few days, I'm not sure I would've remembered to eat at all. My parents are pretty awesome sometimes."

I swallowed hard, thinking about my dad. I would've never expect him to remember such a thing as feeding me, since I'd taken on that role for him, but I missed his quiet support just the same. I had to blink rapidly to keep the tears from accumulating. When I looked up at him again, I caught his confused expression.

"Sorry. Not trying to get emotional on you. Like I said, it's been a rough week."

He must think I was a drama queen, or worse. He hadn't said anything wrong, yet here I was, welling up again. Taking a deep breath, I vowed to be a bit less girly. I needed to focus on the task at hand— getting to the hotel, and praying my dad was there.

"Excuse me. You need?"

We both turned at the irritated voice of a man, standing with his hand palm up, looking at us. He tapped his watch. I guessed he was trying to be polite, but I could see he was verging on losing patience.

Realizing we were holding up the line, I swiftly nodded. Mark replied before I could. "Yes, thank you. We're heading to the Fraser Suites hotel, in the Huitième District."

When the cabbie looked at me, I nodded again. The man sighed and appeared to be searching for luggage until I shook my head. "This is all I have."

"Me as well. Carry-on only." Mark smiled broadly.

The man rolled his eyes, clearly disinterested past whether he needed to throw something in the car, and returned to the driver's seat without opening a door for me. Mark leapt forward, gesturing for me to enter first, and I slid across. Doing up my seatbelt, I gave myself some space by placing my bag on the seat between us. He added his to the small pile, and we used it as a makeshift armrest. He was so casual, but that made me feel even more awkward about how careful I was being not to bump his arm.

It was becoming obvious to me I needed to keep some space between us for my own sanity. Between my paranoia and general ineptness with the opposite sex, I stayed on edge as we drove away from the airport into the heart of Paris.

It had been nearly ten years since I'd last been to this city. When I was fourteen, I'd come with my dad on a business trip. Even back then, I'd been in love with opera, and he'd thought it would be a good opportunity for me to check out what he considered 'the pinnacle' of European culture. He could be surprisingly snobbish at times, and I'd heard him comment more than once about the horrible French spoken at home compared to the dialects in France.

But thoughts of my father led me down that same anxious, fearful road, which I was tired of walking. Hoping to distract myself, I cleared my throat, and turned to Mark. "So, what brings you to Paris?"

He smiled, turning away from the window to answer. "I had a couple weeks off work, and I've been saving my Air Miles for close to ten years. It's the first time I've ever used any," he admitted sheepishly. "It was well past time to have some fun, but I didn't have enough for Thailand or India. I stumbled upon a seat sale to Paris, and I figured it would be easier to navigate solo since I speak French."

I tilted my head. "How come you're traveling alone?"

"My friends are all working or in school. I mean, it's April. Everyone saves their vacation for summer, or winter when it's cold. Without any other strings, I decided to go by myself. Have you *seen* how much cheaper it is to travel off-season?"

He had a point, so I nodded. When he waited expectantly, I realized he was waiting for me to tell him my story. "Oh, I'm in Paris for an audition, for school. That's why I'm here. I'm in my last year of Music studies, opera, specifically, and I'm hoping to make some connections in Europe. If I can get my foot in the door..."

I trailed off, but he appeared to understand.

"That's a good idea. It must be a difficult field to break into. I've been told I can't carry a tune in a bucket, so music was never an option for me. What are you singing tomorrow?"

I debated how in-depth to get. I had tried to explain opera to guys in the past, and in general I'd found if I went into any detail beyond 'I'm a singer', their eyes tended to glaze over. But he seemed genuinely interested, so I gave him the benefit of the doubt. "I'm an alto, but I love the Baroque period of music most of all. The music is richer, and I find it easier to connect to emotionally."

I stopped, thinking that should satisfy his curiosity while hopefully avoiding the unintentional eye glaze, but to my surprise he leaned closer.

"Who's your favorite composer? I don't know much about opera, but I've become more interested after catching a few local chamber concerts near McGill. They were pretty cool, and I'd love to learn more. Where would you recommend I start?"

A warm glow spread over me. I examined his face and could tell he wasn't merely humoring me. His eyes were wide and attentive, and his body language was open as he leaned in. Part of becoming a performer was taking classes on how to move, and body language was something we were taught in order to become better singers, as facial expressions alone weren't always visible to an audience and emotion could also be conveyed through standing, walking, and even arm gestures.

Now, that same training told me more than words could have that he was being honest about his interest. The novelty of the experience caused me to immediately launch into my favorite subject, and as a result, the miles passed quickly.

Before I knew it, the taxi had stopped. I blinked, then disappointment rushed through me when I realized the end of our trip together had arrived, far too soon for my liking. "Well, thanks for listening to me ramble on. I don't get many chances to discuss opera. It's not like the topic is a super popular subject with, well, anyone. Thanks for the ride share. It was nice meeting you."

Mark smiled, and the same enticing dimple winked at me. "I've enjoyed this discussion, like, a lot. If you're not too busy while you're here, I'd love it if you shot me a text. We could you know, maybe, um, go site-see together?" His eyes widened, and he swiftly brought his hands up. "Unless you're busy. Totally fine. I know you've got plans, and you're meeting your dad. No pressure. But, I'd love the company if you're ever between appointments."

I didn't usually give my number out to strangers and managed to deflect most guys the way I had the one at security, but Mark was different. I felt like I knew him now. So despite my long-held, unofficial rule of never giving out my phone number to someone I hadn't known for more than a week, I pulled my phone out.

"What's your number?"

He rattled off the digits and I sent him a text. When his phone rang, I heard a truncated version of the *Star Wars* "Imperial March." Snorting with amusement, I noted his cheeks had turned pink.

He laughed. "You're totally regretting giving me your number, now that you've heard my ringtone, aren't you?"

I bit back a chuckle. "Not at all. Any guy who likes *Star Wars* can't be all bad. You have my number now, so text whenever. I won't answer if I'm auditioning—I always turn my phone off— but otherwise, I promise to reply when I can."

I was closer to the curb, so I slid out first, then waited for him to join me on the sidewalk. After he paid the cabbie, I tilted my head. "How much do I owe you?"

He waved a hand. "Don't worry about it. I would have had to pay anyway. It's my treat—consider it an audition present."

This time, I was treated to the full dimple show. All words escaped me. I could only nod, then wave an awkward goodbye before going inside the hotel. It was the same awkwardness that cursed me on a first date, when it was unclear if the next step was to shake hands, hug, or kiss. Except in this case, we'd only shared a ride from the airport, so even a handshake seemed inappropriate.

Mark waved back easily, and I envied him his confidence as he mimed, "I'll call you," in an overly dramatic, silly fashion.

I smiled, even though I knew tomorrow would be stressful and I still hadn't heard from my dad. Somehow, this stranger had raised my spirits when I hadn't expected anything to do that. Regardless of whether I ever heard from him again, I'd remember our taxi ride fondly.

Chapter 6 Mark

"Hey, how was the flight? Where are you heading? I'm heading to the eighth district, if you want to share a cab and save a few bucks."

She startled, and for a moment, I thought she'd pull out a gun. She had the same wariness I'd seen on the face of ex-military or victims of abuse, and I instinctively tried to make myself appear less threatening. I knew my hair was rumpled already, which hopefully helped with boyish charm, and I hunched over a little to look smaller as I smiled and stayed where I was.

I knew if I moved closer she could bolt, and I didn't want that.

"Whereabouts are you going in the eighth district?"

I tried not to look victorious when she grudgingly replied and made a production of trying to remember the address, scratching my head like I couldn't place it. Maybe if I channeled my dad at his bumbling best she'd relax a little. After all, it worked so well when he did it I'd never even known he was an agent until I was in my final year of high school, after my friend, Paul, had been kidnapped.

"Just a minute. I only booked it a few days ago. You'd think I'd remember the name. Gosh. I'm sorry. You must think I'm crazy. First, I maim you on the plane, and now I can't even remember where I'm staying tonight?"

I shook my head, then opened my phone and pretended to check, brushing away a piece of hair that fell over my eyes. I should have cut it before I left. The locks were getting a little too long. Oh well, I'd see if I had time to find a place this week.

"Aha! Success! I'm staying at the Fraser Suites hotel on Champs-Élysées."

Robin looked at me with wide eyes. At first, she looked suspicious, then her face softened and with the barest hint of a smile she nodded. "Really? So am I."

My relief washed over me more intensely than expected, and I fumbled through introducing myself. She didn't seem to think my questions unusual, but after she mentioned her dad, her face fell.

What was she thinking? From the brief I'd read, I knew she was close to her dad. Had he contacted her since his disappearance? Or was she in the dark as well? Looking at her now, I thought she seemed lost, and I knew worried when I saw it. If I was correct, she was here to find him as much as anything else. And it was my job to keep her safe.

I bit my lip, wishing I could put an arm around her, but settled for looking concerned instead. "Are you okay? You look kind of, well, devastated."

Her eyes shone as she blinked rapidly, taking a few deep breaths before giving me a bright, clearly fake, smile. "I'm fine. There's just a lot going on right now with school, and tomorrow's kind of a big day for me."

I knew what it was like to worry about a loved one who was missing and I didn't have to fake it, but also didn't want her to know that I knew what was going on. "I get that. I was a basket case during finals week my last year. If it hadn't been for my mom bringing care packages every few days, I'm not sure I would've remembered to eat. My parents are pretty awesome sometimes."

I couldn't be sure I'd made her feel better or worse. She looked away, out to the road and across the taxi stand for a several silent seconds, her long, elegant throat moving as she swallowed tears. Now, even more than before, I wanted to take her in my arms and tell her everything was going to be all right. But I couldn't. Biting back a curse, I tried to keep my expression neutral as I waited for her to collect herself.

"Sorry. Not trying to get emotional on you. Like I said, it's been a rough week." Robin exhaled, a deep, shuddering breath, and regained her poise just as a brusque, thickly accented growl came from behind us.

"Excuse me. You need?"

We both turned at the irritated question to see a man, standing with his hand palms up, looking at us with raised eyebrows. He was not exactly polite, and it was easy to discern his impatience. Clearly, not a guy who liked to wait.

"Yes, thank you. We're heading to the Fraser Suites hotel, in the Huitième District."

When the cabbie looked at Robin, she held out her bag with a small smile. "This is all I have."

"Me as well. Carry-on only." I gave him the biggest, fakest smile on purpose, and he rolled his eyes.

My initial impression that he was kind of a dick was confirmed when he got into the driver's seat without opening the door for Robin. So much for French gallantry. When Robin started to the back, I got there first. I opened it for her with a smile then waited as she slid across before setting my bag in the middle beside hers.

It was comfortable, but more than once my arm almost brushed hers. The second time it happened, I glanced at her hand, noticing short but nicely rounded and unpolished nails. The impulse to lace my fingers through hers flashed through my mind, and heat rose, along with a memory.

Was it a memory? Or was it a dream?

It felt so real I had to look away and focus on something outside to keep myself from asking her if and when it had happened. I knew she'd look at me like I was insane, because I felt a little insane. Why would I feel this connection? I'd never had this experience with any other case, but the same tingle in my stomach I got when something needed to be found grew, and somehow, it was connected to Robin.

Between glances at her and the scenery outside, there was a sense we were outside reality. Maybe it was all the images I'd seen of Paris that made me feel like I was in a play, or maybe it was the unexpected reaction I was having being near her. I'd been watching her for a while, but feeling her warmth right next to me was causing my senses to react in a way I'd never felt with any other woman.

It was more than just the way she looked though. She was pretty, but I'd been near beautiful women before who'd left me cold. There was something in her eyes that drew me closer, made me want to touch her, make her laugh.

Damn. Looking out the window, I took a few deep breaths. How was I going to keep her safe if I was already this distracted? I turned when I heard her clear her throat, smiling politely as she searched for something to say. I answered her questions, trying to keep it light, then turned the tables. What would she say her reasons for travel were? Would she confide in me?

For a moment, I thought she was done talking entirely. Then she jumped slightly, as if she'd been somewhere else and just realized I'd been talking. Hardly great for my ego, but it reminded me what I was supposed to be doing and I steered my focus back on the job at hand.

"Oh, I have an audition for school. That's why I'm here. I'm in my last year of Music studies, opera, specifically. I'm hoping to make some connections in Europe if possible. If I can get my foot in the door..." she trailed off, her hands plucking at a thread on her jeans like she didn't know what to do with them.

I knew what I wanted to do with them, but cleared my throat and continued to try to act as unthreatening as I could. "That's a good idea. It must be a difficult field to break into. I've been told I can't carry a tune in a bucket, so music was never a consideration for me. What are you singing tomorrow?"

I could see her assessing my interest level. She must get questions about what she did a lot, but most people probably didn't know a thing about opera or the performing arts. I bet guys would ask without listening, and I didn't want to be like everyone else. Luckily, I'd been thorough with my research and had given myself an unofficial Opera 101 class as part of following her.

"I'm an alto, but I love the Baroque period of music most. The music is richer, and I find it easier to connect to emotionally."

Robin stopped, her cheeks a light pink as she looked down. I wanted to lift her chin up, so I could watch her eyes. They were so full of mystery right, and I wondered what I would find if I peered into them. I leaned in before I could stop myself, forcing myself to pause when she looked up in surprise.

We were so close. If I leaned over a few inches I could touch her, but I knew it was too much, too soon, and she'd spook if I did. With difficulty, I asked about music instead of stroking her cheek.

"Who's your favorite composer? I don't know much about opera, but I've become more interested after catching a few local chamber concerts near McGill. I'd love to expand my knowledge. Where would you recommend I start?"

A warm smile grew on her face, and her blue eyes sparkled as she launched into a more in depth explanation. I forgot everything else as the animation on her face chased away the sadness for the first time in days. When the cab stopped, the bubble encapsulating us from the rest of the world broke, and the moment we'd shared ended abruptly. My chest pinched when she looked away, flustered.

"Well, thanks for listening to me ramble on. I don't get many chances to discuss opera. It's not like the topic is a super popular subject with, well, anyone. Thanks for the ride share. It was nice meeting you."

I smiled, happy I'd been able to distract her temporarily. The sadness was already returning to her eyes, and it didn't belong there. The dolefulness made me forget all my training as I tried to think of something to say to make her feel better.

"I've enjoyed this discussion, like, a lot. If you're not too busy while you're here, I'd love it if you shot me a text. We could you know, maybe, um, go site-see together?" Crap. Too much, too soon. Too needy.

I brought my hands up, hoping she didn't think I was just a stranger trying to get lucky. "Unless you're busy. Totally fine. I know you've got plans, and you're meeting your dad. No pressure. But, I'd love the company if you're ever between appointments."

I could read the pause. I'd blown it. When she pulled out her phone, I didn't know what she was doing at first.

"What's your number?"

Somehow, I managed to give her the number correctly through my elation, but when my phone rang, playing the "Imperial March," I was mortified. When she snorted though, I hoped I hadn't entered unredeemed nerd zone and laughed as well.

"You're totally regretting giving me your number now that you've heard my ring tone, aren't you?"

She bit back a chuckle. "Not at all. Any guy who likes *Star Wars* can't be all bad. You have my number now, so text whenever. I won't answer if I'm auditioning—I always turn my phone off— but otherwise, I promise to reply."

I sighed as she slid out, relieved I hadn't blown my cover or my status as okay to talk to, quickly paid the driver, and turned to Robin, who had waited beside the car for me to finish.

She tilted her head to the departing car. "How much do I owe you?"

I brushed off the offer—she didn't have to know how much I was willing to pay for her company. I wished I could give her a hug or a kiss, but she didn't know me. Not nearly as well as I knew her. Forcing myself to remain relaxed, I kept my goodbye chill and waved as she went to the check in counter. When she looked back, I mimed, 'I'll call you', in an overly dramatic fashion and was pleased to see her smile again.

Not for the first time, I wished I could be completely myself with her. There was something so familiar about her, and now that I'd had a chance to actually talk to her, I knew this assignment wasn't going to be easy.

My abilities screamed there was something here to find. The only question was whether it had to do with the case I'd been assigned to, or if another force was at play. An image of sand, ocean, and sunshine with the feel of her hand in mind tickled my memory again. I knew she was important to me beyond this case, but how?

As she walked away, I swore the faint sound of music followed her out of view.

Chapter 7 Robin

I should be more nervous about the audition, considering how enormous the opportunity was, but the only thought going through my head as I waited in the wings of the legendary Paris Opera House was worry for my dad.

The last time I'd been here I was so young I'd been completely overwhelmed by the architecture and the history of the building and had been unable to take a step. My dad's supportive hands, gently grasping me by the shoulders and squeezing had helped give me the strength I'd needed.

Now, I almost felt like he was with me as I remembered his words. "You're my little songbird, Robin. There's nothing to be afraid of in this building. One day, when you are older, you'll be singing on that stage if you want it enough. I have no doubt you can achieve anything if you believe in yourself and work hard."

I smiled, remembering how firm he'd been. How loving, how completely my dad. I was lucky we were so close. He'd shown me how to achieve my heart's desire, and never once tried to discourage me. As an intellectual, he believed in the power of the mind to reach goals above all else, and I was certain this was the reason he was missing now.

Before leaving Montreal, I'd read up on the Voynich manuscript. Also known as Manuscript 408, it was apparently safe in the Yale library now. The problem was that no one had been able to read it since it had been discovered in a bookstore in the 1920s.

As with any mysterious historical artifact, there were as many opinions as there were people, although most had been thoroughly discredited. The explanations ranged from the mundane, such as researchers who postulated the Voynich manuscript was a journal or a medical compendium. The strangest idea I'd discovered was one man who'd insisted it was an alien textbook, left for humans to learn basic science from. Yet no one, no matter how discredited or boring their theory, had been able to decipher it.

If my dad was on the trail of a book that could crack the code of the Voynich manuscript, his quest was incredibly dangerous, even without adding in the involvement of a backer who may or may not be the single biggest crime lord in the city. In my limited experience, no one was crazier than history fanatics, which made his decision to accept funding from who he had a little less unthinkable.

I sniffed back a prickle of tears, wincing as the tenor auditioning ahead of me missed a note. I knew the song he was singing, and made myself focus. I had about three minutes left until it was my turn, and I began to hum lightly. The opera world could be cutthroat, but I was beginning to wonder if the crowd my dad ran with was worse.

Was that why he'd left me a note buried in a pile of papers? I should have reported him missing to the police, but I hadn't because that would've created a situation where I'd have been stuck in Montréal, waiting for them to do something. At least this way I was free to act. I may not have experience searching for missing people, but I knew my dad. I had a better chance finding and following his trail than a complete stranger, and from his notes, I had an idea where he was heading.

"Robin Locksley." A woman's voice with a thick, French accent called out my name.

I smoothed out my dress, tucking a few loose strands of hair behind my ear and pulled my shoulders back. With my head held high, I strode confidently onto stage. One thing I'd learned years earlier was regardless of how nervous you were, the face you showed the world meant everything.

I handed my sheet music to the accompanist before bowing deeply to the judges. After ensuring the preliminaries were handled, I walked back to the center of the stage and stood still, allowing my eyes adjust to the spotlight. When the head judge gestured to me, I cued the accompanist and began.

The song I'd picked to sing was not a typical one chosen for auditions, but I felt it highlighted my voice perfectly. As an alto, I could sing notes in both tenor and soprano territory. I knew I'd never be able to hit glass-breaking octaves like some of the more famous divas in history, but I was a good, solid cast member with the added benefit of being easy to work with.

And, if I could believe my dad or my friend Melissa, there was even a special quality to my voice they said made them believe in magic. I generally brushed their praise aside as what supportive friends and family were supposed to say, but it gave me confidence now, regardless of the truth.

When I finished I paused for a single dramatic moment, before dropping into a low curtsy, one for each judge. They nodded in return and scribbled on the paper in front of them as the same woman who'd announced me gestured for me to exit stage left.

I curtsied to her as well, then walked off with as much dignity as the queen I'd been attempting to be. On the other side of the curtain, a man waited with a single tulip in his hand. I halted, my hand going to my throat as I recognized him.

Mark stepped forward from the wall he'd been leaning on and bowed, presenting the flower the same way a knight would present a sword to a queen on the occasion of his knighthood.

Instantly, my cheeks warmed.

"Hey," I said, hearing the confusion in my voice. "What are you doing here?"

He stood, still holding the tulip with an expectant look. I bit back a giggle, accepting it with a smile I couldn't contain.

"I remembered you had your audition today. I figured if I showed up early enough I might get lucky and catch you singing. It just so happens I was in time to hear them call your name. So, naturally I thought I'd wait for you to finish so I could congratulate you."

The grin he gave me was three parts mischievous little boy and one part nerves. It had a stunning effect on me. Normally, I had no problem resisting the guys who hit on me but, then again, no one had ever come to see me perform at the Paris Opera house and waited to give me a single tulip before either.

My mouth felt dry, and after a cursory look around where I didn't find any water, I managed to reply without croaking. "Thank you. It's always nice to see a friendly face in a strange city. How did you get here?"

He grinned. "I took the Metro. I figured while I was in Paris I should act like the locals. Speaking of which, you mentioned you've visited Paris before. Any recommendations where I could treat you to a late breakfast?"

I blinked. Was he asking me out?

I looked up at his hopeful face, knowing I would have to crush his anticipation. "I'm sorry, but I have a lesson now." His face fell and I racked my brain for an alternative. For some reason, I needed him to understand it wasn't a rejection. "If you wanted to wait, I could meet you for lunch instead? There's a cute little café I was planning to go to after I finished. You're welcome to join me."

His disappointment vanished. "It's a date!" He paused, biting the inside of his cheek. "Er, I mean, between friends. Unless you want it to be a date?"

I laughed at his awkward attempt at sidestepping. "That's fine. You call it what you want. Either way, I'm calling it lunch. I'll send you a text when I'm done, and we can meet in the lobby."

Mark performed a flowery bow, adding far too much hand movement at the end when I snickered.

"All right, *now* who's the actor?"

He shrugged, but for a moment I thought I caught a hint of guilt flash over his face. It was gone far too quickly to be sure, and I mentally shrugged it off as embarrassment.

He clicked his heels together and saluted. "I look forward to hearing from you, m'lady. In the meantime, I think I shall explore the opera house. Enjoy your lesson."

I bowed as he waved and turned to the front of the building, where the tours generally began. Watching him walk away with a general sense of bemusement, moments passed before I was able to collect myself adequately to prepare for the practice rooms.

When I'd booked my trip, in addition to being excited about the audition, I had been over the moon when I'd found out Natalie Dessay was giving voice lessons that week at the Paris Opera House. She was one of the current European greats, and well known in opera circles, even if the average North American wouldn't recognize her name.

Now however, with the disappearance of my dad on my mind as well as the anticipation of lunch with the intriguing and flirtatious Mark, I was pretty sure my voice hadn't been up to par. She was very kind though and gave me pointers that would be as valuable when I was at my best.

Once my lesson was over, I took a deep breath and texted Mark. He shot back an immediate reply. Moments later, I found him standing at the ornately decorated grand entrance, holding out his arm for me to take.

"Your servant."

I hoped my blush was under control as I took his arm and walked out. The oddest sensation floated through me, as if I truly was the queen I'd portrayed inside the celebrated building and had a trusted knight at my side.

All the worries I'd been holding inside since my dad had left earlier that week lightened, and with my obligations met for the moment, I allowed myself to enjoy holding the arm of a handsome man who appealed to me in a way I couldn't put my finger on. Something about him, his voice felt...familiar, safe. If I had known what the following week would hold, I would have tried to enjoy myself a little bit more.

Chapter 8 Mark

Spending time with Robin wasn't a hardship. In fact, I was having difficulties remembering I was supposed to be working. The restaurant she'd mentioned, Café Cappuccino, was only a few blocks down the street. When she accepted my invitation along with my hand, I'd felt like I could fly.

Fortunately, she'd accepted my invite and arrived at the location I'd expected her to be at, because instead of the boots she'd worn on the plane, she now sported a pair of lacy leather sandals. While they made her ankles look impossibly dainty, no tracker could have hidden in those, no matter how small.

She'd changed out of the sparkling purple dress since I'd seen her, but I didn't want to comment in case it was misconstrued. With the dress and the color she'd worn to make her eyes deepen with mystery, she'd practically glowed on stage. Now, with the make-up scrubbed off and dressed in a loose shirt, jeans, and a jacket with her hair pulled up in a ponytail, she looked fresh-faced and innocent. In many ways, she appeared to be a completely different person.

I was amazed how dramatically she could shift her appearance, and this new insight highlighted my need to focus.

Anyone who could be a chameleon without training was someone to keep an eye on.

Maybe she wasn't as innocent as she looked.

Maybe I was merely letting my hormones get the better of me.

Unable to think of anything to talk about that wouldn't either sound dumb or give me away, we shared a companionable silence during the short walk to the café.

I held open the door, gesturing for her to go first. "Please, after you. Unless you'd like me to order for you?"

She snorted. "Hardly. There's an empty table over there. From what I can tell, it's a seat-yourself facility."

I nodded, following as she wound her way through the half-empty tables. When I looked at my watch, I realized we'd come at a good time. There were a few couples and singles sitting around the room with computers and books, but we'd arrived before the lunch rush.

A harried looking waitress appeared at our table to demand our orders in rapid French. Robin's eyebrows shot up, but she smiled politely, then ordered coffee and a croissant. I followed suit, and the moment the waitress left, Robin leaned forward conspiratorially.

"Well, *she* seems excited to be here. Perhaps it's why the French are so renowned for their *joie de vivre*?"

The sparkle in her eyes made her words come out more cheeky than snarky, and I chuckled, settling into the chair to enjoy being with her, all while keeping an eye on our surroundings.

"So, what are your plans for the day?" I rested my elbows on the table and waited for her to reply.

To my disappointment, it was as though I'd flipped a switch with my words. Her smile dimmed, and her eyes slid away as she bit the inside of her cheek, turning to look out the window to the street.

"Well, I was supposed to meet my dad at the hotel." Her words trailed off, soft and sad.

I could see she wanted to say more, but whether it was natural reticence or fear that stopped her, I couldn't tell. Either way, it was my chance to pry deeper. Maybe I could get her to open up. "You're not meeting him? What happened? Did his plans change?"

She shook her head, but continued looking out the window without meeting my eyes. It was a beautiful spring morning and flowers bloomed in the plant hangers outside. If her face hadn't been so down, she could have been an advertisement for the restaurant. It would have made me want to come in, at least.

Finally, she took a deep breath, and turned to look at me. "Yes, and no." She paused, then as if deciding she could trust me, leaned forward and dropped her voice to just above a whisper. "My dad is missing. He hasn't returned any of my calls, texts, or emails since he flew to Paris. I was hoping he'd be at the hotel, but he wasn't. It's been four days, and it's completely unlike him to not check in by now. I'm worried something happened. I have to find him."

There it was. The opening I needed.

I made a point of looking around and dropped my voice before I replied, "Can I help?"

Her shoulders slumped. For a moment, I thought she would cry, but before she could say anything, we were interrupted by the waitress. She dropped off our cappuccinos, sloshing one over the edge of the cup to the saucer underneath. Acknowledging the spill with an insincere, "Oops," she vanished again, without even offering a napkin.

Robin took two of the raw sugar packets our terrible waitress had nearly thrown down beside the cappuccino and dumped them into her drink, stirring methodically with a teaspoon. For several minutes she stared at her coffee with the intensity of someone expecting it to vanish, and when she finally looked up, her eyes sparkled with unshed tears.

My need to help swelled. "Look, I may not be a pro, but I've got a little experience looking for lost things."

I shrugged, not sure how much to reveal without telling her everything, or lying outright. When her expression turned hopeful, I told her something most of my superiors didn't even know. I could only pray she didn't think I was nuts.

"I can sometimes find missing objects. I know it sounds crazy, but when I was younger, I had a knack for finding missing objects. A few times I found pets, and once, I found my best friend." I caught her startled look and rushed to add, "He'd witnessed a crime and been kidnapped. I don't tell that story often, for obvious reasons, but I can't just sit here and watch your misery. I want to help."

She wiped her eyes brusquely, a stray tear leaving a trail on her cheek. When she looked at me, I was relieved to see she was watching me with more hope than disbelief.

"I am worried, and yes, I'm upset. I've been as strong as I can in order to get through the audition first, but my dad is everything to me. It's been just the two of us for as long as

I can remember. If you want to help, I'm in no position to stop you. I'm grateful for an extra set of eyes. If you think you have some extra-human ability to find things, I'll take that as well."

A bubble of something fluttered in my chest at her half-smile, and my shoulders relaxed. She didn't think I was crazy, but at the same time, it was obvious she didn't believe me.

I shrugged, downplaying my gift. "Look, I'm not saying I have any extra-special abilities or anything, but sometimes I have a knack at putting pieces together. Maybe it's just luck, but either way, I'm here for the next week without a solid itinerary. I'd love to help you find your dad if I can. I've always loved a good mystery."

She inhaled, but this time when she answered her smile was real. Her eyes lit up and I swallowed, hard. Oh crap. I was in deep, deep trouble.

"I'll tell you everything I know. But..." She looked around, pressing her lips together. "Not here. Why don't we go back to the hotel? We can talk more in private."

My cheeks warmed as my body had a knee-jerk reaction to her words. Now I was the one taking a few deeps breaths as I forced my body to behave. Thankfully, the rude waitress showed up at that moment with the croissants, tossing them down as negligently as she had the coffee. It gave me enough time to regain control, but also signaled the end of our serious discussion.

I wasn't sure what the week held in store, but based on my reaction so far, I was in serious danger of losing my heart. Dammit. If only I wasn't an agent assigned to keep her safe.

How was I going to resist her and do my job at the same time?

Chapter 8 Mark

I threw a ten euro note down on the table while scanning to ensure we hadn't left anything behind. While I'd enjoyed the atmosphere and the company, the woman who'd brought our order had one of the sourest faces I'd ever seen, including Agent Derny on the night she'd taken over watching Robin for me while I'd packed. If all the waitresses in Paris were like this one, the downside to the European tradition of not tipping was apparent.

Catching a cab in the interest of time, Robin waved me off when I attempted to pay. "You paid last time. Besides, it's the least I can do if you're serious about helping me find my dad. I'll tell you everything when we get to the hotel— you may change your mind once you know more."

Her frightened eyes darted around the lobby. I held out my arm for her. I wanted to support her and wasn't sure what else to do. When she hesitated, I wondered if I'd overstepped, but when she looped her arm through mine I felt an almost superhuman strength fill me.

It was the first time I'd been this close to her and my heart raced. I wondered if she noticed anything, but we rode in silence in the elevator to the seventh floor with a tinny version of "La vie en rose" playing in the background. Taking her silence as evidence she wasn't thinking about my reactions at all, I scanned the foyer as she stepped out and headed to the left. The halls were empty of people as she scanned her keycard, and I waited for her to enter the room first before stepping in behind her.

The expectant look she'd worn as she opened the door vanished at the emptiness that greeted us inside. I knew she'd hoped to return and find her dad waiting. Instead, the suite was quiet and undisturbed. A brief survey of the entry showed a main living area with a small kitchenette, couch, TV, table, and chairs, and I glimpsed a narrow hallway leading away on either side. I surmised it led to the bathroom and bedrooms, and I let out a low whistle. The room I'd rented was a broom closet in comparison, with a single queen bed and a bathroom. Her hotel room was the size of my entire apartment in Montreal.

Noticing my awe, Robin smiled and waved at the room. "Make yourself comfortable. My dad travels a lot. He likes to make sure his rooms are comfortable when he can afford to. The person he was working for..." Her voice broke, then she cleared her throat and kept talking, as if nothing had happened. "Well, anyway. My dad's contract included an expense account, so he got this suite, in honor of my audition. He said it was his gift to me. I was excited to have my own room." She blinked quickly, a look of regret crossing her face. "We were going to go to the cemetery, Notre Dame, and maybe even Versailles if we had enough time."

It crossed my mind while she was speaking I could potentially stay in the second room. It would make guarding her easier. But when her face fell at the wreckage of her plans, all practical thought left my mind. Without considering whether it was a good idea or not, I strode across the room and gathered her gently in my arms.

I held her carefully, keeping my grip loose so that she could escape if she wanted. She looked so fragile I wanted to press the broken pieces back together and make her smile, but when she stiffened, I pulled back. I berated myself for overstepping and released my hold just as her shoulders began to shake. Before I could react, she rested her head against my chest and began to cry.

Not knowing what else to do, I placed one hand on her golden hair and gently stroked it like she was a baby. Like I used to do when my younger brother was sad, or injured. The fine strands of her hair were as soft as silk and caught on the calluses of my fingers. We stood there for a long time before she pulled back, inhaling with a shudder.

Her face was blotchy and streaked with tears, but she was still the most beautiful thing I'd ever seen. "Thank you. I haven't talked to anybody else about what happened. I'm a little overwhelmed. I'm not usually much of a crier."

Her words were halting, but her face smoothed while she spoke. I could see her internal struggle as she deliberately pushed aside her emotions. It was obvious that she was overwhelmed with worry for her dad, but it was also clear that she had no intention of either giving up or giving in to her fear.

A tingle of awe filled me. She had more fortitude than most adults decades older, and I compared her reaction to how I'd felt when Paul had gone missing. There was no way I would have functioned half as well as she was if it had been one of my close relatives.

"You don't have to explain anything. He's your dad. That alone makes me want to help you however I can. I doubt there's anything you can say at this point that would scare me away. If it was my dad, I'd do whatever it took to get him back."

She stepped back, filling a glass with water from the tap in the kitchenette, before sitting at the small table with a weary sigh. "You may change your mind when I tell you what I know. What little there is, of course."

I shook my head then sat across from her. Resting my elbows on the table, I rested my chin on my fists and watched her. "Try me. I don't scare easily."

She raised her eyebrows, tilting her head. "You're sure? Okay." She took a deep breath, then unloaded. "My father is a professor in the English department at McGill. He often goes on business trips to acquire historical manuscripts, along with other rare books for the university and private collectors. He left as usual earlier this week, but I haven't heard from him since."

I settled back in my chair to listen. While I knew some of the situation, I didn't know anything about why he'd been traveling, or where he'd gone. "You haven't heard from him at all? Not to repeat things you've already considered, but have you checked hospitals, or police stations? Maybe they'd have a report of his whereabouts."

She shook her head. "I thought about it, but I'm not sure where to start. I dropped him off at the airport in Montreal, and got a single text when he landed. I know he arrived in Paris, but that's it. He just vanished. He'd planned to go to a town in the south of France before I flew in, but he was going to meet me at the hotel when my flight landed." She looked around the room, a wry smile crossing her face. "It's silly, but part of me expected to find him here. As you can tell, that didn't happen. I found a few items of his clothing in one of the closets, but his suitcase was gone, and so was he."

I leaned back in my chair and rubbed my chin as I considered her words, discovering stubble I'd been too lazy to take care of that morning. It rasped against my hand, snapping me back to the present. The chair legs dropped to the floor with a bang when I leaned forward. "Where do you think he went?"

Her eyes narrowed. "This is where it gets weird. He didn't tell me much, which isn't unusual for him. If you met my dad, you'd know what I mean. He's basically the prototype of an absent-minded professor type— you know, the guy who goes on about details which aren't important or interesting, but completely leaves out those that are? I chalked the lack of details this time up to normal behavior. Until the day before I left Montreal."

She took a sip of her water, then placed the cup down, keeping it clenched tightly. Her face was tense, and I knew what she was about to say had her spooked. I leaned closer, fighting back the urge to put my hand on hers and loosen her grip.

"The night before I left, I felt like someone was watching me."

Startled, I let out a small gasp. I wondered if she'd seen me or Agent Derny outside, but I pushed the idea away almost as quickly as it arrived. If she had, I wouldn't be here now and she wouldn't be telling me anything. That didn't stop my guilty conscience from waking up again and causing me to nearly miss her bombshell.

She nodded, grimly. "I was in his office, looking for clues to where he went. I found a letter to me hidden in a stack on his desk. He'd deliberately camouflaged it so no one else could find it. I tried to convince myself I was being paranoid. I don't know anyone who'd want to search our house, and the idea was hard to cope with."

"What did the letter say?"

She got up and retrieved her purse, pulling a piece of paper out, and handing it to me. "Maybe you'll get more out of it than I did. I gleaned just enough to feed my fears something has happened to him."

Grateful she trusted me enough to show me, I scanned the details before setting it down on the table. The situation was becoming more complex. I tapped my leg absently, but said nothing of my true concerns. CSIS had been watching the biker gang, and the more I found out, the worse the possibilities became. If her dad had known what he was getting into, he may not be completely innocent.

"Do you think a biker gang had something to do with his disappearance?"

She sat down again, leaning on her elbows and rubbing her face. She looked tired and defeated. "I don't know. It doesn't make sense to me the man who hired him would make him vanish before finding the book he paid him to look for. Why bother? It seems like my dad went missing almost on arrival. That's too fast to double-cross his backer. Even if he was that kind of person—which he's not," she hastened to clarify.

I agreed, not wanting her to think I suspected her beloved dad of wrongdoing. "You're right. There's no point in paying someone to find a book for you, but getting rid of them before they give it to you. Someone else must be involved."

"My thought exactly. If anything, Mr. Lavallee would have a vested interest making sure my father got to the book back to him first."

We locked eyes. Keeping my voice gentle, I said, "Unless your dad did somehow find the book already and changed his mind about giving it to him."

She exhaled shakily. "That, or one of Mr. Lavallee's rivals got to him first."

We sat without speaking for what felt like an hour as we considered both options. I didn't like either, and I could tell she wasn't keen on them herself. Her hand clenched so tightly on her cup I worried she'd get a muscle cramp, so I broke the silence.

"What do you know about the book he was after?"

She shrugged. "I did a little research after I found his letter. He was looking for a book that would translate the Voynich manuscript. Even scholars in the field can't agree on what it says, and no one has been able to read the text since it was discovered, decades ago. I think that's why he was so excited, and so secretive."

I wrinkled my nose. I didn't want to offend her, but needed to ask. "Is it possible your father never intended to hand the book over?"

At first, she just blinked. After a moment, she nodded. "It's not like him to promise something and not follow through, but if he thought the book he was looking for was dangerous... well, it's possible. He's all about sharing knowledge, but if he decided to keep the book, it would be for a very good reason."

I considered what I knew, mulling over her words carefully. So far, my ability seemed to be asleep, and without direction one way or another, I'd have to use my human skills to track her dad. "Do you have a picture with you? Something to give me a better idea what your dad looks like?"

Robin nodded, taking her wallet out of her purse. She handed me a picture and I smiled, unable to suppress my amusement.

"When was this taken?"

She grinned back. "Last Christmas. We were out shopping, and he thought it would be fun."

I shook my head, examining the picture in detail. Her hair was the same style and length, and she was standing between a man with a bushy white beard, red suit, and reindeer and another man with light brown hair. The twinkle in her dad's eye gave the impression of a well-developed sense of humor, showing there was more to the man than just the absent-minded professor she'd described.

Otherwise, as men went, he was fairly average in appearance. His coloring was similar to Robin's with the exception of streaks of white in his hair. Instead of making him look old and frail though, it gave him the look of an old lion; wise and strong. His beard was almost as big as mall Santa's and only a little darker, with only a trace of blonde left. His eyes sparkled with blue ice a few shades lighter than hers were. His face was creased with laugh lines and crows' feet, suggesting time spent outside or smiling, and he was dressed in simple dark jeans and a green flannel shirt.

In short, he looked like a nice guy. I was even more confident in my decision to help her. I wouldn't be the first agent to be tricked by a target, but I didn't think either Robin or her dad were trying to fool me. If he was truly missing under these odd circumstances, it wasn't because of any fault of his own. That meant it was my duty to make sure he was safe and help Robin find him.

"This is great." I looked up. "Any chance you can access his banking information?"

Robin's eyebrows raised. "Actually, yes. Part of qualifying for absent-minded professor includes being horrible at paying bills. Once I was old enough to figure out how to manage finances myself, I took over. I've kept track of all our bills since I was fifteen or so."

I gnawed on my lip. "It might help to follow the Visa charges. How was he being funded?"

She gave me a half-smile, waving a hand at the room. "I'm not sure of the details, but generally he gets reimbursed after a trip. He uses travel points when he can— that's how he got such a sweet room for this trip."

"Perfect. So, if he bought anything with his card between when he landed in Paris and today, we'll be able to see where he's been. If we're lucky, we may even find his current location."

Excitement lit her face. "That would be wonderful. I never thought of that." She pressed her lips together. "Thank you."

I shook my head. "Don't thank me yet. We still have to find him."

But, even as I deferred her praise, knowing I didn't deserve it yet, a warm glow filled me. It was the first time since I started working with CSIS that I felt a little like James Bond.

Chapter 9 Robin

The simple act of sharing my worry lifted a weight off my shoulders. I felt less lost than I had since my dad had vanished, but kicked myself for not thinking to check the Visa.

Why hadn't I thought of that?

After all, I'd always enjoyed detective movies, and one of my all-time favorite characters was Garcia, from *Criminal Minds*. She was the real hero of that show—the things she could find out behind a computer! While my skills didn't extend to hacking, I had all my dad's passwords, so no special skills were required.

Grateful I'd brought my laptop, I pulled it out and opened the banking app.

"Do you need any help?"

Mark settled on the arm of the chair. He'd left a little space between us, but was close enough to look at what I was doing if I said yes.

I smiled at his careful, attentive expression. I couldn't remember the last time anyone had been so considerate. "I should be okay with this part, but maybe later, depending on what we find."

I gestured for him to come closer when I saw the way he was contorted, and he slid from the arm to a spot on the couch that was closer. When I entered my password, he turned his head and the silence in the room grew.

I looked up to find him debating whether to speak. "What's up?"

"I have a computer in my room as well, in case you need a back-up." He paused, pressing his lips together, then leaned back, giving me more space. "It's my last night at the hotel. I was planning on moving to the hostel in Montmartre, but I could move my things into the empty room if you want, just until we find your dad. No pressure though—I can look for another hostel nearby. If you're more comfortable with that."

I hadn't even considered his plans for the week. Wow, conceited much? Shaking my head, I wondered where my head was at. Of course, he'd made other plans before offering to drop everything for me.

He must have read uncertainty in my silence, and he raised both hands, eyes wide.

"Hey, it's totally fine. Maybe the Visa statement will give us a direction. While you're doing that, I'll cancel my reservation for the hostel. I can always crash on a couch somewhere if need be, but I want to be free to come with you if he's out of the city somewhere."

Maybe it was his boyish embarrassment, or perhaps it was my need to have someone at my side through the most confusing episode of my life, but all I saw when I looked at him was someone who wanted to help.

My hesitation melted away. "You know what? It's fine. My dad reserved this room for the entire week so it makes sense to have this for our base. Go ahead and cancel your reservation, and you can use the second bedroom until we find him."

He sprang to his feet, giving me the same dimpled smile I was starting to look forward to. "Cool! Maybe I'll get lucky and they'll give me a refund."

I nodded, waving absently as he left. I scrolled through the last week of the Visa, and my excitement rose when I saw Dad had used the card up to two days ago. That either meant the bank hadn't updated the purchases yet, or that he'd gone silent.

Closing my eyes briefly, I reminded myself it didn't necessarily mean something fatal had happened to him. He could have cash and was in hiding. Maybe he'd thought of someone trying to follow his Visa trail too.

Once I'd collected myself, I re-examined the list of purchases. There weren't many. He'd checked into the hotel and put his card on file, but I already knew that, because I'd had no problem getting a room key. Then he'd gone to the lobby to buy something, but I couldn't tell what. What would he have needed from the store in the lobby? *Hmmm.*

The next few entries were posted the day after arrival. He'd rented a car, which made sense if he was leaving Paris, but it also meant I wouldn't be able to follow train or bus ticket purchases for a destination. I scanned the rest of the list, but nothing stood out.

"Rats."

Jotting down the little information I'd uncovered, I reminded myself it was more than I'd had before. Maybe the car rental agency had information on his destination. And when Mark returned we could check out the store in the lobby. Sighing, I left the laptop on the coffee table and walked over to the window.

I knew my dad had been in this room at one point, based on the items in the closet, but neither of the beds appeared to have been slept in when I'd arrived. Housekeeping had tidied up after he'd left, but maybe he'd left something else besides clothing that could give me a clue to where he'd gone. With that thought in mind, I began to systematically search the living room, digging through the cushions on the couch, even opening it into the hide-a-bed and looking through the mattress part.

Nothing there.

Next, I went to the TV stand, running my hands along the back of the wall-mounted electronic, and opened the drawers on the small hotel desk. It was empty except for a small, blank notepad. With the intrepid Agent Garcia fresh in my mind, I scanned the area for a pencil.

Spotting one inside the drawer, I realized the word McGill was embossed on the side. Was this a sign? Had my dad left me a message? Carefully, I used the pencil to shade the notepad, attempting a rubbing. I'd never tried to do one before and wasn't certain I was doing it right when a knock made me tense up.

Mark spoke from the other side of the door. "Robin? It's me."

I reluctantly stopped what I was doing. Placing the pencil on the paper, I walked over to let him in. He was standing at the threshold with a disappointed look on his face.

"I was too late to get a refund, but I cancelled anyway. I may not have gotten my money back, but at least I'm ready to follow you anywhere." His expression became hesitant, and he shifted to reveal a backpack. "I wasn't sure if you wanted me to stay tonight as well, but figured it would save time. I don't want to scare you, but I started to wonder if someone really *is* watching you. What if someone was following your dad, but now he's missing they've switched to you because they think you know something?"

I hadn't even considered that possibility. Well, I had thought someone was watching me in Montreal, but I'd been so distracted since leaving that some of the more troublesome aspects of dad's disappearance had slipped my mind.

But the question I needed to ask myself was if I trusted Mark when I feared someone was after my dad, and by extension, might be after me.

Without hesitation, I stepped back and gestured for him to enter. "I'd like it if you stayed tonight. I feel safer having you here."

He looked relieved, giving me a shrug as he smiled and walked into the suite. "I'm glad. I get you have to be careful; I mean we hardly know each other. It bothers me no one else has your back. I've always had my family, and I know they'd do anything for me. Sounds like your dad would do the same, but now that he's the one missing..." He trailed off and put his hands in his pockets.

For some reason, the action made me smile. I couldn't think of many people who'd throw away a vacation and offer to help a stranger, girl or guy. Most of the guys I knew assumed everybody thought they were wonderful and should drop everything for them. It was refreshing he wasn't like that.

"Do you have sisters?" Immediately after I asked, I pressed my lips together in mortification, wishing I could take the question back. He'd already told me he had a brother.

Luckily, he didn't seem to notice my lack of attention to detail and laughed. "No, but I'm the oldest, so being over-protective is an occupational hazard. Just ask my little brother, Robbie. I'm sure he'd be happy to tell you how annoying I am, so feel free to let me know if I'm overstepping." He gave an exaggerated grimace. "But, kidding aside, I'll do everything I can to keep you safe. It's kind of my job, you know, as a big brother and all."

Warmth spread in my chest as I gazed at his open, earnest face. I still had the oddest, niggling sensation he was hiding something, but he was being honest with me now. Maybe it was just curiosity, because I wanted to know everything about him. If he was as amazing as he seemed, I was in deep trouble.

Clearing my suddenly thick throat, I abruptly turned back to the desk, creating a space between us before I replied. "I'll take you up on that offer. While you were gone, I found two charges that I thought were interesting."

Mark followed me in, learning on the wall beside me. "What did you find?"

"He rented a car and drove to the hotel after landing. I know what time he got here because he purchased something in the lobby for just under €100. It's a bit much for snacks. Do you think it's a clue?"

Mark rubbed his chin and seemed to be thinking out loud. "So, he got to the hotel, put his Visa on file, and bought something." Straightening abruptly, he scanned the room. "Did you search the room yet? Maybe he left something behind for you."

I jumped at the sudden intensity in his voice. I'd forgotten about the notepad until he jogged my memory. I gestured to the table. "I was about to see if there's something on the paper. The pencil I found beside the stationary is from McGill. That can't be a coincidence. I was hoping the pencil shading thing in detective novels works."

His eyes widened. "Does it?"

"I'm not sure yet. I just started when you knocked."

At the look on his face, I picked up the pencil and began to shade.

Chapter 10 Robin

I paused in my task, pencil hovering over the notepad as a momentary qualm struck me. Was it foolish to trust Mark? Was I being careless, going all Nancy Drew because of his boyish smile and telling myself he was a helpful Hardy boy? Taking a deep breath, I forced my doubts aside and squared my shoulders. It was difficult to decide what bothered me more—the idea the notepad would be empty when I shaded it, or that I was crazy letting a strange, albeit attractive, man stay in the hotel suite with me.

Either way, finding my dad was the only thing that mattered. Bending over the paper again, I was distracted by the faint smell of warm chocolate chip cookies with a hint of spice wafting toward me.

My heart rate picked up as Mark leaned over to watch me gently rub the pencil on the paper. I tried to keep my hands from shaking. It was embarrassing to admit, but I was pretty sure I'd be willing to chance having an axe murderer nearby if they smelled that good.

Giving myself a firm mental shake, I focused on what I was doing with difficulty, then gasped at the writing that had been revealed. I met Mark's equally startled eyes.

"David St. Clair?" He frowned, tilting his head to the side.

It wasn't a name I was familiar with, but that wasn't important. "There's an address here. If I'm reading it correctly, it says 135 Rue de l'Église, Mesnières-en-Bray, Normandy."

He scratched his head, squinting a little as he read the paper again. "Does the name or location mean something to you? I've never heard of either."

I shook my head. "No, I don't know the name, but Mesnières-en-Bray is a village outside of Paris. I've heard him mention it before, and I bet it's where he went to get the book."

His eyes widened. "Normandy? Whoa. I guess we'll be leaving Paris after all."

I frowned as that detail sunk in and looked at the page again. "Yeah, looks like it." Checking my watch, I sighed. "Crap. It's already three, and we still haven't checked out the lobby. The village is about five hours away. Depending on what we find out downstairs, we may decide otherwise."

He nodded. "Okay by me. The more intel we can gather the better."

I stood up and abruptly froze. For a moment, we were so close we were almost touching. The smell of cookies intensified along with a hint of the freshness of mint. Had he brushed his teeth before returning? I caught myself lingering on his lips and blinked, stepping away as I felt my cheeks flame with embarrassment.

I looked down and mumbled an apology. "Oops, sorry. Didn't realize you were so close."

I caught him smile slightly as he backed away, giving me room as he ruffled his hair with one hand. He gestured for me to go first. "Sorry, I was distracted. Er, do you need anything from the room before we go?"

I followed his gaze as he looked around the room.

"Just my purse." Slipping the notepad and pencil in my purse, I grabbed the room key, then hesitated. Taking the other key out of the paper sleeve, I held it out to him.

"I got them to make two, in case my dad had lost his. Why don't you keep this one? That way if I lose mine, or we get separated, you can still get in."

He looked surprised at the offer, but accepted it after a brief hesitation.

He wasn't the only one who was surprised. Something about him was so comfortable, so familiar. From the second he'd bumped into me on the plane, I'd felt I knew him, which was really weird. I'd never had the feeling of instant connection with anyone before, let alone a strange man on a plane.

I watched him take the key and put it into his jeans pocket. My eyes lingered on his hand, and a long-ago memory intruded. I recalled a dream I'd had, right after a mysterious music box had shown up on my door in high school. A flash of beach, and the feel of a man's hand holding mine.

It couldn't be. Could it?

Had he been the stranger in my dream? But how? When I looked up, he was at the door waiting expectantly. I smiled, and pushing aside the odd dreams from so many years ago, I proceeded through. Now was not the time to examine them. Not when my dad was still missing.

Once in the lobby, we headed for the hotel shop. Mark let me lead the way, and his silent steadiness was oddly reassuring. Unlike so many others, he didn't talk just to fill the silence. Perversely, that made me want him to talk even more. When he finally did, the soft, deep timbre of his voice sent a shiver down my back.

"Any idea what we're looking for?"

I paused outside the store entrance, shaking my head. "No. I was hoping to compare the prices of what they sell to the statement. His purchase came to just under ninety-five euros, including tax. If you see anything that stands out, or that you'd want to take on the run if you went AWOL, let me know. I'm trying to think what he'd have bought if he was planning on hiding or thought he was being followed."

Mark nodded, holding out an arm. "Unless you want to split up, it may be less suspicious if we pretend to be together."

I swallowed hard, then linked my arm through his. I was mesmerized by the sight of my small arm being engulfed by his much larger one. The sensation of warmth in my chest doubled, then dropped lower, into my stomach. Standing this close to him was having a most distracting effect on me. Somehow, all the oxygen in the room was being used up at an unusually quick rate.

Telling myself my reaction was due to the stress I'd been under, and not the presence of the hot guy beside me, I focused on my breathing. The last thing I wanted to do was freak him out by having an impromptu panic attack in the middle of the hotel lobby.

Most of the objects inside the store were the usual ones expected in a convenience store anywhere in the world. Snacks, drinks, and objects designed to make people spend money impulsively, or to help a traveler whose luggage may not have arrived with them. But the moment we walked into the store, my attention was snagged by the rack of cell phones along the wall. Not only did the signage loudly proclaim the phone an 'awesome deal', but also mentioned extra minutes were available to purchase at the desk.

Mark came closer and whispered in my ear, "Are you thinking what I'm thinking?"

I looked into his dark blue eyes and forced a nod, telling myself he was looking at the signage and that was all he meant. "It's the right price, especially if he bought an extra card with minutes. But if he bought it, why hasn't he tried to call me?"

My voice cracked unexpectedly and I caught a look of concern on his face. I blinked rapidly, somehow managing to catch the tears before they fell and I embarrassed myself. I let go of his arm, making a show of opening the nearby drink fridge and grabbed a bottle of sparkling water while I collected myself.

Mark followed suit, grabbing a few snacks and drink for himself. We paid and walked back to the room, but this time the silence was less comfortable. Once we were inside the room, he launched himself onto the couch. Using the coffee table as a footrest, he leaned back and opened a bag of chips, crunching on them for a few moments before holding the bag up for me to read.

"It's so crazy how different chips are between countries. Like, these do not exist in Montréal!"

I smiled at what I was certain was an attempt to lift my mood and change the subject, but it faded almost immediately as I put my purchases on the small desk without opening them. I wasn't the least bit hungry.

"Are you okay? I mean, it could be a good thing he bought another phone. Maybe the reason he's not answering your texts is because he's not getting them. And maybe he doesn't remember your number. I know I'm lost without my contact list."

He dropped any semblance of relaxation as he leaned forward, examining me with a slightly furrowed brow, like he was trying to read my mind. Pushing my hair off my face, I sat beside him.

"That would explain why he isn't answering my attempts, but it still isn't like him. He would have made contact by now if he was able to."

He tilted his head. "Maybe. But you've said it yourself. He's absent-minded. Or, maybe he doesn't want to chance calling you even with a burner phone in case he's being followed."

I raised my eyebrows. "Burner phone?"

He grinned. "Sorry. I watch a lot of crime dramas and spy movies. They probably don't even call them that in real life."

I nearly missed the flicker in his eyes as he smiled. Once again, an unsettling suspicion he was hiding something filled me, but vanished almost as quickly. Regardless of what he was hiding, I felt safe with him. I knew beyond any logical reason that he'd never hurt me on purpose. If nothing else, I knew for certain he wasn't in a biker gang because he didn't have nearly enough visible tattoos.

Maybe once he got to know me better he'd tell me what he was holding back, but for now, I needed his help. Whatever his secret was could wait until after I'd solved the mystery of my dad's disappearance.

Chapter 11 Mark

After Robin had relaxed a little, I raised the idea of leaving to check out the other lead. "On the plus side, if we go now, we'll get to the address you found just after dark."

She gnawed on her lower lip, and I had to look away. Focusing on her lips did bad things for my concentration.

"True, but we don't know the area. There may not be anywhere to stay, not to mention the stores will be closed." She got up and began to pace, absently twirling one dark gold lock of hair around her finger. "But if we get there tonight, we may find him right away." She halted and whirled around, her eyes wide. "What if we don't go tonight and miss our chance? What if staying in Paris until the morning is the difference between keeping him safe and something bad happening to him?"

I shrugged, unable to reassure her as much as I wanted to. "I don't know what to say. For all we know it could be, but as you've already mentioned, any store your dad would have gone to will be closed if we arrive tonight. Unless we're planning to break in, going first thing in the morning would be more practical. But it's up to you. I mean, he's your dad. I'll do whatever you feel is best."

I watched her struggle with the decision but knew she'd made up her mind the instant her shoulders slumped, giving her a defeated look that matched the conflict in her sapphire eyes.

I wanted to take her in my arms and tell her everything would be okay, but I couldn't. It may not be okay. The first twenty-four hours someone was missing were crucial. For all we knew, her dad had been missing nearly a week. If he'd been kidnapped the chances of him being alive had already dwindled to the single digits. One more night wasn't likely to change that. And if he was hiding, it would be easier to follow his trail by daylight.

"So, now what?" She searched my face for answers, and I had the strange sensation she was trying see into my soul.

I had to turn to the window and shove my hands into my pockets so I didn't do something stupid, like pull her into my arms. "That depends on you. As much as I'd love to explore Paris, I think it's best to stay here, try to get some sleep, and leave before dawn. Why don't we research the address tonight? Maybe we can get a leg up for the morning."

She nodded, looking less despondent as she focused on my idea. "We should look at the hotels in the area. He must be staying somewhere."

I nodded, turning to smile at her. For someone worried about a loved one, she was doing a remarkable job of thinking logically. Logic wasn't a trait I'd have associated with an opera singer but, then again, music and math were supposed to be linked somehow.

Either way, her perseverance was making me respect her even more. How had I been lucky enough to be assigned to her in the first place?

A faint tingle of my finding ability zinged me. There was something I was missing about her and this mission, but I doubted it was something I could ask my superiors, so I decided to get started. I knew enough to believe the answers would come when it was time, and if we were going the right way, I'd know sooner or later.

"Why don't we get room service? I find it easier to concentrate on a full stomach."

Shrugging, Robin passed me the hotel menu over to peruse, then took a quick look herself before calling in our order. I pulled out my laptop, placing it on the desk.

"It looks like the address you found belongs to a bookstore, but there's a few others in the town as well. Most open at nine or ten."

"If the town is about five hours away, we should leave around four. That way we'll be there first thing."

She looked satisfied with the time but I winced. With the time change and jet lag, five a.m. was not going to be pretty.

"That will give us enough time to get more coffee." When she tilted her head, a confused look on her face, I smiled. "It's a small town. Not only will I need coffee to stay awake if we head out that early, but we might get lucky, and overhear locals discussing unusual events. Early morning gossip is always the best."

She opened her mouth but closed it as understanding sank in. "Which is why old men go for coffee all morning and seem to know everything, even though they never leave their chairs."

I chuckled at the comparison. "Exactly. If France is any-thing like Canada, we'll also get younger locals stopping to grab a coffee before work. We may even see the bookstore owners or employees. I find you can learn a lot from people-watching, especially if you appear to be focused on some-thing else." I winked.

Robin's eyes widened slightly before her eyelashes flut-tered half-closed, a trace of pink coloring her cheeks. I re-alized what I'd done, and cleared my throat before quickly changing the subject.

"Er, also, the town has an old museum. There may be some old artifacts there if the bookstores don't pan out. It sounds like the city was important about a thousand years ago, so even though it's declined since then, it could be worth looking there. Your dad is looking for an old code-book, right?"

Robin nodded. "Yes, one no one knew existed before now. I'm guessing it's at least five hundred-years-old."

"So, bookstores, museums, and possibly antique stores would be the most likely places he'd go to pick up an old book."

She nodded and leaned closer, looking over my shoulder as I scrolled through the establishments in the town that fit the narrow criteria. By the time room service arrived, we'd written down about fifteen places and covered the entire area.

We moved to the table to eat but after a few minutes of watching her push her salad around her plate, I set my fork down. She'd been fine before the food came. Had I done or said something to upset her?

"What's wrong?"

She shrugged listlessly, pushing a walnut from her Waldorf to the other side of the plate without looking up. "Nothing, it's just..."

Suddenly, she glared at me, her eyes practically shooting blue flames as she waved a hand around at nothing in particular. "It's not fair. I'm even more confused now than I was when I started. How could he not use his Visa or phone since leaving Paris? I wish I knew where he was."

I leaned over, catching her hand and stilling it. I wanted to offer comfort, as well as protect myself from her fork, which had already come dangerously close to my face. I squeezed gently.

"It's not fair," I agreed. "Your dad is mixed up with something very dangerous, whether he knew it at the time or not. I believe he's a good man, which is why I'm helping you. Try not to focus on the negatives—we know more now than when you were in Montreal, and more than we did an hour ago."

She sighed, letting some of the tension out of her shoulders, but left her hand where it was. That small allowance told me more than it should have.

When she spoke, her eyes glittered with unshed tears. "Yeah, I know. You're right. I'm frustrated, but I'm also furious with him and feel bad about it. How could he do this to me?"

I didn't have an answer. I didn't know what I'd do if either of my parents went missing, but I remembered how disconcerting it had been to find out my dad wasn't who he'd always pretended to be. What would I have done if I'd found out he was a secret agent because he'd gone missing? I could only hope my parents never got a phone call saying I'd been killed on a mission.

Reminded of the reason I couldn't let my emotions get away from me, I focused on calming Robin down instead of doing what I wanted to. "Look, it's been a long day. With your audition and lesson this morning, not to mention jet lag, you're probably too exhausted to think straight. I'll set my alarm for four and we'll get an early start. The best thing we can do now is get some rest."

Her lip trembled, but she raised her chin. "I know. I'm fine. Thanks again for helping. I still can't believe you're willing to give up your vacation for me."

I could feel my cheeks heat with a combination of embarrassment and guilt. No way could I tell her my vacation wasn't a vacation and I was doing my job sticking close to her. The truth would undo any trust she had in me. How could I explain my reasons without telling her the truth or making her suspicious?

I looked into her eyes and knew there was something I could tell her. If I was brave enough.

"I know it's a little unusual, considering we just met and most people wouldn't drop everything like this..." I paused to look down at her hand, still resting beneath mine on the table. She hadn't made any attempts to extricate it. I hoped it meant she trusted me.

"But?" Her eyes were wide.

A smile crept across my face as I looked at her fresh, delicate features. "But, I like you. When I bumped into you on the plane, I wasn't expecting to meet anyone. The moment I saw you though it felt like I was meant to be by your side. I know it's totally corny and all, but maybe it's part of my gift. Or, maybe it's fate."

I knew how dumb I sounded, but strangely, she didn't seem to care.

Her eyes lit up before she lowered them, looking through her lashes as she shyly admitted, "That's, um...it's kind of how I feel too. Normally, I'd shut down a guy if I thought they were hitting on me. But this—you're—different."

We stared at each other for a long moment. I broke eye contact first to look down at our hands. She'd shifted slightly to link her fingers with mine, and the connection made it impossible to think straight. With our fingers laced together, an image of a beach flashed through my mind. Suddenly, I knew why she seemed so familiar.

This was the girl I'd dreamed of so many years ago. Robin was the woman I'd been meant to find.

Chapter 12 Mark

It was hard to fall asleep after that revelation.

With such close proximity to Robin, I couldn't get her off my mind. Even though I'd been following her for weeks, something about the fact only one wall stood between us now made for a restless night. By the time the early light of dawn peeked through the curtain, I wasn't sure I'd managed to get any sleep at all.

Rolling over, I turned the alarm off before it could ring, and headed to the kitchenette to brew coffee. Once that goal was achieved, I opened the curtains to look out over the city. From the fifteenth floor of the hotel, Paris spread out around me.

I hadn't been lying when I'd told Robin I'd always dreamed of visiting and now the moment was surreal, watching the sun rise over the city was like being punched in the gut by that dream. It was breathtaking; so similar to Montréal, yet completely different. Like an older, more sophisticated sister.

A faint sound caught my attention and I whirled, instantly on guard, but relaxing when I saw Robin yawning as she exited her room, stretching her arms above her head and inadvertently flashing a hint of creamy, white skin when her shirt raised several inches above her waistband.

Averting my eyes, I returned to the kitchen and lifted a cup from the counter, wiggling it at her. "Coffee?"

She suppressed another yawn as she accepted the cup and shambled her way to stand beside me at the counter. "Any milk or cream? Mostly so I don't burn my tongue."

She smiled her thanks when I handed her a creamer, then closed her eyes as she sipped the finished product. When she sighed her pleasure, I forced myself to ignore the warmth pooling in my stomach.

I swallowed hard. "Did you want to grab food downstairs, or find something to eat on the way?"

She opened her eyes again, and they were still soft from sleep. I fought back a groan. Food was not what I wanted to grab right now. *Down boy. You need to focus.*

"My stomach isn't ready for food yet. Maybe later. I didn't sleep much last night. I hope I didn't keep you up with my tossing and turning."

I shook my head, trying not to think about tossing her in bed. "No, you didn't. Sorry to hear that. Hopefully, you'll be able to catch up on your rest after we find your dad. I'm ready to go whenever you are." I pointed out the tiny paper cups beside the coffee maker. "You can bring extra for the ride if you need. I have a travel mug, so I'm good to drive if you want to try to snooze a bit."

She shook her head. "I've never been able to sleep in the car, so I'll take a cup for the ride for sure. Give me five minutes to brush my teeth and pack, then I'll be ready to go."

Moments later, we were maneuvering the streets of Paris with the car we'd had the concierge rent from a nearby dealership the night before. Traffic was light this early, and I was happy for the map function on my phone. How had people ever managed to navigate with old school paper maps when only half awake?

Every now and then, Robin pointed out a landmark as we drove, but otherwise, we traveled in a companionable silence. The farther we went, the more I hoped we'd find her dad the moment we arrived. I wanted my mission to be over so I could get to know her better without hiding anything. As soon as the case was over, I wanted to ask her out, without any lies between us.

She had a quiet beauty that wasn't flashy, the kind I imagined would be equally present at fifty or eighty, but it was her personality that drew me most of all. Although quiet, she'd shown strength and intelligence, and the flashes of humor she'd shared with me were even more impressive under the circumstances. When I realized how my thoughts were straying, I turned my attention back to the road. Luckily, Robin wasn't a mind reader like my godfather, Rob, so she had no idea the way my thoughts were spinning over her.

At least, I hoped not.

I was relieved when she spoke, confirming my theory. "How much longer? Should we try to arrange a hotel before we get there?"

I looked at the time of arrival on my phone. "We should be there soon. Probably best to catch our bearings first. If we find his trail, and he's already gone, we don't want to be stuck with a room we won't use."

She sighed. "Good point. Okay, so we're starting at the café next to the bookstore?"

She raised her eyebrows in question and I nodded, turning my eyes to the road again with effort.

"Yes, we'll go in and get a coffee and breakfast if you're in the mood. Maybe we'll get lucky and overhear something. The bookstore opens at nine, so we'll have a little time before we can check it out."

I glanced over and caught her nod, but she continued to look out her window. She appeared thoughtful, but calm. Considering the level of danger we could be walking into, I was impressed by her fortitude once more.

Soon, we entered the town. It was a challenge keeping to the directions my phone told me, because I wanted to explore the side streets of the old French town. Every building drew my attention but forced my urge to detour down and stuck to the plan. After a few more turns, I parked near the bookstore and we got out, crossing the street to the café without difficulty.

I remained on high alert the entire time, scanning the buildings and street. Nothing appeared suspicious or dangerous, but I restrained an urge to physically shadow Robin, knowing she'd think I was crazy if I suddenly started acting like a bodyguard.

The coffee shop itself was a hub of activity, which didn't help with surveillance, but we found a table in the back. Robin went to save it while I ordered, giving me a chance to examine the faces around me. I relaxed slightly when I saw the usual and nothing but. The early morning crowd composed of schoolteachers, bankers, and a pair of teenagers who were clearly infatuated with each other. They giggled and leaned their heads together while staring deep into each other's eyes. Smiling as I watched them, I straightened up when I realized I was jealous of them. I wanted to sit with Robin like that.

When it was finally my turn, I placed my order, grateful I'd learned French in school and kept it up with courses since. While it was obvious it wasn't my first language, the barista was friendly and seemed to appreciate the effort. Far friendlier than the last café barista had been. I flashed her a smile as I took our order and headed to our table, noticing her faint blush as I walked away.

I repressed a chuckle and tried not to let it go to my head. While I only had eyes for Robin and keeping her safe, it was nice to know a stranger thought I was attractive.

"Is that a chocolate chip croissant?"

Robin looked at the plate I set on the table with an expression of longing and I winked.

"Must be your lucky day. The barista said it was the last one. And here's your cappuccino, m'lady. With two sugars, as requested."

She almost wiggled with happiness as she took a long sip from her cup and sighed. "This might be the best part of my trip so far," she admitted, shooting me a wry smile.

"The coffee?" When I raised an eyebrow, she nodded. "That sucks, but I can't blame you. What with an audition and your dad's disappearance, it hasn't been much of a holiday."

She nodded. "Yeah, I was looking forward to my lesson after the audition, but I couldn't pay attention. I'd really wanted to meet her." Shrugging off her disappointment and taking a bite of the croissant she added, "Maybe I'll have another chance, some day."

I took a bite out of my own Croque Monsieur and watched her sip her cappuccino. My ears perked up when I overheard a man chatting with the barista. They were speaking French, but I was able to catch most of their conversation.

"It's been a long week."

The barista gave him a sympathetic smile. "I'm sure it has. Hey, didn't you say you were meeting a Canadian a few days ago? That must have been a nice change to your routine. What happened?"

The man shook his head. "I don't know. He never arrived."

She shook her head. "Bizarre. I remember you were excited to see him, and I was looking forward to hearing about your visit."

I turned my head a fraction, just enough to catch the man's glum expression without appearing to be eavesdropping. Robin stilled, and I knew she was listening too.

"Yes, it was strange. Not at all like him. But the worst part? Now I cannot even find the book I was going to sell him. It is vanished into the air. *Voila*! I am left with *rien*!"

Her eyes widened. "Do you think...?"

Every muscle in my body stiffened at the look they exchanged. When the man said goodbye without further conversation, I shifted to catch Robin's eye. Without discussion, we finished our food and hurried out after him.

Doing my best to look casual while keeping him in sight, I turned to Robin. "Good coffee?"

She blinked at the unexpected question. "Oh, er, I um, yes."

I draped my arm around her shoulder, which served the dual purpose of keeping her close and hopefully, making us look like an innocent young couple going about their day.

"Great. That means you'll have enough energy to enjoy a stroll."

Her shoulders stiffened when my arm touched her, but when she melted into the fake embrace, it felt real. I swallowed hard and made myself look at the man we were tailing. He crossed the street toward the bookstore at the address on the rubbing from the hotel room. Could he be St. Clair? When he unlocked the door, I decided it didn't matter. He must be the owner or at least a manager. Someone important enough to have a key. That, combined with the odd way his conversation with the barista had ended, made me certain he knew something. We needed to speak with him. Was he the one responsible for the disappearance of an absent-minded professor from Montreal?

Without knowing if we could trust him, I'd have to go with my gut. Right now, I my finding ability was nudging me onward. The way he'd paled in the café had activated a small tingle, and something about the way he'd seemed more confused and bothered about the book vanishing than his visitor not showing stuck with me. I needed to question him and find out how he fit into the puzzle.

We took a leisurely route to the corner, waiting at the lights and intentionally window shopping at a few clothing stores between the café and our destination. Robin did an admirable job appearing interested in a few accessories and I steered her into an open stationary store where we browsed over notebooks for a few minutes.

Finally, it was time.

I held out my arm for her, telling myself it was just for show, but the pink blooms on her cheeks and the way her breath caught softly in her throat almost made me forget the truth.

The smell of old books assailed my senses as a door chime announced our entry. The man from the coffee shop stood behind a desk at the front and looked up with a smile. I assessed him with a quick, clinical detachment, and immediately dismissed him as a threat. With his professorial jacket in tweed, leather patches on the elbows, and wire-frame glasses sliding down his nose, it was safe to say he was unlikely to overpower us.

He pushed up the glasses as he greeted us with a cheery, "*Bonjour.*"

Robin smiled back. "*Bonjour.*"

The man gestured at the shelves around the store as he spoke in French. "Please, look around. We have many objects of interest here. Is there a particular book or genre you are looking for?"

He stepped around the counter, his hands clasped in front of him, an expectant look on his face. How busy was a store like this? It was a nice little town, but I didn't think bookstores were all that popular these days.

"I am looking for anything on the history of music. Particularly opera, or the Baroque period."

When Robin switched to English, his eyes widened before he replied in kind, smiling broadly. "Ah, tourists? Welcome, welcome, nice to see you! I have just received a shipment of books from a private collection. To my great *plaisir*, the estate came from an opera aficionado, and includes several volumes that may have what you are searching for. I haven't finished cataloguing the collection, but you are welcome to look. If any catch your interest, I will need to add them to the system of course, but would be happy to negotiate a price."

"*Absoluement*. I would love to look at them."

While I knew she was playing a role, her interest appeared genuine and I remained silent as the man led us to a table at the back. Several boxes of books were open and spilling out. He moved a small box off the top, placed it in front of himself, and began pulling out several thick volumes with a triumphant look.

"I am sorting according to subject matter, but much work is still ahead of me. The shipment arrived just last week, you see. I am certain I'd seen music books. I was expecting another buyer a few days ago, but he never showed." He frowned briefly then shook his head, and I had the impression he was talking to himself as much as to us. "Oh well. Their loss is your gain."

I leapt at the opening. "I'm sorry, another buyer? Perhaps we should leave them if they're already spoken for."

Robin dropped the eager smile she'd been wearing, replacing it with a disappointed frown. "You're right. I'd feel horrible if I scooped someone else. What if they're still interested?"

We both looked at the man and he shrugged. "Normally, I would give him time, but he was supposed to be here four days ago. I called him the moment the books came in—there was one I was certain he would want, but..."

He paused, looking around with narrowed eyes as if ensuring no one was listening. I followed his gaze, seeing no one. After he was satisfied we were alone, he leaned closer, and with wide eyes, dropped his voice to something just above a whisper. "This man, he's usually a very good customer. Reliable. But I've tried to reach him several times since our appointment on Tuesday, and *rien*. He has disappeared. Even more disturbing— the book he was going to purchase has vanished as well."

I tilted my head to the side. "Do you think he stole it?"

The man's hand flew to his chest and he gave me an affronted look. "Stolen? Hardly! I've known him the better part of twenty years, and consider him a close friend. He's one of my best customers, very considerate. *Mais non*, something has happened. The moment I saw the book tucked in with the others, *Je savais exactement* what I was looking at."

He was barely audible now, and his eyes were as wide as they could get behind the thick lenses as they darted around the room. He looked like a frightened owl.

Seeing his distress, Robin placed her hand on his, and spoke in a soothing voice as if trying to calm a wild animal. "You seem upset. Can we help you? Are you worried whatever happened to your friend might happen to you?"

I managed to suppress a wince at her forthright manner. There was no way that would work on someone so skittish. But to my consternation, the man dropped into one of the chairs beside the table and began to rub his forehead.

"I don't know. Perhaps I imagined everything— the phone call, the book, the meeting." He shrugged helplessly, continuing to stare at the dark wood in front of him. "He was to meet me at *neuf heures du matin*, so I came to open at eight. I placed the book on the table, and went to make *un café*. When I heard the bell, I came out from the kitchen."

He pointed to the door behind him. It was barely visible through the swinging door, but there was just enough light to allow a glimpse of a fridge in the space between the doors.

"By the time I got back to the table, the book was gone. There was *personne ici.*"

Robin shook her head. "Maybe someone else stole the book?"

The man disagreed, waving one hand sharply. "*Impossible*. My bookstore may not have fancy alarms, but I do have security cameras. It takes me less than five seconds to get out from the back to this table, even without hurrying. No one was here. After this, I replayed the tape maybe twenty times. *Une minute* the book was on the table, *le suivant*, it was gone."

An unexpected shakiness filled me at his words and a familiar tingle made me shift uncomfortably as my ability told me the answer I'd hoped not to find. He wasn't a man who joked, or a man who believed in the unseeable. He was telling the truth, which meant that somehow, on the same day Robin's dad had disappeared, the book he'd been after had vanished as well.

Chapter 13 Robin

"**M**ay I look at the tape? From the security camera?"

Out of the corner of my eye, Mark's head jerked. His eyebrow raised as he looked at me. In all fairness, I was a little perplexed by my response as well. It wasn't like me to ask a stranger something so daring, but anything that could help me find my dad, including a second set of eyes on security tapes, was fair game. Sometimes, a second set of eyes could make all the difference.

The shopkeeper blinked then shrugged. "I don't see why not. It's not like the video is highly classified information."

A smile tugged at my lips. He was trying to make a joke but appeared spooked by the odd situation. That fit my mood perfectly. I was every bit as disturbed at the thought a book could vanish all by itself. As I thought about it more, the memory of a long-ago day with my dad intruded.

We'd been reading by the fire, and I had asked if he believed in magic. He'd fallen silent, and at first, I thought I'd made him angry. But instead of answering one way or another, he'd deflected, giving me a vague platitude. That had been around the same time the mysterious box had come in the mail, when the odd dreams of a mermaid had happened. When Melissa and I had first become friends.

I hadn't thought of that conversation in years. Why would a missing book bring back the memory now? I'd long since chalked the weirdness of my last year of high school up to jealousy and stress. Nothing remotely magical or strange had happened in almost four years. Could my dad's disappearance somehow be related to that time? And if so, how? If something unusual had happened to him, I didn't know if I should be more, or less, concerned. Was a magical disappearance a better alternative than one orchestrated by a biker gang? I wasn't confident it was, but hopefully he was safe either way.

I sank into an empty chair. Mark sat next to me, placing a warm hand on top of mine. I looked down absently, appreciating the weight of it as the shopkeeper retrieved an ancient TV with a VHS player.

At my startled look, he took his glasses off and wiped them with a smile. "It's not fancy, but it works for what I need. Until it dies, I see no need to upgrade to a fancy system, which would cost an arm and a foot, *bien sûr.*"

I mumbled something in agreement as he popped the tape in. We watched the small TV screen with the rabbit ears and I was struck by how odd it was to have a TV in the back corner of a bookstore.

He caught my eye and smiled. "Would it surprise you to hear I live here? What can I say—I'm an old bachelor who loves books. A few years ago, I sublet my place to save money. Now I live on the premises when I'm not traveling for work, of course."

Mark leaned forward, his gaze sharpening as he studied the man. "So, with few exceptions, you're always in the building?"

He nodded. "*Exactement.* I usually go to the café across the street to get the paper, along with my morning coffee and croissant." His eyes twinkled under bushy grey eyebrows. "Of course, I could make the coffee here, but I enjoy my morning interaction with the baristas. It gives me a chance to stretch my legs and talk with other people. I tend to become overly focused on my work at times, and small routines are important to keep one connected to the outside world."

I nodded, thinking he had a lot in common with my dad. "I just realized we never formally introduced ourselves. My name is Robin, and this is my friend, Mark. I came to Paris to meet my father, but he's missing. I haven't heard from him since he left Montréal. I think he was on his way to see you."

The shopkeeper blinked. "Your father? To meet me?" Comprehension dawned and his eyes narrowed as he took in my appearance. He moved back in his chair as suspicion replaced his previous openness.

I felt awful and rushed to apologize. "I didn't mean to mislead you. I really am interested in the opera books, and I did have an audition in Paris. My trip was set up long ago, so when my dad got a commission to find a certain book near Paris, we had planned to meet afterward. But he hasn't returned any of my calls, emails, or texts since he arrived in France."

The shopkeeper sat back, his face pale. "Your father is Dr. Brian Locksley?"

I nodded. "I wasn't trying to trick you. His trail stops here, at this address. But I had no idea you knew each other before today."

He leaned back, taking off his glasses and placing them on the table beside him with a deep sigh. "We've been friends since our university days. It is my error. I should have known who you were sooner."

He gave me a weary smile, and then put the glasses back on to take another look at my face. I felt like a bug under a microscope beneath his shrewd examination, which his kindly smile did nothing to relieve.

"My name is David St. Clair. He has spoken of you over the years with pride, but the last time I saw your picture you were a still young girl. You've grown into quite a lovely young lady, if you don't mind me saying."

I smiled at the awkward compliment, trying to rein in my excitement upon hearing his name. He *was* the man my dad had been coming to see. At least we were on the right track, even if he didn't know where my dad was now.

"Thank you. He's never mentioned you to me, but then again, he rarely speaks of his book contacts, only the books." I snorted, amusement unexpectedly bubbling up as I recalled how secretive my dad could be about his book finding excursions. "In fact, as a child, I sometimes thought my dad was like Indiana Jones, but for books. He was always jetting off between classes to search for rare and unusual editions, often coming home with some new injury, or no suitcase. Of course, he never said what he'd been up to, so I was left creating my own, admittedly wild, explanations."

David laughed. "Well, knowing your father, it's possible some of your explanations hit rather close to the mark. He was a bit of a wild man in his younger years, but he's mellowed since becoming a single parent."

Before I could process his words, Mark interrupted. "Why do you think he wanted this particular book?"

I'd almost forgotten he was there, even with his hand protectively on top of mine. Somehow, during the conversation, it had begun to feel like it belonged there, and with effort, I forced myself to consider the question Mark had asked. It was something I wanted to know as well.

David considered it momentarily, shrugging as he replied. "He didn't say anything other than it was a rare book he'd been after forever. I didn't think much about it. Truthfully, it's a small and rather boring item, and I didn't expect it to fetch much. I hadn't done a thorough examination of it prior to its disappearance though, so perhaps I underestimated the value."

I slumped in my chair, disappointed he didn't know more. I'd hoped he'd say it was a spell book, or something equally bizarre. Given the situation, almost anything would have seemed reasonable.

My eyes landed on the TV. I gestured to it, feeling it judging us as it sat there; forlorn rabbit ears twisted to either side. "Do you have the security footage from when the book went missing?"

He shifted in his chair. "*Bien sûr.* Of course. Let me get the tape to the right place."

I watched as lines of static crossed the screen, reminding me of old VHS movies I'd watched as a kid.

He stopped it and hit play. "See here? This is when I opened the box and put all the books on the table. Then I went into the back," he pointed. We watched as he retraced his steps. "Now, *regarder*. It only lasts a second."

I squinted, but didn't see it the first time. He rewound the tape and played it again. Then again. Finally, on the fourth viewing, I saw it. The book was dark blue, plainly covered, and about the size of an ordinary paperback. One moment, it was on the table. David placed a few other books down, then turned and went into the back through the swinging doors. Between one blink and the next, the book vanished.

In the place where the book had been was the faintest hint of shimmer in the air, almost like dust sparkling in sunshine, but there was no sun lighting up the table. Two seconds later, the video David returned, looked around, then began shouting soundlessly before racing to the front door.

He let the rest of the video play. It was apparent when the video version of him walked back to the table he was utterly confused. Without knowing more about doctoring tapes, I didn't see anything obvious suggesting it been faked. There was also nothing to explain why David had heard the bell chime, as no one else had been caught on camera.

"So? Is this helpful? I'm open to your ideas. I was there and still have no clue what happened." He looked at me, then Mark, waiting for an answer.

What could I say? Other than I agreed no one appeared to have been present, I had no idea what had transpired.

"Yes, actually. This has been most helpful."

I was relieved when Mark answered, but I wasn't sure seeing the video had helped at all. Other than meeting the man my dad had written on the paper, we didn't know anything more than when we'd entered.

David nodded, giving me a smile tinged with sadness. "I wish I could assist you further, but as I said, it isn't like Brian to miss an appointment. If he hasn't contacted you, I am certain something significant has happened. I hope for his sake, and yours, young lady, that he is in hiding. It is truly the strangest occurrence I can recall."

What had my dad discovered? After meeting David and viewing the tape, I was starting to think something far more mysterious than a simple kidnapping was at play. But if something paranormal was at work, what chance did I have of finding him?

"Is there anywhere he may have gone if he was in danger?"

I was grasping at straws now, but maybe he'd discussed other findings with David in the past. Otherwise, the bookstore was another dead end.

He thought for a moment, humming lightly under his breath before shaking his head. "Maybe. There is one place he mentioned once, long ago. He told me he wanted a cottage by the ocean, close to where his ancestors are from. He mentioned the town, but I've long since forgotten it." He looked mildly embarrassed as he admitted, "It was one of those conversations you have late at night, after a bottle or two of red wine. He may have said more, but that's all that comes to mind."

I stood up from the chair, extending my hand. "Thank you for being so helpful. If I leave my number, will you call if you remember anything else? It would mean a lot."

He stood, coming around the desk. "Of course. Pardon me for asking, but have you reported this to the police?"

I looked at Mark, uncertain what to say, feeling grateful when he smoothly stepped in.

"Of course. But I recommend being cautious if anyone else comes looking. The benefactor who wanted this book is not a nice man. He might send someone else for the book who is less... amiable than Professor Locksley. It might be a good time to close the store for inventory."

David's eyes widened, and I watched a look pass between the two men before he agreed, as if he'd been planning to do just that. "Yes, in fact, I need time for processing all these new books. And since it's midweek, it's slow right now. In fact, I'm closed until Saturday. How remiss of me to forget to change the sign."

His words were hasty, and a smile flickered on Mark's face.

"Perfect. Give us a call if you hear anything. Here's my number, for good measure. Be careful."

David nodded and escorted us out. "I will. Take care. Robin?" I turned to the aging man, finding him solemn. "I hope you find your dad soon. He's been a good friend, and I know him well enough to be certain there are very few reasons he'd keep this from you, the main one being your safety. Or, if he couldn't tell you. Remember, not everything is how it appears." He tilted his head toward the TV. "Especially when it comes to old books."

I nodded, walking out into a fresh morning mist as the cheerful tinkle of bells echoed behind us, as if mocking me for leaving with more questions than answers.

Chapter 14 Robin

The air was heavy and pressed down with a sense of foreboding. Was there a storm coming, or was it what I'd learned inside the store which made the sky look so gray? I turned to Mark, hoping he had another idea. I was spooked and had zero ideas left. "Now what?"

He looked down, and for a moment, I thought he was somewhere else. Finally, he blinked, cocking his head a little. "Where are your ancestors from?"

David had said something about ancestors earlier, but all I knew was what my dad had told me, which wasn't much. "I'm not sure. I mean, I've always considered us to be British origin, with the last name. Scotland, somewhere."

He shook his head. "Mr. St. Clair said near the sea. Could it be somewhere near here?"

I nodded. "Perhaps, if you go way back. Our ancestors went with William the Conqueror to Scotland in 1066 from Normandy, but far as I know, I haven't had relatives in France for a thousand years. Maybe longer."

He frowned. "Do you know where in Normandy they were from?"

I looked around, gesturing to the street. "Technically, they could have been from here. But wouldn't he have told

David he wanted a cottage somewhere in Normandy if they were from here?"

When his eyebrows drew together, giving him a perplexed look, I explained. "Some of our ancestors took the last name Mesnières because they were from this exact region. They were the ones, according to the scant bit I know of my family history, who took part in William the Conqueror's invasion of Britain. Most went on to live in the Scottish Highlands before moving to Canada and the US in the 1850s during the Clearances."

"Huh. So do you think he's somewhere by the ocean in France, or did he mean other country?"

It was my turn for confusion. "Like where?"

"Maybe your dad isn't in France anymore. Maybe he went to Scotland, where you say your ancestors were last known to reside."

My eyes widened. "It never crossed my mind he'd leave France, but then again, everything about this is weird. Knowing my dad, if he was having a rambling conversation with a friend while drinking, he'd want to retrace the entire journey of our ancestors from Normandy right to where they left Scotland for Canada."

Mark raised an eyebrow. "Should we be looking for evidence of his departure in that case?"

I clenched my hands, trying to keep my impatience at bay. It was a valid question, but I had no idea where to begin. "His Visa trail ended the day after he arrived in France. There's been no purchases since, except for one cash advance, which was hardly enough to cover the cost of a plane ticket, let alone everything else he'd need after leaving Paris. I hate to admit it, but I think we're at a dead end."

I fought the tears that threatened to spill over as Mark looked around. He gestured to the rental car, then put one arm around me as he gently guided me over to the passenger's side.

"Let's talk in the vehicle. I've got an idea, but I'd rather speak where no one can eavesdrop."

At the look in his eye, my paranoia crept back in. With everything going on it was hard to believe I'd forgotten, even for a second, that people could be after me. A thought struck, and caused me to pause with my hand on the door. "Is it possible someone bugged the car while we were inside the store?"

He glanced at me, nodded his head yes, and answered in the negative. "Absolutely not. We weren't gone long enough. Hey, what do you say to a bit of sightseeing?"

I narrowed my eyes as I tried to understand his mixed message. Yes, he did think it was possible? No, he didn't, and this was an attempt to humor me? I gave up and decided to follow along. "Um, sure. I think the guidebook said there are a few historical monuments nearby."

This time, his body language and words were congruent. "Perfect. We can get food after we check them out. I'm getting hungry—I'm a growing boy, after all!"

I couldn't tell if he was trying to reassure me or deliberately going out of his way to sound cheery, but if the vehicle had been bugged, his answer was tailor-made to deflect a listener from any of my paranoid musings.

"All that walking is making me hungry too." I smiled, but didn't attempt to match the *joie de vivre* in his voice.

As much as I was burning to discuss what we'd learned, I buckled up in silence as Mark googled the local tourist attractions with his phone. Then, still without a word, we began to drive, traveling without speaking to a small bridge with a historical plaque beside it. Mark parked the car and got out, issuing another cheerful invitation for me to join him.

I wasn't surprised to see we were the only ones there, but curiosity won over concerns of getting rained on. I followed him to the bridge, wrapping my arms against the chill air. The sky was still as gloomy as it had been when we'd left the bookstore, and despite the fact it was technically spring, it wasn't an inviting day for exploring the countryside.

Once we reached the midway point on the bridge, Mark stopped and rested his arms on the wood, leaning over and gazing out at the river as if he had no cares in the world. Maybe he didn't. Had this been his plan for the day all along? I drew my eyebrows together and crossed my arms tighter as I watched him, a trickle of unease growing at his nonchalance.

Abruptly he spoke. "I don't think the car was bugged, but how would you feel about trading it in anyway?"

I frowned, even more confused by the mismatch between his relaxed posture and unexpected question. "What do you mean?"

He turned his head, giving me a mischievous smile. "One of the things I discovered on the way to our fascinating tourist destination." He gestured at the quaint but hardly exciting view. "Is that the rental agency we got this car from has a local branch. I believe our car obtained a flat tire on the bumpy road to this old bridge, and we're on such a tight schedule we need to have it replaced for something sturdier."

My frown deepened. "Changing a tire is pretty easy. I'm sure they could do that in about twenty minutes. Hardly worth doing the paperwork for."

He nodded. "They could, true, but I'm thinking an SUV would be better if we're driving to Scotland today."

I almost choked as I drew in a breath. "Say what now? Scotland? Is that even possible?"

"Well, I was thinking of ways your dad could have gotten away without creating a paper trail. Driving is one. Unless I'm mistaken, you can now drive the channel between France and England. I'm warning you now though— it's a long drive. At least fourteen hours without stops."

The idea hadn't crossed my mind before he said it, but now I recalled a movie where Matt Damon had been a spy fleeing from people. Driving did seem like the most under-the-radar way to go. Once I remembered that movie, several other examples of spies driving through the night to escape pursuers came back to me.

"I guess. Unless, of course, he got there using magic."

I'd meant it as a joke, so when Mark straightened abruptly, turning a solemn face toward me, I wasn't prepared for the wave of uneasiness that hollowed out a pit in my stomach. I wanted to take the words back.

But before I could, he nodded thoughtfully. "That's another possibility of course. But unless you're holding back some serious family secrets, you don't have that ability, and neither do I. So, if your father did somehow manage to teleport himself, either with the book or via some other method, it isn't an option open to us."

I shook my head, bewildered by the turn in the conversation. "Magic? What? Don't get me wrong, things are really freaky right now, and I can't explain what happened to the book or my dad, but did you seriously just say magic?"

I rubbed my palms up and down my arms briskly, telling myself I was feeling chilled by the weather, not the discussion. For some reason, I was reminded of the book on curses and magic I'd found in my last year of high school. Some unexplainable things had happened then, too, but I'd managed to put those events behind me, chalking them up to anxiety dreams related to graduation. Everything had been so normal for the last few years I thought I'd been overreacting.

But now, as I looked at Mark, something in his eyes made me wonder. Deja-vu swamped me as I asked him a question I was pretty sure I didn't want the answer to. "Are you saying you believe in magic?"

His gaze slid away. He stared at the river for several long moments, two unexpected spots of color dotting his cheeks. Feeling awkward and unsure, I hugged my arms tightly hugged to my chest, but wasn't sure if it for warmth or protection now.

In the space of a few short hours, I'd gone from thinking my dad was at the mercy of violent criminals to wondering what the hell I'd stepped into. Magic? Disappearing books? Disappearing fathers? For the first time, I thought I preferred the idea of my dad being kidnapped by a biker gang. At least that could exist in the real world. This new scenario was something I didn't have a map for. How would I find my way if magic was involved?

After an interminable silence, Mark rubbed his forehead. He turned to search my face before he replied slowly, as if preparing himself for how I would react. "Yeah, I do. Believe in magic. Well, in the paranormal anyway. I don't think it's the way we see it in the movies or anything, but I like to keep an open mind. I've dealt with more than one situation in life I'd have a hard time explaining any other way. After watching that video and seeing the book vanish on camera, I'm willing to entertain the possibility that something I can't explain may be happening."

I shook my head. I didn't want to believe what he was saying. "There's got to be another explanation. I mean, magic? Surely, if magic existed, we'd know about it by now."

I heard myself pleading, and as if called back by my confusion, memories of my last year of high school intruded again. I'd never been able to figure out if those dreams had been real either, and apparently, they'd been lurking in my subconscious, waiting to rear up again.

He shrugged. "I'm not so sure. Maybe it's like everything else. Some people are great athletes, others are better at math. I imagine magic would be the same. And, like everything to do with humans, if people can't understand how something works, they fear it. Maybe the paranormal is on a 'need to know' basis, and you only need to know if you're involved, or can sense it. Or, maybe it's just a kind of science we don't understand yet."

I looked away, embarrassed. I wanted to discount this idea not only because it contravened the safe and sturdy framework of how I thought the world ran, but also because I was scared about the implications. If magic did exist, it meant everything I knew was different, and the comfortable framework I'd created for my life the way it was completely fell apart.

"Hey, being scared is nothing to be ashamed of."

Mark's warm, calloused fingers gently touched my chin. He tilted my face up and I stared into his sympathetic face, not sure what to say, but wanting to explain myself to him.

"It's just –" I stopped, unable to find the words.

A crooked grin crossed his face. "I get it. It was like that for me the first time I realized what I can do isn't 'normal.'"

I stared into his deep blue eyes. "I don't understand."

My words were hardly more than a whisper, but he'd heard me. He hesitated, dropping his hand as he moved to step back. Without thinking I grabbed it, holding him there. I needed him close while he told me whatever he was about to say.

"I mean, the things—and people—I've found...I shouldn't have been able to find them. There's no way I could have done it without..."

I looked at him, certain my expression was blank. I had the same gut sensation, the same suspicion I remembered having when Melissa had become ill. There was something in the background, beyond my understanding at work. Despite my misgivings, I poked at it, wanting to know anyway. "What do you mean? You can tell me. I promise, I'll believe you."

He rubbed the back of his neck, sighing deeply before reluctantly meeting my eyes. "I get flashes sometimes. Of things I've never seen, sometimes of places I've never been. I'm sure you've heard of police departments using psychics in missing persons cases?"

I waited for him to continue, knowing it was difficult for him to share. I'd never told anyone what I'd seen in my dreams, even if I had tossed the idea of a curse around with Melissa at one point. I'd done my best to brush them away as a vivid imagination, but something told me Mark hadn't been able to do that.

"When my friend went missing, I had a dream that woke me up. But it was more than a dream; I saw him being kidnapped, knew exactly where he'd been taken. I was lucky." A half-smile flickered, then disappeared. "When I told my dad we needed to go to the police, he didn't question me. And that was when I met Rob Avery."

When he paused, I whispered, not wanting to interrupt his narrative, but worried he'd stop before he told me the rest. "What happened next?"

He shrugged. "I told him everything. He said I was something called a 'finder,' whatever that is." He gave a wry smile, this time looking genuinely amused. "I'm not sure I can explain it any better than that. I can find things, but only if I'm supposed to."

"They found your friend?"

He smiled. "They did."

While I had many new questions I wanted answered, like whether he was helping me because he was meant to find my dad, suddenly the only magic I was could focus on was the way my hand tingled. At that moment, I realized I was still holding his hand. Without thinking about the consequences of what I was doing, I stepped closer.

His eyes were so beautiful, I wanted to swim inside them and get lost. I tilted my head for a better view. He stared back for an indefinable moment, and then as if in slow motion, his head lowered.

He stopped when his lips were level with mine. I felt the warmth of his breath against my face and threw caution to the wind. Raising my chin, I captured his lips and the world spun around me.

Chapter 15 Mark

Had I made the first move?

Had she?

The only thing I knew with certainty at that moment was how amazing it felt to have her pressed up against me, her lips moving against mine, her arms around me. I slid my hands around her waist and deepened the kiss, feeling her passion rise to meet mine.

A cool breeze off the river reminded me where we were and I pulled back reluctantly. As amazing as it was to have her in my arms, as much as I yearned to take the moment deeper, now wasn't the time or place. I kept her close as I looked down, watching her eyes flutter open as if she'd just woken up from a dream. I saw the moment she remembered where we were, and her cheeks flushed as her expression sharpened.

When she pulled back, my entire body felt cold, missing the heat of her beside me. I settled for capturing her hand and trapping it between mine. "I'm sorry, I've been wanting to do that since you tripped me on the plane."

I smiled, using humor as a shield. Maybe it could lighten any feelings of awkwardness that inevitably followed a first kiss, not to mention provide a safer path forward than the attraction which had roared to life inside me at her touch.

Her eyes widened, then narrowed as she realized what I'd said. She began to sputter. "I never! Well, I didn't mean... it was an accident!"

I laughed, and just like that, the tension between us melted. She smiled back, and as I continued holding her hand carefully, I hoped she could see the truth in my face.

"I want you to know I won't push. My emotions may have gotten... erm, a little carried away just now, but I'll plead guilty because of the company and the beauty of the surroundings."

She shook her head, managing to maneuver her hand so that she was holding mine back, and gave it a squeeze. "You didn't do anything wrong. I started it. But I can't promise anything. Not until..."

Her voice trailed off and we exchanged a solemn look. I knew she was thinking about her dad and wondered how much more complicated this was going to get. Biting back a sigh, I tried to reassure her.

"I know. We'll find him, I promise. After we trade in the car, we'll head—where did you say your ancestors were from?"

Robin's hair was lifted by the breeze and she brushed it off her face. "All over the Highlands, really, but there is one place my dad speaks about often. Something about it seems to fascinate him, even though I'm not sure we have relatives from there. But I wonder..."

I waited for her to continue, but her gaze slid away. She looked down at the water, her pensive expression telling me she was somewhere else, far away. Finally, she shook her head.

Wrinkling her nose, she gave me a self-deprecating smile. "You'll think I'm crazy."

"I just told you I get visions and find things I shouldn't be able to. Of all people you could tell something to, I'm probably the least likely to think you're crazy."

She chuckled. "Oh, right. That's a fair point. But to be honest, your ability doesn't sound that abnormal. In fact, I'd love to have it—it would come in handy in my house, the way my dad is always losing everything, up to and including his marbles." She gave me a wry grin. "There's an old castle on the Isle of Skye that belongs to Clan Donald, one of the extremely remote ancestral lines on my mother's side. It's said a fierce warrior woman named Scáthach lived there and trained legends, but details are scarce, and mostly written a hundred years after she was supposed to have lived."

"Scáthach? I've never heard of her. How does this relate to your dad if it's your mother's side?"

Robin shrugged. "I'm not sure. It's just a feeling. I've no idea how many of his stories are even remotely accurate, but that one always gnawed at me. He's usually full of more details than I can tolerate, except when it comes to her. But I know it's a place he's always wanted to go, because it has come up repeatedly over the years. I always got the impression he was hoping to find her there, but that's silly." She shook her head. "Nah, you're right. He probably wouldn't head there if he's on the run."

I watched as she turned to gaze out over the water again, trying to hold back a smile at the feel of her hand in mine. It was nice standing together like this, even under the circumstances that led us here.

"Is there somewhere more likely he'd go? Do you have any family currently living in Scotland?"

She didn't answer, seemingly intent on watching a family of ducks passing underneath the bridge. When a few of the ducklings flipped upside down, showing only their little feet and tail feathers, she chuckled. Once they had passed by, she turned and shook her head.

Her eyes were full of doubt. "No one I know of. Other than Skye, my only guess is Scotland in general. Maybe your abilities will kick in when we get closer."

I nodded, wishing it worked like that. "Maybe. For now, it sounds like the Isle of Skye in Scotland is our destination. I find intuition is generally a reasonable substitute for scant information so, if nothing else turns up along the way, we may as well head there."

She straightened from her perch on the bridge, but when she tried to take her hand back I tugged on it gently.

"Is it okay if I keep this while we walk to the car?" I hoped I didn't sound as eager and immature as I felt, but I wasn't ready to let her go. If all I could have right now was her hand, I didn't want to give it up.

"Um, sure. I'd like that."

Her shy smile made me feel ten feet tall and I pulled her closer to my side as we headed back to the car.

WE STOPPED AT A GAS station to fill the tank, buying bottled water and snacks for the road. When we were a block from the rental agency in front of a construction site, I stopped and got out again. Looking around to make sure no one was watching, I planted a nail from a loose board I'd picked up on the bridge into the sidewall of the back passenger tire.

It was the best I could come up with on short notice. I hoped it was enough to allow us a replacement without being dinged too much for damages. In the short distance from where I'd stabbed the nail in the tire until we reached the rental place, the tire deflated just enough to be almost flat by the time we arrived.

I parked and turned to Robin. "Ready to trade in the car?"

She nodded, pressing her lips firmly together, a determined glint in her eyes. "Of course."

We took our belongings with us. Less than twenty minutes later, we'd completed the customary red tape and were on the road with a brand-new Toyota built for the Highlands. Apparently, driving to the islands of Scotland was a life-long dream for the woman behind the desk. When Robin had mentioned the possibility of a road trip to Scotland to see castles, the employee had become excited and almost insisted we trade in the vehicle we'd been driving for a more rugged four-wheel drive, completely glossing over the nail damage in her excitement.

I offered to let Robin take the reins, but when she deferred, I settled in for the long drive. We headed along the coast toward the ferry, and I thought about the soldiers who must have traveled the same route. With those solemn thoughts in mind, I glanced at Robin. Her face was drawn and introspective, and I elected not to share my war thoughts. It was unlikely talking about death would take her mind off her missing father, and possibly make things worse. Searching for a more neutral topic, I tried to sound casual and broke the silence.

"What happens after you get home? I mean, are you all done with university? Or are you planning to continue on?"

Turning with a start, she smiled apologetically. "What? Sorry, I didn't hear your question. My mind was... somewhere else."

I waved away her explanation. "As it should be. What's next for you with school? Are you completely finished, now your audition is over?"

She exhaled. "Well, for the year at least. Exams are finished, but I have a concert in two weeks I need to prepare for. I've been accepted for a Masters' for next year, so there's that."

I nodded, wondering if it was wise to keep prodding her. She still seemed distracted and sad, but I couldn't think of anything safer to talk about, and fourteen hours of silence felt like an eternity without conversation of some kind.

"What's your end game then? Masters'? PhD? Or world opera domination, perhaps?"

I did my best to keep the tone of the questions light, hoping the domination bit would get a rise. When I saw a spark of animation in her eyes, my spirits lifted.

"Well, once I've finished with my Masters', I'm hoping to apply for a PhD in a few major opera cities. The more contacts I make, the easier it will be to carve out a career. I'm not a soprano, which counts both for and against me."

She turned, leaning in slightly at my noise of interest. "See, if you're soprano with an amazing voice, lead roles are yours for the picking. There are fewer opportunities for altos in that way, but on the other hand, there aren't as many of us around. In some ways that means less competition. It's the same as for guys, except in reverse. Lots of famous tenors out there, but few good enough to make a name for themselves. I'd love to become the next Lili Chookasian."

She looked at me expectantly, and I grimaced.

"I'm sorry, the name doesn't ring a bell." At her crestfallen expression, I backtracked quickly. "I'd love for you to tell me more about her though. Who is she?"

With that small nudge of encouragement, she was off. I listened with more interest than I'd expected, mostly due to her animated explanations. Her love of the subject was easy to recognize, and I was glad I'd been able to lift her out of her sad contemplation.

By the time we stopped at the port where France looked across the sea, we'd passed several hours in an abridged history of opera class, and her mood was the sunniest it had been since I'd first met her. Getting such an in-depth look at her passion for singing had done nothing to dull my interest in her, and if anything, made me crave more.

I cleared my throat as I looked at the choppy sea. I'd heard you could see England on a clear day, but it was far too cloudy right now. The waves crashed on the shore and I had to raise my voice to be heard above them. "Are you okay to stop here? We need gas and I'm getting hungry. I thought we could grab a bite somewhere after I fill up."

Robin looked at her watch and blinked when she saw the time. "Sure. I could eat. I didn't realize it was already noon."

We pulled into the first gas station I found, filling the vehicle before perusing the limited selection of fried and prepackaged foods available inside. Robin turned up her nose at the options, and I couldn't blame her. Some were extremely questionable. One looked like it might grow legs along with the faint green moustache I saw forming on the cheese.

Robin mimed begging. "I know we're kind of on a time crunch, but could we look for something a little less... greasy?"

I laughed. "That's kinder than the word I was thinking of. You don't have to twist my arm. I'm pretty sure this stuff could kill us. There was a café about two blocks back. Want to swing by and see if they have sandwiches less likely to kill us?"

Relief flooded her face. "That would be amazing."

We paid for the gas, and I held the door as she exited. We were halfway to the car when I felt a prickle on the back of my neck. It was a feeling I knew well.

Doing my best to make sure it wasn't obvious, I scanned the parking lot. Nothing except a few parked cars. A sudden flash of movement next to the building caught my eye and the prickling sensation intensified. I blinked. Was there a man watching us?

I couldn't be certain. If someone had been there, they were gone now. I briefly debated exploring, but that meant leaving Robin's side. No, it was wiser to keep moving. If someone was following us, we'd see them again. The sensation didn't subside though, which made it difficult to head to the vehicle, a fact which Robin noticed.

"Is everything okay?" A faint tightness beside her eyes betrayed her apprehension.

I shook my head, scanning the lot again and not meeting her eyes. "Everything's fine. I'm just a little hypoglycemic. I'm in the mood for some tartlets. Hopefully they have some at the cafe."

She chuckled. "I thought you said sandwiches. Maybe we should look for a bakery instead?"

I laughed along with her, trying not to sound fake as I turned on the car. I didn't want to worry her, so I did my level best to stay upbeat as my neck continued to prickle. I knew someone was nearby, watching, and it was the first time in years I hadn't followed the urge to find them. I had to keep Robin safe, and I couldn't be sure I wouldn't lead us into more danger. So, as much as it pained me, we drove to the cafe.

To our shared delight, we discovered it was attached to a small bakery. We were able to get both sandwiches and the tartlets I'd hoped for. Even though I couldn't place my full attention on food with the persistent urge to look for our hidden watcher, I splurged and got a variety.

The drive would be long enough to justify the volume, and my expense account could handle it.

Robin couldn't keep the judgmental look off her face when she saw the amount I'd purchased, but when I shrugged, she sighed.

"I wish I could eat like that. If I did, I would be living up to the opera stereotype. You know, the 'it ain't over until the fat lady sings,' thing?"

I scoffed and gestured at her. "Oh, come on! You can afford to eat whatever you want once in a while. I mean, it's not like you're in France all the time. Besides, I get the feeling you've skipped more than one meal this week. You have some catching up to do." I immediately regretted my words when her face fell. I'd made her think about her dad and crashed her mood without even trying. Cursing inwardly, I turned to pay the woman behind the counter, then guided my tartlets and songbird back to the car.

The moment we were outside though, the insistent prickle returned. I focused on it carefully and in seconds was able to hone in on a man hiding behind a blue Peugeot a few cars away from our rental. I didn't recognize him, but something about him was familiar. He didn't appear to be a gang member, yet my talent confirmed he was indeed the man who I'd felt watching us.

Acting on reflex, I pushed the bag of food into Robin's hand and bolted at the man.

Startled, he hesitated for a moment before he took off, but only managed to run a few steps before I tackled him at the knees.

As I took him down, I thought of my dad. He'd be so proud of me. I hadn't shown any interest in football at school, preferring hockey instead, but this was textbook.

Maybe that was why we landed so hard.

For a moment I laid there, adrenaline pumping through me as I struggled to catch my breath. Once I'd collected myself enough to continue, I rolled him over and pinned him as I'd been taught at the academy.

"Who are you? Why are you following us?"

"Mark? What are you doing? Who is that? What's going on?"

Without looking at Robin, I kept the man firmly in my grasp and said, "That's what I'd like to know. He was at the gas station too, but he was too quick for me to get a good look at him. How long have you been tailing us?"

When the man groaned, I eased off some of the pressure my knee was putting on his back, but only enough to let him speak.

"Please, don't hurt me. I mean you no harm. I'm here to give you a message."

"A message? From who? My dad?" Robin's eyes lit with hope.

I eyed the man suspiciously. At the moment, he didn't appear to be a threat, but I couldn't take any chances or let my guard down. With both the book and her dad disappearing mysteriously, not to mention my senses screaming at me this man held answers we needed, I didn't want her getting hurt; either physically, or because of a lie from this stranger.

"From Scáthach."

I frowned and glanced at Robin, finding her looking at the man with an expression every bit as confused as I felt.

"Scáthach?"

The man's eyes were earnest and full of fear. With the way he was lying pinned beneath me, I had a chance to examine him closely, and for the first time, I realized something about him was different.

His speech and his manner were foreign, but not in a way I could pinpoint. He was dressed simply; wearing a long-sleeved, baggy cotton shirt that appeared average until I noticed it had no buttons or zippers. The stitching was neat, but different than anything I'd seen or purchased in stores myself. A glance at his pants and his boots cemented the ludicrous idea that sprang, fully formed, into my head.

"Where are you from?"

The man licked his lips and swallowed hard, as if his throat was dry. "From another time. But my message is important, so I need you to heed my words. You must hurry. Head to the stronghold of the Clan Donald. Bring no one. 'Tis a dangerous path you must walk if you wish to save your father and find the truth behind the lies."

Robin leaned over the man. Tears filled her eyes, making her voice thick and hard to understand. "You've seen my father? You know where he is? Please, tell me he's okay."

The man's lips tightened. I got the strangest feeling he wanted to comfort her and released a little more of the pressure. I wanted to hear his reply, and now was certain he meant us no harm. Surely, he wouldn't care about her feelings if he intended to hurt us.

"Aye, I know where he is. But I cannot say more. You would nae understand. Do as I bid, and head to Skye. You'll get the answers ye seek there, if you move quickly, and with purpose. If you show bravery in the face of the unknown, you may yet rescue him from his fate."

Any doubts I had vanished at his earnest expression.

I may not be able to read minds the way my godfather could, but I knew the truth when I saw it. Easing my weight all the way off, I left him lying on his back unrestrained and held out a hand to him. He hesitated a moment before accepting, then allowed me to help him up.

Our eyes met and it struck me again I knew him, yet at the same time, he was a complete mystery. He looked to be in his fifties or sixties, with long brown hair streaked with grey that contrasted with his neatly trimmed beard. The tan skin and wrinkles bracketing his eyes and mouth suggested a man of intellect who spent a lot of time outside. But it was a feeling beyond what I could see with my eyes that made me pause.

A sense of kinship, a knowing in my bones that he was someone I should know.

Someone important.

"Who are you? You haven't told us your name. How do we know we can trust you?"

His eyebrows raised as he shrugged. "How does anyone know who to trust? I can only tell you I am here to help. You wouldn't believe me if I told you who I was; not now at least. Maybe later, after you've been to Skye. Perhaps we shall get the chance to speak again one day."

While I stood in silence, unable to think of what to say that wouldn't come off as belligerent or stupid, Robin looked between the two of us. As she did, the man stepped forward, placing a hand on my shoulder and smiled.

"I'm proud you are here helping. The decisions you make now will change both of your lives forever, but if you stick together, I promise, you'll never regret a moment."

He smiled at me then turned his gaze to Robin. "There's so much ahead of you. Never give up. The world needs you.

Your quest to find your father is only the beginning. T'will be challenging, and there are many who mean you harm. Be careful who you trust."

Robin shook her head, reaching out a trembling hand to him. "Please, tell me who you are. How do you know us? The way you're speaking it's as if—."

I finished her thought in my head. *As if he knows the future.*

But, even as the idea came to me, I knew it was wrong.

It wasn't the future he knew. It was the past.

Chapter 16 Mark

It was increasingly obvious to me this man was not from my time. There were so many questions I wanted to ask, but instead, I just stared at him. Then as if someone had rung a bell in the distance, the stranger's head jerked up. For a moment, I had the feeling he was listening to something I couldn't hear, then he turned back to look at me with an odd smile.

A sad smile?

"I'm sorry, it is time for me to depart. I have delivered my warning, and wish you luck and good health. Remember—things are not always what they seem. Your intuition may be the difference between failure and success."

He stared into my eyes until I nodded, then stepped back, giving Robin a smile that made his eyes crinkle. "Never stop dreaming. One day, the world will know your name."

I reached out to stop him, but when I extended my hand, the sidewalk shimmered beneath him like asphalt under the midsummer sun. I blinked at the disorienting image. When my vision cleared, the man was gone. I scoured the parking lot, certain my eyes were playing tricks on me, but he was nowhere to be seen. It wasn't possible for anyone to move that fast. If I could believe my eyes, he'd disappeared into thin air.

Just like the book had disappeared on the security tape.

"Robin, I'm not sure if I want you to tell me you saw that or not. It's totally cool if you tell me I'm crazy."

I spoke slowly, still staring at the place the stranger had vanished from. When she didn't answer, I turned, finding her pale and looking as shaken as I felt.

"Maybe it's a shared hallucination? Because I'm pretty sure I watched that guy disappear too. That is what you're talking about, right? And if I say you're crazy, does that mean I am as well?"

Exhaling, I clicked my tongue. "Let's get in the car. We can drive and talk. I'm not in the mood to hang around to see if anything else weird will happen."

Robin's eyes shifted nervously around the parking lot before she nodded. She'd somehow miraculously kept hold of the food during the strange encounter, which I appreciated. While my appetite was on a temporary hiatus after our encounter with the vanishing man, I was certain I'd be hungry soon enough.

We drove in silence until we were back on the highway and for several long moments after while we tried to collect our thoughts. I was less disturbed by seeing the man disappear than I was by the niggling feeling I'd knew him from somewhere.

As if reading my mind, Robin broke the silence first. "Who do you think he was?"

I shrugged, not taking my eyes off the road. "I'm not sure, but I felt like I should know."

I saw her nod, an odd, faraway look in her eyes. "Me, too. He felt almost like family, but his clothes and speech were strange—he didn't sound French or English. Did you notice that?"

"Yeah, that was odd. Some words had a trace of English accent, others were more French, but it was like he had another accent beneath that and was trying to pronounce things in a neutral way."

She sounded hopeful. "Hey, you're right. Now that you mention it, the way he spoke reminded me of a few people I know who attended British schools in a foreign country. Their English always sounded faintly British to me, except for the underlying accent of their native tongue. Do you think he's from another country?"

Our eyes met, and I could tell she didn't believe her idea either.

"No, that's it," I laughed and shook my head. "Call the guys with the straight-jackets, but to be honest, I got the idea maybe he was from another time. The past, specifically."

She nodded thoughtfully "I don't think your idea is all that bizarre under the circumstances. Did you notice the way he disappeared? It was the same way the book at the bookstore did."

I paused, biting my lip. "I did notice. But, I honestly don't know what to make of it."

Robin's eyes lit up, hope burning bright. "Do you think my dad could do that? I mean, disappear like that man did?"

I shrugged, letting one hand fall to my side helplessly. "I don't know. Before seeing him vanish, I would've said it was impossible for a human to do that. Now? I'm starting to think anything is game." At her crestfallen look, I changed the subject. "At least it sounds like we're heading the right direction."

Robin looked out the window. A ghost of a smile flickered on her face. "Yeah, there isn't very much left for the Donald's to sit on. Dunscaith is a ruin, but it is on the Isle of Skye."

When she didn't elaborate, I prodded her. "What do you know about the history of the castle and area?"

She shrugged. "It's an old ruin. Nobody's lived there for hundreds of years, but apparently it's a popular hiking destination. There are several legends, most of which were written down long after the fact and are likely apocryphal, including those about Scáthach."

I jerked my head around to stare at her. "Scáthach? That guy mentioned her. Seems a little coincidental, doesn't it?"

She grimaced. "Maybe. But that doesn't make any sense. She lived hundreds of years ago, even before the first accounts of her were written. My dad's been looking for information on her for as long as I can remember and hasn't been able to prove anything. And he's an expert."

I scratched my chin absently while I thought about the timing. "Don't you think it's a little strange your dad found a book you say he's been searching for as long as you can remember and both him and the book go missing, and then, when you try to follow his trail, a strange man disappears after giving us cryptic information? It's obviously connected."

Her eyes widened, and I thought I saw a hint of fear flash in them. "Do you think it's time travel?" She shook her head. "It can't be. That isn't possible. It can't be."

"I don't know, but it's all connected. Whether it's magic, or a technology we don't understand, we both watched him disappear. It makes me think your dad might be okay, wherever he is."

"I hope so." She bit her lip, looking torn between hope and worry.

I reached over to take her hand, keeping the other one on the wheel. "It would explain why he hasn't used his Visa or called you. It wouldn't surprise me if his phone doesn't work wherever... whenever... he is."

Robin's eyes welled with tears. "What if he's stuck somewhere and can't get back? How are we going to save him?"

I squeezed her hand gently, wanting to share my strength with her. When she placed her other hand on top of mine, sandwiching it, warmth filled me.

"We will. That man was sent to guide us in the right direction." I hesitated, adding something I hoped wasn't a lie. "I have a feeling when we get to the Isle of Skye, I'll be able to tell where he is."

Robin tugged my hand closer to her. "Really? You aren't just saying that?"

I shook my head, giving her what I hoped was a reassuring smile. "No. Something tells me when we get to the ruins, I'll get a flash. When I'm meant to find something, I'll sense it. The trail is too cold this far away, but I felt the stranger there before I saw him, and once we get to the ruins, I have faith it will happen again."

My stomach twisted as she blinked back tears, and I felt even worse when she sniffed and squeezed my hand, like she was trying to reassure me. Her watery smile solidified my guilt. I hoped I wasn't leading her on.

"I'm glad to hear that. I know you can't give me any reassurances, but after what I've seen today, I'm going to keep hoping we find answers to my dad's disappearance in the ruins of a thousand-year-old castle."

BY THE TIME WE REACHED the crossing from the mainland to Skye, it was evening. The last shuttle Ferry from Mallaig had already come and gone, and it had been dark for well over an hour. We were exhausted and disappointed, but hadn't been keen to drive the extra distance north to cross the bridge at Kyle of Lochalsh by that point anyway.

When I spotted a nearby bed and breakfast, I made an executive decision to get rooms for the night. Robin was nearly asleep and didn't put up much of a fuss, even though I knew the delay bothered her. Neither of us were any good in our current state, but that didn't stop me from wincing as I handed over my credit card. Part of my discomfort was due to the painful conversion from British pounds to Canadian dollars, but most of it was in response to the age of the slide machine the elderly woman used to copy it. I hadn't seen anyone take carbon copies of a Visa since I was a kid.

There was only one room left, but luckily, it had twin beds. With the first ferry departing at eight the next morning, we had few options except to try to get some sleep. Out of habit, I scanned for points of access as I entered the room.

I saw one window large enough for a person to fit through in a pinch, in addition to the door we'd entered and another door, which I suspected was the ensuite bathroom the grand-motherly owner had been so proud of.

The entire room was a nightmare of pink; carpeting, flo-ral wall paper, even the bedspreads. While the decorations likely hadn't been updated since the early eighties and it wasn't a style I was particularly fond of, it looked clean and welcoming. In a strange way, the room reminded me of childhood visits to my eccentric great aunt's farm in rural Ontario.

Robin cleared her throat, and spoke in a hesitant voice. "Which bed would you like?"

I swallowed hard and reminded myself this was work. It was my duty to ensure her safety and comfort. But, despite my inner chatter, the beds loomed larger and closer together in the small space than I'd expected, and it was challenging to think of sleeping so close to her. I knew she was trying to sound casual, so I kept my movements easy and tried to light-en the mood.

Placing my bag on the bed closest to the window, I added a wink for good measure. "I'll take this one. That way if any-one tries to climb in they'll land on me."

She smiled, and I was glad to see some of her tension drain away. She was still on edge, but at least she didn't look as scared.

Trying hard to keep my thoughts off the idea I'd be close enough to reach out and touch her in my sleep, I offered her first dibs on the bathroom. "You go ahead. I'll make sure the door and window are secure while you run through the bath-room."

She threw me a quick, nervous smile but bobbed her head and tucked her toiletry bag under her arm and took a bundle of clothes with her. The moment the door closed, I hid the more incriminating items from my suitcase, sliding the gun I'd picked up after landing under the pillow moments before the door clicked open again.

I whirled to smile, hiding what I'd been doing with my body in the process. "All done? Everything's good here; we're secure for the night. You can turn off the light if you want—I'll only be a minute."

I deliberately kept my eyes only on her face and caught a faint blush. I caught a glimpse of something soft and pink below as well, but did my best not to stare. What I could see of her pajamas wasn't particularly revealing, but the air of sadness and fragility she wore like a cloak made me want to draw her into my arms.

Before I could either embarrass myself or frighten her, I closed the bathroom door behind me.

AFTER ANOTHER FITFUL night, we woke with the sun to repeat our nighttime ritual in reverse. The same averted gazes and general state of awkwardness lasted until we were dressed, and I had time to wonder how she'd slept and what she'd dreamed of.

My dreams had been full of the smell of frangipani. It'd taken me a while to realize it was her perfume I'd been dreaming of, but once I'd placed the scent, I knew I'd never forget it, regardless of how long I lived and whether she remained part of my life or not.

Once we were ready, we went downstairs for the breakfast included in the price of the room. It was delicious, if somewhat unusual from my Canadian perspective. Fish, grilled tomatoes, porridge, and toast with lard and a homemade blackberry jam to round out the meal. Considering the toast seriously, I wondered if it would encourage me to change my allegiance to butter. Wincing after chewing the first bite, I revised my plan. Perhaps not.

Glaring at the bitter betrayal, I put down my toast and looked at Robin. "You all set for a ferry ride? I'm not going to lie—I'm more excited than I should be. I've never been on a ferry before."

She took a deep breath, looking a little wan as she nodded. "As ready as I'll ever be. I've never been on a small ferry either, so I can't guarantee how I'll react to it."

She let out a rueful chuckle, and I couldn't help smiling.

"Don't worry, there's an equal chance you may end up being the one to hold my hair back while I heave over the side." Our eyes met, and my heart rate rose. Clearing my throat, I pushed back from the table and stood. "I'll grab my bag. Do you want me to get yours while I'm up there?"

Shaking her head, she stood as well. "No, I like to take one last check around when I stay somewhere, to make sure I didn't forget anything."

After a quick inspection to ensure we had all our items, we thanked the elderly hostess and drove the short distance to the ferry. Neither of us were prepared for just how small the ferry was. Even though the crossing was supposed to be close to an hour, the boat hardly looked large enough to fit the posted maximum of ten cars.

Praying for a calm crossing, the prickle of anxiety creeping up on me made me work on both my breathing and staying alert. The idea of being stuck on a ship crowded with vehicles didn't sit well with me.

Especially if someone was following us.

Chapter 17 Robin

I'd always dreamed of visiting Scotland, but the reality was so different from what I expected. It felt like I was still dreaming even as saltwater sprayed my face. I was more energized than I'd ever been from a cup of coffee or a long run in the dark, yet it was an odd sensation too. I felt at home in a moment and place so far from everything I knew. With Mark beside me and the Isle of Skye ahead, peace filled me for the first time in many days. A bubble of laughter escaped me.

"What is it?"

I turned to smile at Mark. "Laughing at myself. I was thinking how content I feel."

His answering chuckle stirred something in my chest, a sensation that somehow reminded me of hot chocolate. It was delicious, warm, and decadent all at once.

The corner of his lip quirked up. "I agree. I didn't expect to hear you to say it, but I feel something similar myself. Except my thoughts were more along the lines of feeling this was meant to be. I'd say it feels like destiny, but that's cheesy, even for me."

I snorted before I could stop myself. "Who am I to tell you what sounds cheesy? I was thinking I felt safe, which is ridiculous. My dad's missing, I'm travelling with a stranger—no offense, and we were, and maybe still are, being followed by one or more people with unclear motives. But, now that you mention it, I feel a sense of purpose behind all this as well. Like I'm following a path I was meant to follow."

I tilted my head, waiting for his reaction. When he nodded, his face thoughtful, relief filled me. I may not have known him long, but there was something about him which resonated with me. I wanted him to understand me.

He stepped close enough for our shoulders to brush, but looked over the water instead of at me. "I know what you mean. I've been thinking about the man from the bakery."

I wrinkled my nose. "You mean, the disappearing stranger? What about him?"

Mark shook his head, and continued to look out over the railing. We were only a few hundred meters away from the island now, and I expected to hear an announcement from the crew any minute.

"I felt like I knew him. He was familiar, like a distant relative or something." He shook his head but kept staring down at the dark water, looking so deep in thought I wasn't entirely sure he was speaking to me.

Biting the inside of my cheek, I considered his words. I hadn't recognized the man, and he didn't resemble any of my family, except perhaps his coloring. I had noticed he didn't fit in with his surroundings though. "What makes you think that?"

Mark dragged his eyes back to me. "I don't know. Something about his eyes maybe. I'm sure I knew him." His eyes sharpened, suddenly intense. "Whoever he is, he's related to your dad's disappearance. And the book your dad found. Or the other one—what's the name of it? The Vo-something."

I nodded. "The Voynich manuscript."

He nodded. "That's the one. Everything started when your dad was commissioned to retrieve the code book."

I had no doubt he was right. Even before he left, my dad had known this would be different from other trips. Why else had he have left me that letter? He'd never done that before, and he'd never ever been out of communication for this long, no matter what kind of cell service he had.

But without more to go on, I could only pray answers lay ahead on the green island shrouded in mist.

If we did find answers, I hoped they would make sense.

DISEMBARKING FROM THE ferry in the beautiful town of Portree was the matter of a few minutes. Even with my inner turmoil, I felt surprisingly at home. If I'd been more of a romantic, I would have said I could sense the blood of my ancestors calling to me, telling me I was where I was meant to be.

At any other time, I would have brushed those thoughts aside. But given how my week had gone so far, I acted on a sudden, inexplicable urge.

Turning to Mark, I blurted the idea which had popped into my head out of the blue. "I know where to go."

Without question, he nodded and held out the keys. "Okay. You want to drive?"

I almost said no, but the same insistent inner voice pushed me. "Actually, yes."

Tossing me the keys without hesitation, he got in the passenger's side.

From that moment on, I let my subconscious drive, literally. Without consulting a map or getting directions from Mark and his ever-handy phone, I let my feelings guide me. Each branch, every fork in the road was decided by the same gut instinct. We drove for hours like that, stopping twice for fuel and a pit stop, but otherwise allowing the strange navigator inside me to lead. Mark was quiet, seemingly content to go wherever the road led until after our second stop.

I could tell his curiosity was beginning to outweigh his calm, and I almost told him what I was doing. But then I felt it. Pulling over onto the shoulder, I turned the car off, pausing for a moment until I was certain.

I turned to him. "We're here. We need to walk from here. Oh, and bring your bag. We'll want our things with us where we're going."

His eyebrows shot up, but he waited for me to explain. When I didn't, he placed his hand gently on mine. "Are you okay? Have you been here before?"

I thought about his question, not sure how to answer it. It did feel like I had, but when? To my knowledge I'd never set foot on Skye. I looked at Mark, wondering if he could see my confusion.

"Maybe?" I said at last, taking a deep breath and exhaling with a shudder. "The minute we stepped onto the island, I felt something calling to me."

Mark looked at me thoughtfully, but I saw no judgement in his eyes.

In a quiet, contemplative voice he asked, "Does that surprise you?"

It was his easy acceptance which allowed me to admit the truth. "I'm more frightened how at home I feel. Do you think my dad did this? I mean, let this kind of illogical emotion guide him? It isn't like me at all, but I wonder..."

Mark undid his seatbelt and gave me a smile. Warmth washed over me. None of this seemed to faze him, and I hadn't realized how much I depended on his steadiness until that moment.

"I don't honestly know. You'd be a better judge of why he'd do something than I would, considering I've never met him. But for what it's worth, I'm fine letting the illogical lead sometimes. It's basically how my finding ability works."

He leaned over to brush a strand of hair away from my face, letting his hand linger on my chin, as gentle as if I was made of glass. I felt both fragile and supported in that moment, and my heart thundered so loud it almost blocked out the rest of his words.

"If it makes you feel better, I think you're brave. We're working with a new set of rules, and until we figure out what's going on, we'd be wise to listen to these feelings."

Relieved he didn't think I was crazy, comforted by the way his hand felt against my skin, I closed my eyes and soaked in the sensation. When I finally, reluctantly drew back and undid my seatbelt, he leaned over and grabbed his bag out of the backseat. We got out, and together started down the narrow hiking trail that led off into the mist.

Chapter 18 Robin

The harshly beautiful landscape looked nothing like the Trip Advisor pictures I'd seen, but everything like the strange flashes of what felt like a vague, inborn memory told me it would. Rocky ground coated with heather and wild grass made the short hike to the ruins slower than it should have been in distance alone, but I was spurred on by the faint outline of a ruin against the misty background of green and blue.

Was it always like this here?

I'd have to look when we got home. Memories of the musical from grade twelve intruded, but not the play I'd starred in; the original movie version. The similarities were uncanny. In *Brigadoon*, two American hunters became lost in the Highlands, stumbling across a mysterious village, which appeared once every hundred years out of the mist. Now, looking at the scenery around me, I could almost believe it was based on a true story.

I squinted, trying to make out the building in front of me, then shook my head. I'd do better to watch my step. Tripping and breaking my ankle so close to Dunscaith would suck. The next time I looked up, the ruins loomed larger.

When we reached the next small roll of hillside I paused. Mark halted behind me. We'd had to walk single file from the car due to the narrowness of the footpath, but had mostly walked in silence. The mist made the morning's atmosphere feel somehow sacred, and neither of us had chosen to break it.

Mark spoke softly, the quietness of his voice reinforcing the sensation. "It's quite impressive, isn't it?"

"Yes." When I glanced at him, I found him staring at the ruins with wonder, mixed with something else I couldn't decipher. "What is it?"

I could tell something had changed, and alarm instantly shot through me. His eyes were shadowed and pinched at the corners, as if he was about to share something painful. Was he going to cut and run? Shocked by the intensity of my fear of abandonment, I swallowed hard. I hadn't realized I wanted him at my side so much. Maybe I simply didn't want to be alone—I couldn't afford to have actual feelings for him on top of everything else.

Either way, I braced myself for the worst.

"Before we go any further, I need to tell you something. I'll understand if you don't want me to come with you, and if, after I tell you the truth, you never want to talk to me again." He looked at the castle again, shaking his head almost absently. "I need to be honest with you before we arrive at the castle. You remember the ability that helps me find missing objects?"

My breath caught in my throat. What was so important to tell me now, and why did he seem so anxious and sad? "Yes. What about it?"

Taking my hands in his, he squeezed lightly before meeting my eyes with a half-smile. "My gift has always been part of me, but before my last year of high school I'd suppressed it. My dad thought I had done it unconsciously to protect myself. I guess I didn't want people to think I was a freak show, or a thief. You know?"

His lips tightened and I wondered who'd hurt him. I squeezed his hands back. "Mark, there's nothing you could tell me that would change my opinion of you. I admit I don't know you well, but anyone can see you're a good man. Not many people would have helped me, not to mention believed anything that's happened since then."

He let out a short, mirthless bark of laughter. "I really hope you still feel like that after I tell you the truth. Before I destroy any good impression you have of me though, I want you to know that from the minute I first laid eyes on you, I've done everything I can to keep you safe. I care about you, and about getting your dad home safely."

He stopped abruptly. He looked like he'd been about to say more, so I stepped closer, drawing his hands up close to my chest, where my heart was pounding. I needed to know what he was he holding back.

"Can you feel that? I know you wouldn't hurt me deliberately. Get it over with. What secret is so bad you think I'd react by throwing you out of my life?"

He looked down at our hands, then at my face, emotion swirling in his eyes. "It wasn't an accident we met on the plane when we did."

My eyes widened reflexively, and his shoulders slumped. He tried to pull away but I refused to let him, tugging him closer instead. "No, you have to tell me everything first. You owe me that, now that you've started. What do you mean, it wasn't an accident?"

"I've been following you since before you left Montréal. I work for CSIS and was assigned to watch you. I promise. Everything I've done has been to keep you safe."

My mouth dropped open and my hands slackened, allowing him to move away. I snapped back from my surprise, but it was too late. Free from my grip, he began to pace back and forth on the path, running a hand through his hair and messing it even further than it already was.

"Mark, stop. I'm not mad, just confused. I don't understand what you mean."

Something in my voice must have broken through his self-flagellation because he finally stopped, dropping his hand to rub the back of his neck for a moment before allowing it to fall to his side.

"How could you not be mad at me? I met you under false pretenses. I'm basically a stalker, even if I am getting paid to do a job."

I thought about what he said. He was right. Under normal circumstances, I probably would have been upset. But for some reason, maybe because of the ruins of my ancestors and the strange atmosphere of the mist, I wasn't. In fact, I felt like the final piece of a puzzle had just clicked into place.

His admission explained why he sometimes seemed far away, or wouldn't meet my eyes. He was such an open book otherwise that every time he'd pulled back, I wondered if I'd done something wrong. But if it was because he'd been assigned to follow me without my knowledge and had been feeling guilty, it all made sense.

"How long have you been following me?"

He stared intently at his feet as he kicked the ground, and spoke so quietly I almost missed his mumbled reply. "About two weeks."

I shook my head, impressed despite myself. "I never saw you. It's weird, because I noticed you immediately at the airport."

It was true. Something about Mark had stood out even before I'd boarded the plane, but I was practical enough to admit he'd probably snagged my attention because I'd thought he was cute.

He smiled sheepishly. "They train us to keep out of sight when we're undercover. I'm happy you didn't see me earlier; it means I was successfully doing my job. I've been following you since your dad got the commission from Mr. Lavallee. CSIS has been watching the bikers for a long time, and the connection worried them. It was out of his usual pattern. Why would a gang leader contact your dad about a book? You have to admit, it's odd."

My head snapped back as other things I'd brushed off before began to make sense. "You mean whenever I thought there was a car following me, or had the sensation someone watching me, someone actually was?" I snorted. "Huh. And all this time, I thought stress was getting to me."

He shook his head. "No, you were probably feeling me or another agent. A lot of people notice if someone is watching them whether they know it or not. When your dad went missing, we became concerned you would be the next target. My boss thought it prudent for me to stick close. And by then, I couldn't let anyone hurt you. I wanted to tell you so many times, but..."

He trailed off, but he didn't have to explain further because I understood exactly what he was trying to say. I searched his face, the same handsome, open face I'd felt I could trust on sight, and threw caution and anger to the wind.

Closing the distance between us, I reached up and drew his head down, wanting to show him the only way I could that I forgave him. My eyes fluttered shut and I met his lips tentatively. Heat flared, and his surprise disappeared as passion overcame us.

I could have stayed in his arms forever, but a sudden loud crack split the silence. Whirling around in unison to face the unknown, Mark placed himself protectively in front of me, hiding me from whatever or whomever had made the noise.

Chapter 19 Mark

I wasn't sure if lightning had struck or someone had shot at us.

One minute I was in heaven; now my heart raced from a different kind of excitement altogether as I searched for the origin of the sound.

There was no one else on the path.

If Robin hadn't also been looking around with a worried expression, I would have thought I'd imagined the noise.

As if she'd read my mind, Robin asked, "You heard that too, right?"

"Yeah, I heard it. It sounded like a gunshot."

She nodded, her expression grim. "That's what I thought. But there's nobody here."

Ahead of us were the empty ruins and windswept, rocky cliff edge. Behind us was the empty trail. I couldn't see a vantage point for a sniper, and nothing seemed out of place. But as I turned back to the ruins, something shimmered on the path ahead and caught my eye.

"Wait—did you see that?"

Robin followed my direction, gasping when she saw it. An almost invisible curtain shimmered in the air ahead, like sunlight rippling on the bottom of a pool.

She wrinkled her nose, looking embarrassed. "Okay, I know this sounds like a leap, but what if it's a rip? Like, in time?"

The idea caught me off-guard, and for a moment, I stood there blinking at her while I processed. Then, with a sigh, I held out a hand to her. "I've got nothing. Maybe?"

When she took my hand and curled up closer, I was relieved. She still trusted me, even after I'd revealed my duplicity.

"Well, if I'm going to get any closer to it, I don't want to face it without you. You're still with me, right?"

The simple question made me swallow hard, but my decision was easy. "I'll follow you to the ends of time." The second the statement left my mouth I winced. Did I sound as cheesy as I thought?

But she didn't laugh. Tucking herself further under my arm, she gave me a look. I felt a million feet tall in that moment. Then, jutting her chin toward the shimmer, Robin looked at the ruins with mixture of fear and determination.

"I'm ready when you are. I've got a feeling our answers lie just beyond whatever that is."

Chapter 20 Mark

The castle was a brilliant bone white, rising starkly against the sky on the edge of the cliff. The ocean crashed against the rocks below. Everything was sharp and clear now. Somehow, that made what was happening even more confusing.

I looked over my shoulder and saw the place we'd walked through moments earlier completely walled off by a strange fog where the shimmer had been. When I turned to look ahead again, the day was still as sharp and sunny as my first glimpse.

But the weather wasn't the only contrast. The castle itself was altered. When we'd left the car, we'd been walking toward ancient ruins. Now, a well-fortified castle greeted us instead, standing proudly at the edge of land like a sentinel preparing for invasion.

My attention was caught by the odd appearance of several posts sticking out of the water below. Squinting to see them better, I realized they were the size of entire trees. Standing about four feet apart at regular intervals, I counted ten in total. At some point, someone had evidently placed them there, and when I saw two people sparring with wood staffs on the two posts furthest from the beach, I knew why.

We obviously were no longer in the same place we'd been a moment ago.

But *when* in the hell were we?

I tapped Robin on the arm, drawing her gaze to the scene below. "Robin, look down."

Her eyes widened. "Is it just me, or are they fighting with bo staffs?"

I nodded. "That's what it looks like to me."

Although they were at least a hundred feet away, it was easy to make out the features on the fighters below. One was a youth, maybe fifteen or so, narrow in body and without a hint of whisker to shadow his determined face. His opponent was a woman with night black hair that had been braided and coiled on top of her head, and who currently wore an amused expression as she regarded the youth.

Before I'd processed the scene below, the woman's eyes flicked up, locking on me. As I stared into the chilling ice blue of her gaze, I was overcome by the uncomfortable sensation she could read my mind. Regardless of whatever I'd been considering we should do next, it became crystal clear to me our only option was standing in front of us. I took one hesitant step toward the cliff.

Robin squeezed my hand, matching her steps to mine. "We have to meet her, don't we?"

"Yeah. Pretty sure she's the boss here, *whenever* here is."

Robin sighed but didn't protest. A few steps closer to the edge, I spotted steps carved into the side. Squeezing her hand once, I let go. We were going to need both hands to climb.

"I'll go first. Try to step where I do. Unless, of course, I fall to my doom. In that case, feel free to find other places to step."

She smiled weakly, but her face was serious as I slowly picked my way down the side. Without my attention having been captured by the people below, I didn't think I'd have seen the faint crack of the hidden staircase. The rock steps were nearly invisible from above, but as we descended, it became obvious someone had carved the path into the rocks, as rough as it was with handholds and barely smoothed boulders.

Once we were both safely on the beach, the water appeared darker, almost indigo, and dark, angry clouds loomed on the horizon. I shivered, not wanting to imagine the beach in a storm, and hoped I wouldn't find out for myself.

When I glanced at the woman, I saw she'd tucked the staff across her back and was nimbly jumping between the poles. She made the task look so easy I began to consider maybe it wasn't as hard as I thought, until the youth attempted to do the same. He almost fell trying to keep up and flailed his arms wildly for a few moments before regaining his balance.

Her eyes met mine again briefly, and I paused. She was clearly heading to meet us. Was I supposed to bow? How did one greet a formidable warrior woman in whatever time we were in that wouldn't earn me an ass kicking?

Because I was pretty sure we weren't in our time anymore.

Deciding discretion was the better part of valor, I waited until she was on the beach, then attempted a bow as she came closer.

Her hands were open and without a weapon, but I wasn't fooled. She had the same tough and sinewy look most of my self-defense instructors had. Like she was both capable and comfortable killing an opponent with her bare hands. She didn't need a weapon because she was the weapon.

When she stopped a few feet away, I slowly stood from my bow with a cautious smile. "Hi. Sorry to bother you. We were looking for the ruins of Dunscaith Castle, and somehow, we've ended up here." I gestured to the beach with one hand, then waved it toward the castle. "While this castle is lovely, it isn't the same as the ruins we were heading to before a shimmering curtain appeared in front of us. I think we may be a little lost."

That was an understatement.

My words hung in the air for several moments as the woman's expression changed from cool and unreadable to shocked. She turned to search Robin's face. In the time it took me to blink, the fierce warrior vanished. Her eyes darkened to the shade of the ocean behind us. Tears filled her eyes as she lifted a hand to her mouth and choked back a sob.

Taking a step toward Robin, she stopped with the other hand outstretched. In a shaky voice, full of heartache and hope, she said one word. "Robin?"

I felt as if I'd been slapped as Robin paled and stepped back, shaking her head as she moved with a dream-like slowness.

"No, this isn't real. I'm not seeing this. You're dead. Mom?"

I looked between the two women, now able to recognize the obvious similarities. Our journey had just become a lot more complicated.

Chapter 21 Robin

I stared at the woman whose face still haunted my dreams. How old had I been the last time I'd seen her in person? Five? Everything I remembered was fuzzy, except for the way I'd felt with her nearby. I'd always known I was safe, never doubted she'd destroy anyone who tried to hurt me. But this warrior -- this stranger— there was no way she could be my mom.

Even if she hadn't died so long ago.

Yet, the ferocity I'd seen in her eyes while she'd been fighting had vanished the moment her eyes landed on me. Eyes so much like my own.

She took another tentative step toward me. I waited, standing motionless. I didn't know what to do. Even though it didn't make sense, my heart was screaming the truth. So, when she continued to inch closer I moved without thinking. Her arms closed around me and I shut my eyes. Inhaling the clean smell of wind and water, along with the faint underlying scent of flowers, I was thrown back to my childhood.

It was really her.

I stepped back, numb. It took a second to recognize the wet patch on her shoulder for what it was and I wiped my face, vaguely amused to feel tears streaking my cheeks.

I hadn't realized I'd been crying. Warmth enveloped me as Mark draped a cautious arm around my shoulder.

He cleared his throat, his voice polite, but a little stilted. "I gather you two know each other?"

Shifting on his heels as if trying to find stable ground, he waited, looking at me for direction. I took his hand, hoping to draw in some of his strength. Some of the odd numbness dissipated as his solid presence steadied me—enough so that I didn't feel I was about to pass out anymore.

What was the socially appropriate reaction to finding out a loved one you'd thought dead your entire life was alive? Anger? Happiness? Unable to decide, and not in any mindset to examine my actual emotions, I fell back on politeness.

"Remember when I told you my mom died when I was a child?" He nodded slowly, and I could feel the tight, brittle smile on my face tremble when I shifted my eyes to the woman in front of me. "Well, it appears I may have been wrong." I frowned now, giving up the attempt at pleasantries. "I was told you died in a car accident. For years I worried every time my dad left on a trip he wouldn't come back either."

I knew my accusation had struck the mark when she looked down, blinking rapidly. I immediately felt like a jerk and sighed.

"I'm sorry, but this is the last thing I expected. If you're my mom, where have you been for the last twenty years of my life?"

Her lips tightened as she returned my gaze. Her eyes were clear, and for a moment, it felt as if nothing had changed; as if no time had passed.

Her voice was soft, but didn't waver. "Yes, I am your mother. I know it's difficult to believe, but I had my reasons for leaving. I've missed you and your father so much. Seeing you here, now...." She swallowed hard. "Let's just say I hadn't expected to be gifted with the sight of you again, at least, not in this lifetime."

I shook my head. "So, why did you leave? If you loved us, why didn't you ever call, write a letter, something?"

A faint, sad smile curved her lips. Even in my confusion, I could read regret on her face.

"It was to keep you safe, of course. Your father and I should never have met. When he showed up in my life, appearing from nowhere in strange clothing, I knew I'd been waiting for him. But even then I knew our time together was borrowed." Her smile faded. "While I wished otherwise, there was too much time and distance between us."

"What do you mean, time and distance?"

At my question, she gestured in the direction of the castle. I followed her movement, noticing the young man she'd been sparring with waiting several paces back, near enough to hear our conversation, but far enough to be unobtrusive.

"He was from a Canada of the future, and I exist here, in this time and place, in a fortress of shadows. There's nearly a thousand years between us." She turned to the ocean, her strong cheekbones cutting an elegant, haunting profile against the backdrop of the roiling waters. "I have been given many gifts in this world, but the responsibilities that come with them bind me as tightly as any chains. When you know the future, the way is both clearer, yet more difficult."

"You can see the future?"

Mark's sudden intrusion was startling, but she appeared to have been expecting the question. She merely shrugged one shoulder.

"I would think you of all people would understand. After all, Mark Notting, you are no stranger to the difficult choices talent brings with it."

His eyes widened as she spoke his name and he nodded, wide-eyed. She chuckled, then sobered as she turned to me again. Her eyes roamed my hair and face.

"I see much of the future, but I can honestly say I never expected to see you here. Now that you are here, however, you will face a decision about the path you must travel." Shaking her head, she laughed quietly under her breath. "I cannot believe you are already grown. Such a beautiful child I was blessed with; always singing and happy. Even then, I knew where your powers lay. Your name suits you well."

My stomach clenched painfully, and unconsciously, I brought my hand up to hold it. "You named me Robin because of my power? But... I don't have any power. I'm a singer, that's all."

It was too much. I was in Scotland with my dead mother, who was standing in front of the ruins of a castle that looked brand new, telling me I had power. But, even as my mind worked to deny her words, I recalled Melissa, and the way her sudden illness had resolved after I'd sang to her.

Shaking my head, I spoke too loudly, hoping it would somehow make me believe my own words. "I don't have any power."

"Ah, but you are mistaken." She glanced at the water, frowning slightly. "Come. There's a storm fast approaching.

This is a conversation that would go better with food and drink. I'm certain you are hungry from your travels."

"I am," Mark agreed, raising a hand.

As if released from his quiet deference, the young man stepped forward, speaking to my mom in a language I didn't understand. I did catch one word—Scáthach—and my head whirled. My mom was the sorceress from the legends?

My mom laughed and ruffled his hair then winked at Mark. "Connor agrees with you, even though he has no idea what we're talking about. He asked if I was done with his lessons, so that he could leave and get something to eat."

When she laughed again, arrows shot through me. I thought I'd never hear it again, outside of my dreams. I had so many questions to ask her, but she was right. A stormy beach wasn't the best place for what would surely be a long conversation. We started up the hill behind Connor.

Mark gestured for me to walk in front. "You go ahead. I'll follow, to make sure you don't stumble." His eyes crinkled at the corners.

I knew he was teasing me to lighten the mood, and it was nice. Somehow, he'd become the only constant in my life after the craziest week ever, and I knew without question he would catch me if I fell. Picking my way up the stairs, the thought occurred to me I couldn't say the same thing about my own parents. My mom was back and my dad was missing. A horrible idea pierced me. Had my dad known she wasn't dead?

Everything was all upside down.

I faltered, but Mark's hand caught my elbow as he'd promised, narrowly keeping me from falling off the step.

Thanking him absently, I stepped more carefully, feeling more off-balance than before. What other bombshells were going to be dropped on me before my life settled down? Would it ever settle?

As I watched the woman who'd given me birth pick her way up the rocky cliff ahead of me, I braced myself for the possibility my entire life had been a lie.

Chapter 22 Robin

I hadn't been inside a real castle in years. Sure, I'd gone to Casa Loma in Toronto last year after a concert with my dad, but it was nothing compared to this. Casa Loma was a testament to the vanity of a wealthy businessman, but Dunscaith was a fortress, meant to be defended by warriors from anything that came their way.

A large portcullis, wide enough for several horses to walk abreast and tall enough for an average-sized man to stand up on the back of said horses, stood half-open, gaping like a sharp-toothed mouth. Unease at the image filled me. It seemed unusually large, but without a frame of reference, I couldn't decide if the structure was typical of the era or not.

The courtyard curved around a large central building and extended far beyond it, confirming my suspicion the castle was meant to house hundreds of people. I couldn't tell if there were other entrances. Regardless, the castle was sturdy and likely the most secure one could get during the time.

The stones were a whitewashed gray that sparkled in the sun, drawing my eyes to the windows, where bars interspersed the rock. It reminded me of the old *Robin Hood* movie with Kevin Costner.

Maybe Hollywood had gotten something right for a change.

My thoughts instantly switched gears when my mom halted without warning. "These are the external walls of Dunscaith, built to withstand the might of all enemies. But it takes more than bricks and stone to make a castle powerful."

She waved her arm as she spoke, and I followed her demonstration, fascinated despite myself. Mark had been surreptitiously tapping on a lever beside the gate mechanism and dropped his hand with a guilty look when she caught him.

She smiled and pointed to it. "That lever drops the portcullis, which is the first line of defense. You can't see them right now, but the walls have guards stationed at the top at each corner armed with bows and arrows. While we have little to fear from the ocean except weather, it pays to be prepared."

Mark moved closer, the sparkle in his eyes and eager expression making him look like a little boy at Christmas. "What other defenses does the castle have?"

Apparently, my mom agreed with my assessment and laughed gently. I wondered if she wanted to ruffle his hair as much as I did at that moment.

"I'll tell you all about the castle once we're inside. First, I need to notify the servants we have guests. They'll prepare a room while we discuss things."

My mouth fell open when I realized what she meant. "Stay? But I must find Dad. He's still missing."

My mom's eyes were pinched with sadness as she apologized. "I know. We shall speak about that as well. For now, you should prepare yourself to stay a few days. It will be tricky, but not impossible, to return you to your exact time. We need to plan, and in the meanwhile, you'll need somewhere to sleep. Before you leave, I'll give you as much information as possible."

My shoulders slumped. There was no reason for her to lie, but it was frustrating nonetheless. I hated the uncertainty of not knowing more than anything else. Was my dad okay? How had we ended up here? Had everything else in life come so easily to me that even being reunited with my mom wasn't enough to calm the burning I felt, just beneath my heart?

As if sensing my inner turmoil, Mark slid his arm around me. "I know how you feel," he whispered. "I wish things were normal, too. The one good thing about being stuck here, in the past, is that time isn't moving ahead without us, right? I mean, we haven't been born yet, so your dad isn't missing yet, either."

The simple logic of his words hit me and gave me hope. "You're right. I hadn't considered that." Turning to my mom, I smiled. I hoped I hadn't come across as an ungrateful child. "Thank you for the offer, Scáthach... Mom. I do want to catch up; I'm just worried. And... it's a lot."

She stepped closer. With a hand that seemed too hesitant for her powerful presence, she gently pushed a strand of hair off my face. "I know. Don't worry–we'll find him and put a stop to this. While I cannot see everything related to those I love, I have my own suspicions about what has happened. Once we've had a chance to discuss the situation, we'll plan a rescue together."

The warmth of the smile she turned on me softened the doubts bombarding me, even if part of me still wondered if I could trust her. She was my mom. I knew she loved me, despite everything. Feeling more hopeful than I had since boarding the plane to France, I nodded. "Thanks again, for everything."

We headed up the grand set of stairs, leading off a large room. Based on the way the staff rapidly and graciously filled her commands she was evidently not only some sort of warrior queen, but a well-respected one to boot. The congenial smiles they gave as we passed suggested she was also kind and well loved.

I could almost convince myself I was in a five-star hotel, the way we were guided to our rooms. In pantomimes of gestures and smiles, we were directed to put our bags down in a set of rooms that faced each other. Once we'd complied, we were led back downstairs.

The next room we were shown to was different from the others we'd seen. The first thing I noticed on entry was a long hall with open windows, allowing both sunlight and fresh air to enter and making it the brightest room of the castle. It seemed out of place compared to the fortifications of the rest of the castle until I recognized the central courtyard through the windows. I stepped closer, intending to look out, when my mom appeared.

"Robin, Mark. Please, join me. I wished to speak with you in less formal settings than the main dining room, and thought you would find this room a comfortable alternative."

She directed us to join her at a small seating area near the large fireplace that took up most of the wall across from the windows. Beside her was a small table set with food and a large silver pitcher next to crystal goblets. Beads of moisture dripped off the belly of the pitcher. Suddenly, I was parched.

Picking a seat with the best view of the window, Mark sat on my other side as my mom poured a glass of water for me then another for him. "Please, help yourselves. It is not the same as what you are used to eating at home I know, but I had them bring food I thought you would enjoy."

Mark raised an eyebrow, inclining his head to one of the covered dishes. "They do mac & cheese here?"

She laughed. "Not exactly. A little more 'homemade' than that. Fresh bread, churned butter, and the best jams and spreads we can make. There's an assortment of cheeses and meats as well. Basically, I had them make tapas. You always enjoyed nibblies when you were little."

I snorted, shooting Mark a grin. "Really? Macaroni and cheese? Please." Giving my mom a nod as I took a small plate, I thanked her. "It looks wonderful. I'm unexpectedly starving, but since I'm not sure I can remember the last time I ate, that isn't surprising. Speaking of which, how does it work?"

The moment I asked it, I knew my question didn't make sense. Heck, I wasn't even sure what I was asking, but for some reason, my mom seemed to understand. She shook her head, giving me a thoughtful look.

"Traveling between times? I wish I knew. When I traveled to your time, it was as quick as a blink, but it is not something to be undertaken lightly. Every time one travels beyond one's own life span, the risk of changing important events cannot be known. Even if one is careful, it is nigh impossible to remain unseen and alter nothing."

Mark leaned forward, his food completely forgotten. "Like the butterfly effect?" When she squinted, he explained. "It's a movie I saw. The premise is that a small change can make a big change. Like if a butterfly flaps its wings, it could cause an earthquake somewhere else in the world."

Her face cleared, and she nodded. "Ah yes, exactly. I had to travel between eras to return your dad to his time after he came here. Imagine the damage that could have been done to the timeline if someone from the twentieth century remained in the eleventh?" She gave me a wry smile. "Like you, my dear. You were never supposed to exist, but at least by having you in the future, the past remained stable. Could you imagine how things would have changed? If you had children, and your children had children? How would human history have been altered by ten centuries of people who were never meant to exist? The implications are enormous."

I sat back in my chair, barely feeling the lumpy cushion on the straight-backed wood beneath me. If I had grown up in this time, I wouldn't be an opera singer. Opera didn't exist yet. But how many other ways would my life have been different? I swallowed hard at the enormity of what she was saying.

"I never thought of that. But, if I wasn't supposed to exist..."

My mom left her chair and knelt at my feet, taking my hands in hers and looking at me earnestly. "Your father was the man I had been dreaming of. He is in the prophecies; we were meant to be. But I never saw you until you happened. I would have given anything to bring you both back with me, but it was not safe." She closed her eyes tight for a moment. When she opened them, they sparkled with unshed tears. "'Tis easy enough to say you would nary change a thing until faced with having to choose between love and responsibility."

My voice was small. I could hear the child I'd been as I asked, "Why did you leave us if you loved us?"

As she looked up at me, I saw the pain. She'd clearly wrestled with the decision since leaving, but her answer was quick and certain.

"To save your life. To save your father's life. I would give my own life and happiness to keep you safe. You shall understand someday. Perhaps, you already do."

Her eyes flicked to Mark. I followed her gaze and found him listening attentively. When he spoke, his words were soft, but they hit her as hard as any blow.

"Someone came after you, didn't they?"

She nodded. "Yes. My sister and I, well, let us just say we are very different people and have not always gotten along. We have never gotten along. Unfortunately, Aífe was determined to pass her grudge against me down to her descendants. They will stop at nothing to get what they feel is their inheritance. That is the reason I left, in the end." She twisted her mouth, bitterness nearly dripping from her words. "There were too many close calls after we moved to Montreal. I was forced to leave to keep you and your dad safe after an accident nearly claimed my life."

"What do you mean? What grudge? What inheritance?"

She let go of my hand and stood, then began to pace across the carpeted area by the chairs. The loss of contact made me realize how much I'd missed her. I followed her with my eyes, still unable to process having my mom back in my life.

The long black hair, which had been pinned on top of her head earlier, was now in a simple braid. It tapped lightly against her back as she walked, but even though the hair was different, her shadowed eyes made her look like the mysterious warrior we'd seen fighting on the water again. At that moment, she barely resembled the mother I'd known in childhood.

"Aífe was always jealous of my gift. She wanted me to share what I saw with her, but when I discovered she was using the information to her own advantage, I stopped." She paused at the window and looked out into the garden, a deep sigh escaping as she leaned on the wall.

"She wasn't happy." Mark spoke with certainty.

She nodded. "No, she wasn't. Somehow, she found out I had been keeping track of my dreams and visions in a journal. I hid it, but it was too late. She became obsessed with finding my prophecies. Unbeknownst to me, Aífe passed the obsession to her son, and left him in a time and place beyond my reach."

Wait, I had an aunt? Cousins? I stood up, taking a step toward her without registering the drops of water that spilled from my cup onto the wood table. "Who was her son?"

She faced me, pressing her lips into a thin line. "How much do you know about history? He was a force to be reckoned with in his time, although few in the future see him as anything more than an oddity."

I shook my head. "I've taken a few history classes, but mostly involving music. Sorry."

The corner of her lip twisted. "My sister loved a man with power. Something she had always valued more than family, a facet of her nature I did not comprehend until it was too late. Aífe pretended to be something other than what she was for a time; long enough to fool the rulers of England, and bear a child who was not supposed to exist. A child who rose to prominence as an advisor in the court of Queen Elizabeth the First, John Dee."

"Wait, I don't understand. She raised him in Elizabethan England, like you raised me in my time?"

She nodded. "Yes, and when he was old enough to carry on her search, she left him there, figuring correctly there was nothing I could do to prevent him from finding and using the prophecies for his own purposes in a time where I did not exist."

A trickle of icy certainty flowed down my back. "Dad was looking for *your* book, wasn't he? You wrote the Voynich manuscript."

A smile crept over her face, and I felt her approval wash over me.

"I did. What you know as the Voynich manuscript is my journal, which contains everything I have ever seen—doodles, and all. My sister's descendants were poisoned by her desire to control it, and I believe they still want it badly enough to search the entirety of time to find it."

"If this all revolves around your prophecies, how do we stop them from getting the book? How do we save my dad?"

Her eyes clouded, and she suddenly seemed far away. When she spoke a few moments later, her voice was deeper, and somehow eerie. "I have an idea, but much risk is involved, for both of you." Her eyes moved between us, making my hair stand on end. Was she having a vision right now? "I have a second copy of the translation text for my manuscript."

Caught off-guard, my eyebrows shot up. "You do? I thought it was one-of-a-kind."

The darkness that had spooked me left her face as abruptly as it had appeared, replaced by a mischievous grin. "After getting trapped in the future with your father, I managed to make a copy, with the help of an old friend." The corner of her eyes crinkled with the memory. "That was when I discovered the books are tethered to a particular time. The one I made must stay in the future, in your time."

"So the book her dad was searching for *can't* travel through time?" Mark sounded excited.

I shared his feeling, but if that was true...

"Correct," my mom said. "Two books exist. One remains in my time, with me, and one remains in Robin's time. They remain in the time of their creation, and can only move forward from there, in the way things normally move. The book is not a living creature, and only the living can swim the streams of time. I was able to travel to the future because my manuscript already existed there, and I can go as far into the future as my book abides." She chuckled at the expression on my face. "My existence is quite literally bookended. I can travel anywhere my creations endure—but no further. I never dreamed my life would turn out to be so varied, or so complicated."

I sat down in chair as comprehension flooded in. "The book really is a time-machine."

"Yes, although the furthest back in time it can take someone is when it was created, only a few decades before the time we are now in. As for the future?" She shrugged. "I do not know how far the book will abide."

Mark sounded thoughtful. "If the book exists that means we can get back to the present, right?"

I thought about the book disappearing from the store on camera and stood again. "What if the codebook is gone? We watched it disappear."

She smiled again, crossing her arms. "If you did not see it destroyed, it still endures. I have personal experience that these codebooks can be a little tricky."

She didn't explain further, but for the first time, I knew why my dad hadn't lost his fascination with searching for this book, and by extension, the Voynich manuscript. Unlike every other scholar in the world, he'd known about the codebook all along. Had he been trying to find the book, or had he really been hoping to find my mom?

I thought back to the way he'd gone quiet every time I'd asked about her. The way he'd quietly freaked out when I'd bought a book on magic in high school. We needed to have a long conversation after I found him, but I thought I understood why he'd kept this from me all this time. Had I not currently been living in the past, there is no way I ever would have believed him.

I walked over to stand next to her at the window and looked down at the courtyard. Where everything else in Scotland had a harsh and rocky beauty, someone—her, perhaps? — had gone to great lengths to make the inner sanctum of the castle peaceful. A multitude of plants and small fountains adorned the area, and walking paths meandered off beneath towering trees in full leaf.

I looked at her profile, so familiar and strange. "Dad was looking for you, wasn't he?"

She let out a mournful sigh. "I do not know. Probably, knowing him." Her mouth twisted, but I couldn't tell if it was with sadness or love. "It is also possible he was searching for the book, and the book simply disappeared on its own. It seems to know when someone is getting too close and vanishes at will, only to turn up again, years later. Possibly, because I designed it to do that."

A self-satisfied smirk crossed her face, and I raised an eyebrow.

"Possibly?"

She smiled back, unrepentant. "You cannot be too careful when people wish to know the secrets of the universe, especially when they plan to use them to undo the balance between darkness and light. I may be known as a shadow warrior or a sorceress, depending on which version of my story you read, but I am firmly on the side of the light. It is a never-ending battle. The dark pushes ever onward, trying to undo all of our hard work, and those of us who can fight a tireless and unending battle."

Mark came to stand with us, placing his hand loosely on my shoulder. "Are we here because of this battle? Is that why I'm part of this now?"

She nodded. "I am both saddened, yet grateful to have you at my side, Mark. I believe you're meant to help Robin find the way. While your powers are not yet fully developed, your mind is open, and she will learn much from you. One day soon, I believe you will achieve your full potential."

He looked shaken but curious. Then she turned to me, and her eyes seemed to bore into mine.

"Robin, you have trained your gift to the best of your ability in the way of ordinary mortals, but there is more power in your voice than you know. Once you unlock your true nature, you will be both weapon and savior."

It sounded unbelievable, yet somehow, I believed every single word. I had power? I thought back to when I'd sung to Melissa. Her words were a confirmation I hadn't imagined the healing wave I'd felt then, and it stirred something in me.

I squared my shoulders, looking back without flinching. "How do we use our abilities to save my dad, and keep the codebook safe from those who want it for dark purposes?"

Tilting her head, she gently stroked the side of my face before letting her hand fall to her side. "You will discover what to do next as you go. No matter how confusing this is right now, I know you will succeed. This is merely the beginning of what I see for you. Many will guide you along your path, and even without using my gift, I can see you are intended to walk this path together. I am happy you will not be alone."

She included us both in her words and I shrank back, a blush roaring painfully across my cheeks. Mark reflexively stepped away from her, and I tried to salvage the situation from complete and utter awkwardness.

"Oh, um, we really don't know each other well. It's too early to, you know, um, you know."

My smile was more of a grimace, and when I glanced at Mark, he wore a similarly pained look. It was amazing—I hadn't had a mom for years, but in an incredibly short amount of time, she'd embarrassed me as thoroughly as any teen with a crush had ever been embarrassed by a parent.

Clearly, mage-level mothering in action.

Mark softened the edge of my mortification by squeezing my shoulder lightly and smiling down at me, his eyes twinkling as if he knew what I was thinking.

"We'll take it one day at a time. I'll be glad to have a friend at my side if I have to travel down such an unusual road."

As swiftly as if he'd laid a cold cloth on my face instead of spoken, the heat in my cheeks subsided. I wasn't sure I believed in soulmates or not, but despite having met him only a week ago, I felt a sense of rightness with him I couldn't explain.

It was nice to think that maybe one day we'd end up together, but I wasn't ready to commit to a happily ever after just yet.

Not until after I figured out what the hell I'd gotten myself into, and what my mom meant when she said my power would be enough.

Chapter 23 Mark

Everything Scáthach told us rang true, even though I saw the indecision and conflict on Robin's face. I had no problem believing her, but then again, after magically traveling to the past, the explanations of a legendary sorceress made more sense than anything I'd been able to come up with.

Once Scáthach explained things, the pieces began to line up. Scáthach said my finding ability was needed. Finally, something that made sense. But finding out Robin possessed abilities she was unaware of added a new dimension to the puzzle, setting my ability buzzing. I thought of the few times I'd heard her sing. At the time, I'd thought the prickly feeling on my skin was just her voice touching me the way good music did—that sensation of power created when a song resonated with your soul. But now, I wondered how much was her voice, and how much was *true* power.

Power aside though, I was having a hard time understanding how we were going to get back to the present. I'd listened when Scáthach explained her heartbreaking departure from Montréal; not wanting to interrupt what was clearly a private, family moment. I could see her love and pain and knew she hadn't left due to a lack of love, but because she'd truly believed it was the only way to keep her husband and child safe. But as she spoke, I began to wonder about the mechanics of traveling through time using the books.

If the codebook was still in our time the way she said it was, and she had hers here, then logically, the portal should be available for us to go back. So why and how had we crossed through to this time without using it in the first place? A sudden wave of fatigue washed through me before I had a chance to ask, and I attempted to hide a yawn.

Scáthach smiled and stood, raising her arm and gesturing to the door. "I believe we have said enough for now. You need rest after your long journey. Come, I will guide you back to your rooms." Robin opened her mouth to protest, but Scáthach shook her head once. "I promise we will talk more tomorrow. I will teach you what I can to prepare you for your return trip home after you sleep."

Robin bowed her head, accepting the words meekly. "All right. I am pretty tired. Maybe sleep will help me process." She tilted her head, raising her eyebrows as she looked at me. "Mark? What do you think?"

"I could do with sleep," I agreed. "There's a lot to think about. Hopefully, things will be clearer in the morning." I hesitated, pursing my lips. I looked between the two women then asked the question that had been gnawing at me. "If the books were how you traveled to Robin's time before, how did we get here? We didn't use them."

Scáthach waved off a servant who had arrived to guide us to our rooms, giving them quiet instructions in a language I assumed was Gaelic. The small woman curtseyed and scurried away, and Robin's mother smiled in a self-deprecating fashion.

"Everyone in the castle is so helpful it sometimes feels like I'm tripping over people." When I raised an eyebrow, she elaborated. "Everyone in the castle was either sent here for training or escaped from danger elsewhere. Many have power of their own and were persecuted for it, while others are orphans, or those who had fallen on hard times. Dunscaith is a sanctuary of peace in a tumultuous world. No matter how much I reassure them they do not need to earn their keep, many of the newer residents feel otherwise."

I realized she'd avoided my question, but didn't press, making a mental note to ask in the morning. There was so much we still didn't know, and it was late. I considered the woman leading us through the winding halls. According to Robin, little was known about the legend of Scáthach or her castle. How much of what was recorded was based on fact, and how much had been omitted, wasn't clear. After meeting her it was obvious to me she was more than just a fierce warrior or the shadow sorceress history spoke of. If people came from all over to join her and stay, there must be more going on in this castle than she'd told us so far. The familiar prickle of my talent told me I was right, but now wasn't the right time to explore that line of thinking.

Scáthach paused between the doors to our rooms. Giving us each a smile, she bowed her head slightly. "Sleep well. Wake when your body tells you. You are safe here."

"Thank you," I nodded to both women as I entered my room, giving them a chance to say goodnight privately.

For the first time in weeks, I was able to let down my guard completely. The sensation of a weight being lifted was almost enough to make me collapse into bed. Nothing would harm Robin in her mother's castle. Within seconds, my eyes closed and the next thing I knew, sunlight reflecting from metal bars on the stone window pierced my heavy eyelids.

Metal? Stone?

I sat up abruptly, the strange events of the day before returning in a rush. Swinging my legs over the side of the bed, I stood and walked to the small table in the corner of the room where I found a hand towel and bowl of water already waiting. I tested it, finding it the perfect temperature. When had the bowl been placed there?

I glanced around, but saw no one. It was another one of those magical events my life seemed to be overflowing with lately I guess. Deciding not to dwell on questions I couldn't answer, I washed my face and upper body and toweled off before dressing. Although it had seemed strange at the time, I was grateful Robin had made me bring my bag from the car. It wasn't quite as good as a shower, but a change of underwear was a blessing and I felt relatively clean by the time I left my room.

My heart rate ticked up in anticipation when I knocked on Robin's door, and I was rewarded almost immediately when it opened to reveal a halo of honey gold hair wreathing a bright face that softened into a smile when she saw me. My mouth went dry. I cleared my throat, feeling like an awkward thirteen-year-old talking to a girl for the first time. "Good morning. Um, did you sleep okay?"

She didn't appear to notice how dumb I sounded, which was good. I'd planned to open with something more clever, but the moment she'd smiled, I had nothing.

"Actually, yes. I had an amazing sleep, thanks for asking."

And she must have. The dark, bruised look beneath her eyes had softened, and there was a faint blush of roses in her cheeks, like I'd woken her from an enchanted slumber with my knock. The urge to pull her into my arms was almost overwhelming. She was even more beautiful rested.

A long moment went by where she stared at me before I realized she was waiting for me to reply, not sweep her off her feet, and I started with embarrassment. "Um, sorry. I'm still half-asleep. What do you think the odds of finding a cup of coffee in this century are? Any idea which decade it came to Europe?"

She pursed her lips, wrinkling her forehead as she considered the idea. "You know, I'm not sure. I doubt it was before Columbus, though. Pretty sure we're out of luck."

Sighing dramatically, I agreed. "You're probably right. Can we check anyway? Maybe we'll get lucky. I mean, this place *is* magic."

I let myself look as miserable as possible, earning a giggle for my efforts. I held my hand out for her to take, my palm tingling slightly when she accepted it after shutting the door.

We retraced our steps from the day before, returning to the window-lined room overlooking the courtyard. It was empty, but the sun lit the chairs in a cheery fashion. I spotted a door that looked like it led to the garden and pulled on her hand.

"Come on; let's go check out the courtyard."

She gave me a bemused smile but didn't resist as I headed to the stairs leading down into an open area. Paths shot out from the bottom like spokes of a wheel, and in the center, beneath a large tree groaning under the weight of apples, was an ornately carved wooden bench. I led her toward the bench and sat down, breathing in the beauty around me for a moment before turning to her.

I caught her with her eyes closed and her face turned up, soaking in the morning air in much the same way I had, but she reminded me of a flower basking in the sunshine. For a long moment I sat, appreciating the peace and the company.

My mind wandered back to what Scáthach had told us the night before. While I hadn't been able to find anyone able to specifically train me on how to use my gifts, I also hadn't felt they were suppressed. Sure, I didn't always get a chance to use them in my job, but I'd been as true to myself as I could be in the world I lived in. Of course, as soon as I started to think about that, I thought about what I would tell my boss when I got back, if anything. I didn't even know where or when we'd return to.

I was in the middle of considering how our trip to the past could affect the future when Robin opened her eyes and caught me staring at her.

Her mouth curved into a smile and she raised an eyebrow. "You have a funny look on your face."

I bit my lip, unable to keep from grinning back sheepishly. "Well, I started off thinking how beautiful you are, but then I got distracted wondering what we're going to tell people when we get back."

Her smile faded. "Yeah, I've been thinking about that as well. Ideally, we'll return to the exact moment we left. If that's the case, we don't need to say anything. If we return too early, we'll have to stay put until we get to our time to avoid changing the future." She winced then asked, "Is it wrong to base everything I know about time travel and alternate realities on graphic novels? Yes? No?"

I laughed. "I don't think it's necessarily the best scriptwriting, but it's better than anything I can come up with. I'm sort of hoping we return to the same time we left as well, because it will be hard to explain if we show up months later."

She winced again. "Not to mention the repercussions on us with school and work."

We fell silent as we considered the ramifications. Would she graduate if she returned after the fact? Would I get fired? Neither were great possibilities. When she finally broke the silence, her voice was hesitant.

"So... I've been thinking about the way the book disappeared. If my mom is right, and the codebook must stay in the same time as the manuscript, it has to be somewhere in the present. Er, future?"

I bought time, scratching my chin as I considered her words. The rasp of stubble was harsh against my skin. How long had it been since I'd shaved? I wasn't certain anymore. "Okay, if we say the book is somewhere in our timeline, then the questions remain; where is it, and why did it vanish to begin with?"

She pressed her lips together, now looking frustrated. "That's what I can't figure out. I was dreaming about the book when I woke up the morning we left the hotel. About my dad *and* the book."

I felt my neck prickle at her words and allowed the sensation to expand. Something about what she'd said made my gift sit up and pay attention. But, which part? I leaned closer, searching her face. "You were dreaming about the book the morning we went to look for your dad?"

She nodded. "Yes, I tossed and turned most of the night, but right before waking up, I had a dream about a book identical to the one we saw in the video from the bookstore. My dad was there, and he told me I was connected to the book because of who I was, and because of who my mom was. But I figured I was just having another stress dream. I'd completely forgotten about it until now."

I tilted my head, closing my eyes and allowing her words to wash over me. Following the buzz of my gift, a sense of rightness coursed through me, and when I opened my eyes, I knew.

"No, you weren't having a stress dream. I'm certain you saw your dad. Based on what we've learned here, if you're connected to the book...."

Her eyes widened, and a hand flew to her mouth. "Do you think the book disappeared because of me?"

I nodded. "I do. And, if I'm right, the missing codebook should be in the same place you saw it last."

She frowned. "In my dream it was at the hotel, but we've already searched everywhere. The book wasn't there."

I shook one finger. "We didn't search before we left; we searched the night before you dreamed about the book."

Her mouth fell open. "Oh my God. You're right!"

I stood and held out my hand, giving her a half-smile. "I think the codebook disappeared from the bookstore for whatever magical reason it had, and somehow your subconscious found it afterward. The only way to know if I'm right is to find out when we return to our time and look again. Good thing you kept the room, hey?"

Excitement flooded her face. "We need to get back to Paris." She paused. "What do we do about the rental car?"

I waved the question aside. "The car is the least of our concerns. I can make a phone call to another agent if we return in a different location." I winked. "One of the perks about my job is having the ability to deal with small annoyances by calling in backup. Some may call it dumping, I call it awesome."

She didn't look entirely reassured by my joking reply, but she didn't argue. "In that case, I'd like to find out what my mom meant about powers. Okay, that sounds weird." She halted, shaking her head before continuing. "I hope she can teach me something, but the sooner we can leave, the better. I'm not comfortable staying here any longer than necessary. What if we accidentally change something in the future?"

As I had similar concerns, I easily agreed. "Absolutely. The more people we contact from the past, the more chances we take that something will change. We'll talk to Scáthach, find out what she knows, and get her to send us back. From the sound of it, she's the only one who can."

Chapter 24 Mark

With the help of a servant who was able to speak an odd dialect of English well enough for us to communicate what we needed, we managed to locate Scáthach. When we found her, I was pleased to discover breakfast as well. I wasn't used to eating the type of breakfast food offered to us, but it was close enough not to confuse or frighten me, which I counted as a win.

Conversation while we ate involved the two women circling each other carefully. For the most part, I listened, unable to imagine how I would feel if reunited with a parent after such a long time, not to mention under the odd conditions. To Robin, her mom had basically returned from the dead. The same thing wasn't true for Scáthach though, and if I'd harbored any doubt her mom loved her, it evaporated long before I'd finished eating.

It showed in every word and every glance, the way she'd go to touch Robin's hair, face, or arm, as if she was trying to convince herself Robin was actually there, but pull back just before she did, remembering she shouldn't. The longing in her face was so strong at times I had to look away. It was obvious she'd suffered from the separation, and after watching her, it looked like the most painful non-physical torture anyone could go through. But without ever having had a child of my own, I was certain I was underestimating the reality.

Once our plates were empty, a servant entered and bowed.

Scáthach's eyes widened, and a hand flew to her throat. "My goodness! Look at the time. You said you wanted to be on your way as soon as possible. Now that you are full, let us adjourn to my chambers. I will tell you everything I can there, away from potential eavesdroppers."

She tilted her head deferentially toward the servant, giving the woman a slight smile of apology.

"As much as I trust everyone within these walls, some information is on a need to know basis. I have never shared certain details of my journal with anyone else. But as my daughter, everything I am about to tell you is your birthright. Whether you will consider the knowledge a burden or a blessing is up to you."

She dismissed the servant who offered to accompany us, instructing them to stay behind. She led us to the door and down a long hallway I hadn't seen earlier. After several twists and turns, we arrived at a hidden staircase where she stopped, pausing in front of a door with a large brass lion for a handle.

"What I am about to show you is a secret. Prophecies can be vague, misinterpreted, and manipulated. If altered, it is hard to know if, or when, things have been changed for the better. Sometimes, the very thing you are trying to prevent can occur because of good intentions and tampering."

While her words weren't entirely clear, the warning in her tone was.

When Robin remained silent, I replied as honestly as I could. "I understand. I'll do everything in my power to protect anything you share today, along with keeping your daughter safe. But, as you've already pointed out, knowledge is power. Without more information than we have now, our enemies have the upper hand."

She nodded with approval. "Well said. Once we are inside, feel free to ask anything, but remember—I may not have the answers you seek, or if I do, they may not be the ones you want to hear."

With that last warning, she turned and pushed the door open. Robin's hand crept into mine. I gave it a squeeze, trying to give her courage, but her weak smile in return wasn't much stronger. We ascended a short, dimly lit staircase in silence, entering a surprisingly well-lit, circular room at the top. Instead of the room of potential horrors I'd half-expected to see, it appeared instead to be a comfortable bedroom.

A large bed took up most of one wall, while a nearby wardrobe and small sitting area took up most of another, but my attention was drawn to the other wall when Scáthach headed to a small library that was partially shielded by a large bookshelf. To my surprise, she pushed the spine of one of the books. The bookshelf slid forward, revealing another room.

I didn't know if it was an optical illusion, or if there actually was an entirely separate room in front of me. Behind the bookshelf was an archway that led to another section of tower. Three windows only as wide as my head extended from waist height to ceiling in front of me. They must have been ten feet high, and on either side of the windows, a sconce flickered with a torch. The fire didn't appear to have any visible fuel source, nor was it the usual color of fire.

Without asking, I knew it wasn't a natural fire, but even as the idea crossed my mind, I was distracted by the podium in the center of the room, in front of the middle window. An ornate book lay open on top, reminding me of pictures I'd seen of the *Book of Kells* that was in Trinity College in Dublin.

Could it be? No. Because if it was, that would mean...

I shook my head, pushing the thought away as I looked around the rest of the room. Figuring out if Robin's mom had an ancient book of mysteries in her private study wasn't my main goal right now.

A tingle coursed down my spine when my eyes landed on a small bench underneath the far window.

Innocently decorated with cushions, the bench was arranged beside a small table with two books neatly placed on top, as if someone had been reading there a second ago and would be right back. There was nothing particularly special about the seating area, and visually, it wasn't nearly as interesting as everything else in the mysterious room, but in the space between heartbeats, my finding ability sprang fully awake.

The books right in front of me were at the root of everything happening now.

Scáthach glanced my way and, catching my gaze, smiled. "Good. You've spotted them. Your gift *is* strong, even if mostly untrained. I am grateful you do not use it to persecute others with magic, the way so many of your ancestors did."

When I jumped, she gave me a sad nod. "You've perhaps heard of witch finders?" Shaking my head, I began to apologize, but she waved a hand. "It is okay. In a way, I am glad you have not. Other finders have existed before you, and many have used their magic in ways nature never intended. Unable to accept the premise that anything unexplainable could be good, they instead believed God had given them their own gifts as a way to rid the world of witches and demons. Many innocent lives have been lost at their hands during the course of history. Luckily, the time you were born into and the people who raised you were different, and have guided you better."

I looked at her, unsure if I was in trouble or being praised, and she sighed.

"Well, go on. Look for yourselves. As you have already surmised, those books are the reason the game pieces have been set in motion. It is okay for you to peruse them."

For a moment, she looked tired and frail, and so much like Robin had back at the hotel that I wanted to say something to comfort her. I took a step toward her, but before I could work up the words, her attention shifted to Robin.

"Sometimes, I wonder if I'd have done better not writing anything down. But whenever I think that, I remember how much love and happiness I received from you and your father. It may not have been as much time as I wanted, but it gave me hope for the future. I have dreamed of seeing you again, one day. And now, here you are." She smiled, but it had the same bittersweet sadness as before.

Robin must have seen it too, because she crossed the distance and gave her mom a hug.

I stood back as I watched the women, able to bear watching the strength and the pain of the love between them. Even with the shock of finding her mom alive, Robin hadn't taken long to forgive her mom for the years of distance. The trust may be shaky, but I didn't doubt they loved each other.

When Robin relaxed her hold, I cleared my throat. "Um, Scáthach? You said you have the codebook, but that a copy also exists in the future. How can we be certain we'll return to the correct time? And how did we get here without using it to begin with?"

Scáthach sat on the bench, patting the space beside her. Robin sat next to her and I gingerly followed, careful to leave enough space not to crowd either of woman while I waited for an explanation.

"I cannot explain how it works with physics or science," she began, apologetically. "But from what I can determine, travel by the books has to do with the bloodline of the one using it. Because I had to create a new book to return to my time from Montreal, the book is tied to me, and through me to my children. I don't know if it can exist in a time where my blood does not. So, I know the book will exist as far in time as when Robin or any children of hers were last alive. Does that make sense?"

Robin shook her head. "I don't know. Maybe? It sounds plausible, but it still doesn't explain how you can be sure we'll return to when we left, especially if I'm here now."

Scáthach grimaced. "It is not an exact science, as I have already mentioned. The Highlands themselves are known for their abilities to warp time and space. I'm sure you've heard tales of people witnessing battles from centuries ago?"

She chuckled dryly. "They have even made plays about the phenomena—you are familiar with *Brigadoon*?"

When Robin's eyes widened, she smiled and took her hands.

"I cannot be certain you will return to one place, but I have seen some of what is to come. I have faith that, between my magic and Mark's finding ability, you will return exactly to when you are required in your time line. 'Tis no' exactly a guarantee you can hang your hat on, but..."

Her accent thickened into a more Scottish brogue as she half-shrugged, and I leaned forward. Since entering the room, my finding had been humming to a low tingle, but now, it blazed up fiercely.

"I think I know where the book is. But if I'm correct, we'll return to Paris, not Scotland."

Scáthach turned to me for a moment, and once again, I felt she was peeling back the layers of my skin, searching my soul. Then just as abruptly, she leaned back and crossed her arms, the satisfied expression on her face giving me the feeling I had confirmed something for her.

"I believe you *do* know. That is why you were assigned to watch my daughter and the true reason for your mission."

"What—?" I croaked.

She narrowed her eyes, holding up a hand. I stopped instantly.

Her words were mild, but firm. "I do not need details. But you need to know that this information is classified, particularly from the people you work for. No government should *ever* have information allowing them to connect the Voynich manuscript to my codebook. Humans have come a long way, but there are too many cogs in a government for me to trust even an honest one with my prophecies."

I hung my head. For the first time, I was almost ashamed I worked for CSIS. She was right—how many times throughout history had powerful information ended up in the wrong hands? Was it possible my organization already knew about the books? Was that the *real* reason I'd been assigned to watch Robin and her dad?

I couldn't be sure, which meant I had to keep what I knew a secret from my organization. Looking at her, I crossed my heart. "I won't tell a soul. When I tie up loose ends, I'll omit any specific mention of the books from my report, beyond what is expected."

Scáthach's expression eased slightly. "Good. I am relieved to hear that. Now, before you return, Robin must learn to access her power."

She stood and strode over to the podium, beckoning for Robin to join her. Surprise flashed over Robin's face, and with a combination of curiosity and apprehension, she joined her as directed.

"I believe Mark knows the basics of his power, even if he is somewhat out of practice." She raised her eyebrows.

I blushed. It felt like I'd been scolded by a Victorian schoolteacher for not handing in my homework. "Yes, ma'am. I promise, once I get back, I'll use it more."

She nodded her approval. "Good. I recommend setting aside a minimum of one hour a day from now on. Something tells me you may require more from your talent in the future. A combination of meditation and practice locating objects and people should be adequate, I think."

"What about me? I mean, you said my power is in my voice, but I'm already practicing daily."

Scáthach shook her head at Robin's question. "Yes, but you practice as if you have an instrument, not as if you have an *ability*. There is a fine distinction. If you were an ordinary human, what you've been doing would be perfectly sufficient to become one of the best opera singers in the world."

Robin's eyes widened. "Really? You mean it?"

Scáthach's clapped a hand on her daughter's shoulder. "I'm proud of how far you've come. In fact, I would like you to sing now. I need to see what is missing."

Robin looked confused, but with a shrug, launched into an aria I'd never heard her sing before. Once she'd finished, Scáthach pursed her lips and turned to the book on the podium. She flipped the pages until she came to a picture that looked a little like a mermaid on a rock.

Not wanting to miss out on the action, I left the bench and came to stand behind Robin. Up close, the picture was beautiful. The image was a mermaid, but she was placed in front of a castle, floating with birds surrounding her. It looked almost like a choir with a soloist, but the strangest thing about the image was its uncanny resemblance to Robin.

Seeing the look on my face, Scáthach explained. "This book did not make it to the future; at least, not to my knowledge. There are a few other illuminated manuscripts like it, but if I can be impartial, I think mine is the most beautiful."

Robin leaned closer to the picture. "What is it? Why does she look like me?"

Scáthach voice became hushed and almost reverent. "This book was left to me by my teacher. Remember when I said prophecy is murky? Well, when the vision involves those closest to a seer, we must use other mediums." She waited for Robin to nod her understanding before continuing. "Any time I have been able to see you, it is due to what I have interpreted from these pictures. Therefore, I know you need to reach deep into your soul to find the spark that powers you. I caught a glimpse just now, when you sang, but your magic is buried. You need to unlock your abilities to use them as intended."

Robin's eyebrows shot up. "You saw something when I sang? But... I didn't feel anything different."

Scáthach's face took on a mischievous look. "You may not feel your power, but it's there."

Robin frowned, causing Scáthach to chuckle. By now, I was completely lost. She seemed to be speaking in circles, and my internal finding compass was spinning.

"Sometimes, when something is innate to us, we are unable to recognize it. If you did not have a mirror, how would you know your eyes are blue? This is a similar concept. No one has ever shown you what your magic looks like, and it is as if you have never seen your eyes. That doesn't mean they aren't blue."

Robin's frown deepened. I was beyond confused now, and Scáthach let out a small snort then changed tack.

"Have you ever lost time singing? Or found people more receptive after you've sang for them?"

Robin thought for a minute before shrugging. "Maybe? I just assumed I'd sang well."

Scáthach nodded. "Perhaps. Any song is better with a touch of magic, whether you used it knowingly or not. You have the power to influence others with your voice; to make them do, and believe, what you want them to."

Robin's mouth dropped open. "Wait—are you saying I have some kind of mind control powers?"

Scáthach's face smoothed out. "Exactly. You have been given a great and terrible gift, my dear." She turned and took Robin's hands in her own. "A gift of this nature has the potential to be used for both good or evil. You must learn how to control it, and always, always use the power with caution. Never change events unless absolutely necessary."

Robin looked troubled. If I were in her shoes, I'd be wondering if continuing to sing was safe, but she merely pressed her lips together for a moment as she processed.

When she looked at her mom again, her eyes were clear. "So how do I access my power? And how do I guard against hurting others?"

Scáthach took Robin's hand and paused, guiding it to hover just over the image of the mermaid who could have been her twin.

"This is a special book, and over the years, I have read it from cover to cover. When a page is meant for me, I merely need to touch it for the answers to reveal themselves. When I look at this page, all I see is the image before me. I believe this page is meant for you. But be warned—once you touch the book, you can never go back to the way things were. Once you choose to know, you will not return to the way you were before."

For a moment, Robin hesitated with her hand just over the page. But as I watched, determination steeled her expression. In that instant, she reminded me of her mother the first day I'd seen her. She was a warrior, ready to meet her destiny.

"My life has already changed beyond anything I ever expected. I may as well know the full extent of what I'm capable of."

Chapter 25 Robin

I looked at Mark, a tendril of anticipation curling around the fear rushing through me. My mom's face was intent, waiting for me to lay my hand on the picture. With the weight of anticipation pressing down on me, breathing took all my effort. I couldn't focus on either my curiosity or fear though.

I needed answers, and I needed them a week ago. I had to save my dad.

If finding out more about myself will help find him, I couldn't turn my back on the opportunity just because I was terrified.

Taking a deep breath, I let my hand drift closer to the page but stopped again an inch away. What if this changed me, but not for the better? If my mom was right, and I did have a latent power to influence others, what would happen?

Did I even want it?

In high school, I'd worried I'd made Melissa sick somehow by being jealous of her, but when she'd improved, I'd wondered if I'd healed her. Both ideas had been crazy and unprovable, so I'd done my best to push the memory down, chalking events up to stress and the germ theory of disease.

But what if it had been real? The curse, as well as the possibility I'd cured her with my singing?

I glanced at Mark. How had he coped with discovering his talent? He had an ability to find things, but I didn't see much in the way of a downside. No potential for becoming really evil. But what if my powers twisted me? What if I wasn't as good as my mom thought, and I started to use them for my own benefit?

Yet, on the other hand, if I didn't find out more, would I ever be able to find my dad?

That thought gave me the strength I needed to take the next step. I'd worked my butt off to achieve my goals in life, and this was no different. If I could spend years training to be an opera singer, I wasn't about to cheat myself now.

Without further hesitation, I put my hand on the page.

At first, nothing changed. My hand rested on dry paper, but as it did, a faint warming sensation grew beneath my fingertips; as if the book was heating up beneath my touch, or my hand was touching the skin of a living person instead of the drawing of a mermaid.

I leaned closer, squinting at the page to see if something had changed. But as I did, my vision darkened. Everything went black.

BLINKING, I FELT SOMETHING cold beneath me. I didn't remember falling, but somehow, I was lying face down on a rock. Had I passed out? Pushing myself up to a seated position, I briefly scanned my body. Nothing hurt or felt injured, but when I tried to open my eyes, cold water splashed against my face. I inhaled the spray, as shocked as if someone had just slapped me.

I opened my eyes again, more cautiously this time, to find I was sitting on a rock in the middle of the ocean, with water lapping against my feet. No, that wasn't entirely correct. I looked down, and discovered that not only was my clothing gone, but there was an iridescent, greenish-blue tail draped over the side of the rock where my feet should have been.

My eyes widened. The shimmering tail came all the way up my torso in something resembling an evening gown, and ended in a point just below my throat. My hair fell loosely around my shoulders and in front of my body like a cape. I touched the area where my legs should have been and felt the chill of my hand. This was no dress.

"What the heck?"

My words were swallowed by the crash of the waves, and the only answer I heard was the far off sound of seagulls. I pinched my arm, forcing myself to breathe through my nose instead of hyperventilating the way I wanted to. *Think, Robin, think!*

A second ago, I'd touched a page with a mermaid that looked just like me, and now... I looked down at my body again. I was one hundred percent the mermaid in the book. "Holy crap. I did not see that coming."

Forcing myself to think about why I was here instead of how crazy it was to have a tail, I spent a moment admiring it before looking at the horizon. How could mermaids be related to my powers? Was it because they were supposed to be good singers?

I whirled at the faint sound of laughter, almost losing my perch on the rock when someone spoke nearby.

"It *is* one of the more well-known legends. Although in those stories, we are generally called sirens."

Leaning against the other side of the rock as if she was waiting for a bus was a woman with startlingly red hair and pale, mother-of-pearl opalescent skin, watching me with twinkling emerald green eyes. She was arguably the most beautiful person I'd ever met and was now watching my reaction with a grin.

My hand went to my throat, but I quickly gathered my wits. Maybe she was here to provide answers. "You startled me—I didn't see you there a moment ago. Who are you? Wait – us? Are you a...?"

I tried to peek over the side of the rock to get a better look at her undercarriage, but she threw her head back and laughed, then slipped over the side into the water. I almost cried out in panic when I thought she was gone, but a splash in front of me caught my attention.

I turned again and caught her playfully flicking water onto my tail. I shook my head. My *tail*. Surely, I must be dreaming.

"You may call me a siren, others say mermaid. In the islands of Greece, I am usually known as Circe. That is my name, by the way."

"Circe? You mean..."

She tipped her chin, looking suddenly disgruntled. "Try not to believe everything you read. Jason and his Argonauts... well, normally I would be charitable, but they were the worst kind of dumb. Not only did they exaggerate everything in their famous 'adventures', but they more than earned the privilege of turning into pigs. Not that I did that." She rolled her eyes, and her expression became bored. "That was my sister."

For moment, I was speechless. Jason? Pigs? Mermaids? The incongruity overcame me, and I began to laugh. When I heard an edge of hysteria in the sound, I stopped abruptly and forced myself to take a deep breath in an attempt to regain control.

Once again falling back on manners, I smiled at the mermaid in front of me and pretended she was a famous singing coach. "I don't understand what's happening. Can you help? The last thing I remember is touching a picture of a mermaid who looked like me..."

I bit my lip, suddenly wondering how much to tell her. She waited, watching me with a calm, implacable expression, and I decided it didn't matter if this was a dream or not—I needed to trust someone if I wanted to get back.

Sighing, I shared everything. "I need to understand how to use my powers to save my dad. Until yesterday, I believed my mom was dead and he was kidnapped, but now everything is so much stranger. Somehow, I've managed to time warp hundreds of years into the past, and now I'm a mermaid. So, basically, I have no idea what's going on and it's possible I am hallucinating."

A smile spread over her face at my disjointed mishmash of questions and details, and it gave her a look of such radiant kindness it made me blink. "I do not know your father, but your mother and I are acquainted. In fact, I owe her a great debt. As for you, let us say I have been waiting to speak with you again. Do you remember our last conversation?"

She smiled again, and it struck me that she looked familiar. Where had I seen her before? Frowning, I examined her more closely. Surely, I couldn't have forgotten meeting a mermaid. Maybe she mistaking me for someone else. But she merely waited, the same mysterious, small smile playing around her lips. Just when I was about to give up trying to place her, she began to hum the lyrics of an old song.

My hand went to my mouth. "You—you're the mermaid from the music box. You were in my dreams!"

In grade twelve, the same time the odd events with Melissa had been unfolding, I'd received a mysterious music box in the mail from Scotland. It had a return address that was from the Isle of Skye but no sender, and I'd never discovered why it had appeared when it did. Following its arrival, I'd had odd dreams every night for weeks until one morning, when I'd looked at it and found a bland ballerina figurine instead of the mermaid. That was when the dreams had vanished completely. I'd chalked everything from that time up to stress, and had completely forgotten about the music box—until now.

Circe bowed. "Indeed. I am somewhat surprised it has taken so long to encounter you in person, but on the other hand, I was not expecting to find you in your true form yet, either." She gestured to my legs. "Oh well, some things are delayed, while others arrive early."

I tried to match her calm but was certain I was failing miserably. She had the coolness of a Hollywood star, and it made me feel as if I was in the presence of royalty.

"I'm pretty surprised myself," was all I managed to croak out.

To be fair though, one moment I was in a castle with a new crush and my long-lost mom, and the next, I was a mermaid in the middle of ocean. Such a change would be an adjustment for anyone.

She nodded slowly. "I can see how the situation would be disorienting. But, as we do not have much time, we should get started. Why don't we begin by determining if you are able to function in your new aquatic form before we work on exploring the essence of your magic."

I leaned forward, eager to finally get some answers. "What do I do? Do I just dive in?"

She shrugged. "No reason not to. But remember, the way humans swim is not how you will move as a mermaid. You can use your arms, but the real power comes from the tail. It will take time to coordinate your movements, so do not panic. It may be helpful for you to know that mermaids cannot drown."

I nodded then launched myself inelegantly into the water with one of the worst belly flops I'd ever performed. The slap against the water caused me to inhale sharply, but I held onto her words like a lifeline as I struggled. Knowing I wouldn't drown went a long way toward keeping me calm, particularly since it felt like someone had tied my legs together.

It took several minutes, but once my head was submerged beneath the waves and I didn't die, I was able to relax. After a few minutes longer, I began to get the hang of it. I was pleasantly surprised to discover the water wasn't as cold as I'd expected. Maybe my new form adapted to the ocean temperature as well.

After a few more tentative movements, where I discovered breathing underwater was exactly like breathing air, I gradually improved. Soon, I was able to lift my head above water again and, while not nearly as graceful as Circe, I was surprised how much easier it was to swim with a tail than I'd imagined.

I surfaced to find her smiling at me with approval. "Easy, right?"

I shook my head, laughing at myself. "Easier than I thought, but I have a lot of practicing ahead of me."

When her laughter rang out like bells, the ethereal sound was as striking as her beauty.

I narrowed my eyes. "Your laugh – is that part of the magic I'm supposed to learn?"

She stopped laughing but still looked amused. "Part of it, yes. There is a reason siren are said to have the power to sing men to their death. Not all the stories are true, of course." She paused to shake her head. "Sailors in general are a superstitious lot. Not to mention after months at sea many men would jump overboard at even the ugliest, vaguely female-shaped creature. Oh, and don't forget all the vitamin deficiencies." She shuddered delicately. "Bleeding at the gums, and crazy to boot."

I smirked, thinking how many encounters I'd had in the past with odd men. "Yeah, I'm not surprised. Tell me more about the connection between mermaids and singing. Does the magic lie in the music, or is the voice where the magic lies? Like, if you talk to someone, would the magic have the same effect?

She considered my question for a moment then shook her head. "Yes, and no. It's not about the music or the voice. It is because we can harness the power of our soul; the thoughts, feelings, and desires within us, and then use that energy to influence those who hear us. We can make others feel happy if we are happy, or sad when we feel sad. Whatever we experience is present in our song, if, and when, we wish it to be so. In extreme cases, it is possible to wound, or even compel others to end their own life."

I drew back with a hiss, and she nodded, her face solemn.

"It is a great power, and one not to be taken lightly. Once you understand all the implications, you will know how important it is to use your voice wisely. There is one more thing you should know about sirens before you return."

My eyebrows went up. "Only one? But I don't know anything, yet."

She inclined her head. "True. But this part relates to the origin of your abilities. For you to possess this type of magic, you must have mermaid blood in your family tree somewhere." She narrowed her eyes, tilting her head to the side and considering me closely. "Normally, I would guess your power came from your mother, as this magic usually travels through the maternal line, but I know Scáthach's background. You must get your siren magic from your father's side."

My eyes threatened to pop out of their head. "My dad? But... he's human. He teaches at a university. He's a completely average dad, well, for a professor."

"Maybe. What about your paternal grandmother? Or aunts?"

I shook my head, unable to believe my dad could have contributed in any way to the magical weirdness in my life beyond than his recent disappearance. Finding out my mom was alive was enough of a shock. Now Circe was saying my dad had mermaids in his family tree?

The image did not fit the tweed-wearing, professorial stereotype he exemplified.

Yet, even as I as I tried to deny it, a small voice whispered inside my head. He hadn't told me everything about my family, and he hadn't been honest about my mom's death either. Based on everything I'd learned this week, there was a high probability he'd neglected to share other important information as well, like a mermaid or two in the family tree. But, to find out, I had to find him and demand answers. For now, the origins of my power would have to wait.

Because first, I had to learn everything Circe could teach me about being a siren.

Chapter 26 Robin

Something about the way I moved in the water made my thoughts more fluid than ever before. Maybe the sensation was what athletes called a flow state, but as I tapped into the qualities Circe was trying to show me, I experienced more than my usual, simple joy at singing. I realized I'd taken my voice for granted as something to polish and perfect with practice. Now, it was so much more.

My voice wasn't different—*I* was different.

"You seem to be picking this up nicely. Does everything make sense so far?" Circe waited for me to nod, and when I did, she clapped her hands. "Wonderful! Now, in order to verify you are using your voice correctly, we need an audience."

An audience? I crossed my arms, not keen on using my newfound ability with anyone else present, but my concern didn't seem to faze Circe.

After examining me for a moment, she pointed toward the ocean. "There."

I squinted, following her gaze. I saw nothing an empty, blue horizon in front of me. "There's nothing there."

A mischievous grin spread across her face. "You are mistaken. In fact, there is a very important ship ahead, which I would like you to try to inspire."

Feeling uncomfortable, I hesitated. Circe noticed and swam closer, resting a hand on my shoulder.

She gave it a quick squeeze. "Worry not. I would not ask you to do anything to change the future, nor the past. All I wish you to do is sing. The ship heading toward the coast is meant to conquer England, but they have gotten a little off course. I want you to simply encourage them to head southward, to the location they are meant to land."

Circe cocked her head and listened.

I strained my ears but heard nothing. "Should I hear something?"

A faint smile crossed her face. "No, not hear, not with your ears at least. This is about what you can feel with your soul. You see, the ship is off track because of your mother. When she traveled to the future, it caused ripples in time, and some events were thrown off kilter. We have been correcting them here and there as needed, but I would like you to set this one to rights so that history may unfold as is meant."

I bit the inside of my cheek. "Won't things change in my time if I do?"

A dreamy look replaced the one she'd worn earlier. "Time is fluid, much like the great waters of the earth. As a mermaid and the daughter of a sorceress, you will develop the ability to understand those waters better than most."

When I opened my mouth, she shook her head, as if already knowing what I wanted to ask.

"No, you will not be able to tell the future, not like your mother, but you *will* be able to sense the ripples as changes spread out. When they deviate from where they are meant to be, you will know. It will be as obvious as a pebble thrown into a pond. Soon, you will learn what to avoid, and what to change."

I could already sense the currents she spoke of, both literal and figurative. I closed my eyes. Awareness rushed through me. I felt dark the undertows in the sea where creatures became stuck, mired in the layers of silt that preserved the bodies of hapless victims for the ages.

I gasped and opened my eyes, overwhelmed by all the knowledge.

Her hand was still on my shoulder, but I didn't feel reassured by her touch any longer.

"I know. It's too much to handle at once. The only solace I can give is that learning is better here, with me, than returning home and stumbling upon the darkness without forewarning."

I looked at her, almost mesmerized by her emerald eyes. How much of what I felt was due to her power? Was she controlling me, even now? But as I looked at her, memories of the cryptic dreams in high school returned, and my worries subsided.

"How will I learn enough to avoid the darkness? And why are you helping me?"

I wasn't sure what I was asking, but she brightened, her smile seeming to make the clouds part. The sun was so strong now I was almost blinded. I blinked against it.

"We are linked, you and I. All creatures with the magic of water in their blood are. As much as a school of fish senses when they are together, a siren can always find another siren once they are connected. Only a few of us now remain, but you will encounter other sirens, along with others with and without magic who will help guide you on your way. No matter how stormy the waters of life may become."

Was it her words, or her magic that made me feel better?

Perhaps there was no difference. Whatever the case, I knew I would do what she'd asked of me. Taking a deep breath, I looked out into the empty ocean, searching for the ship she wanted me to try my power on.

"Now what?"

Removing her hand from my shoulder, she pointed southeast. "Just beyond the horizon is a ship of soldiers who've been blown off course. The waters they have entered are unfamiliar. If they attempt to land there, they will be dashed upon the rocks, thus changing the future." She raised one eyebrow. "Your mother may have mentioned the rocks around Skye do not provide many safe harbors?"

I remembered her saying something to that effect when we'd first arrived, but it hadn't seemed important at the time. Now, I understood, and struck out toward the shore. After a few lengths, I realized I was alone. Circe was nowhere to be seen.

Shoving down my uncertainty, I pretended I was auditioning for a lead role. There, I was used to being on my own. At least now I was able to sense the ship on the surface of the water ahead of me. I couldn't be sure which time period I was in, or even where I was. The castle wasn't visible, and there were no recognizable landmarks. All I knew was what Circe had shared with me. The ship needed to land somewhere south of where I was now.

She said the men needed inspiration, so I chose to sing "The White Cliffs of Dover." I knew the song wasn't historically acute, but I hoped it would draw them toward me and the safe beach where they were supposed to land anyway. As I sang, I did my best to infuse adventure, excitement, and hope into every word of the lyrics. I allowed my emotions to spill out into the song and as I did, I sensed the ship turn toward me. I was filled with rush of *knowing*.

At that moment I was certain the men would land safely on the beach and fulfill their duties to history.

I kept singing, heading south and turning every so often to make sure the ship was still in sight, and left them before they reached the shore, feeling a change in the spirits aboard the ship. I couldn't be certain why, but what had felt turbulent before was now a smooth ripple, eager to make land.

I stopped singing, slightly breathless from the effort of swimming and singing at the same time, and watched the ship head to shore. Circe had been right. The song didn't matter so much as the soul that was put into it. I felt the power in my bones, and knew I'd left the men full of inspiration, just as she'd said I would.

The wind began to pick up and as the sky darkened, I fought back a trickle of fear. I could breathe underwater, and I was safe in the water. No storm could change that. When the water began to move, swirling into a small vortex in front of me, I felt no fear. The shimmer in the water was identical to the shimmer I'd walked into with Mark when we'd gone into the past.

Taking a leap of faith, I swam directly into the whirlpool.

Chapter 27 Mark

I caught Robin as she collapsed to the floor in a faint, my body reacting appropriately, even though my heart stopped when I'd realized she'd lost consciousness after touching the paper. Once I'd reassured myself her breathing and pulse were strong, I carried her to the small bench we'd been sitting on earlier.

Her mom trailed after us, her expression strangely calm considering Robin had collapsed after touching the book she'd told her to touch. I glared, not trying to hide my suspicion. "Did you know that was going to happen? You don't seem surprised."

She flinched, and I felt satisfaction my words had hit the target. She exhaled, shaking her head. "Yes and no. The page does nothing when I touch it, but I had a similar experience in my youth, which led me to my own path."

Some of my anger faded as I watched her look down at Robin's sleeping form, her lips pressed together in a tight line.

Suddenly, I felt like a jerk. Sighing, I extended an olive branch. "Do you think she's okay? What happens next?"

Scáthach shrugged. "It depends on her. If she passes the test, she will simply wake up."

I caught her brief hesitation. "*If* she passes the test?"

Her face became even more solemn. "Yes. There is the chance she may fail. If she does..."

She didn't complete the sentence. I wasn't sure if she'd paused out of concern or for another reason, but suddenly, I didn't want to know.

"Okay, I'll proceed with the assumption she'll succeed. How long until she wakes up?"

Scáthach shrugged again. "I have no idea. You may recall my lecture earlier about time being fluid? As someone who sees into past and future, I'm not always able to put a specific time stamp on events."

My shoulders slumped. There wasn't any point being angry at a clairvoyant who didn't have answers. Robin had accepted the risks, and there wasn't anything I could do other than wait for her to come back. I needed to trust she was strong enough to do this herself and would come through.

I just hoped it would be sooner rather than later.

But as Scáthach had so cryptically warned me, time is relative. Eons passed while I watched Robin's motionless body. My stomach was no help at all, remaining in a giant knot the whole time. It could have been lunch or supper for all I knew. I looked to the window, where the sun still shone brightly. It had only moved a few inches when a movement in my peripheral vision caught my attention.

I turned to see Robin's eyelids flicker, then she gasped and sat up, looking around wildly like someone waking up from a nightmare. When she saw me standing in front of the window, she relaxed back on the bench. Closing her eyes and placing a hand on her forehead, she took a few deep breaths then opened her eyes again.

They seemed different—a sharper, clearer blue, if possible, and were even more beautiful than they'd been that morning. I wasn't sure if it was my imagination, but the shade reminded me of the color where the sea meets the sky and you can't tell them apart.

I glanced at Scáthach, who had closed her eyes briefly, betraying the anxiety beneath her smooth facade before she spoke in the same calm tones she'd used with me earlier.

"How did it go, my dear?"

Robin swung her legs over the side and turned to her mom with a smile. "Mind-blowing is an understatement. I met Circe. Did you know she was there? I mean, in the book?"

When Scáthach nodded, Robin stood up and turned to me. I waited, eager to hear everything she'd seen, but didn't expect her to throw herself at me. My arms sprung up reflexively, but when she tightened hers around me, I gathered her closer.

Relishing the feel of her heartbeat next to mine, I knew at that minute I would have been lost if she hadn't returned to me. Long before I was ready, she pulled back, eyes sparkling with a new vibrancy. *What had happened while she'd been gone?*

"It was amazing." Robin tilted her head to the side. "Mom, does Mark have a page in the book?"

Scáthach looked startled. "No, at least, not one that I know of. Then again, I didn't look specifically for him before, so it is possible..." Her eyes narrowed and she walked over to the book, humming to herself as she began to flip the pages.

"Oh, I'm not sure I need to know anything else. I'm happy not to have any more out of body experiences."

Robin's eyebrows shot up. "When have you had an out of body experience?"

I bit my lip. "Well, sometimes, in my dreams. When there's something I'm supposed to find. The first time it happened was when I found my friend. It was terrifying, and not just because of what happened to Paul. I couldn't touch or interact with anything—it was like being a ghost. I hated it."

I shuddered at the memory, and she laughed when I made a face. I was deliberately downplaying my terror, because I didn't want her feeling sorry for me. I'd come to terms with the memory a long time ago, as much as I could. I was drawn to her as she laughed and wanted to get closer. But, when I took a step toward her, she abruptly clapped a hand over her mouth.

She looked at her mom with wide eyes, then back at me. "Did you sense something when I was laughing?"

I felt heat warming my cheeks and blinked, confused. Did she want me to say how hard I was falling for her? As embarrassed as I was, I could tell it was important by the way she was searching my face. "Um, yes?"

She looked elated as she whirled around to her mom. "Circe taught me how to activate my magic. I think I just used it unintentionally!"

Scáthach looked pleased, as if Robin had passed some sort of test, but I had no idea what she was talking about.

My confusion overrode my normal wait-and-see personality. "What's going on?"

Robin was almost bouncing with excitement, but her explanation didn't help my comprehension in the slightest.

"It has to do with how I use my diaphragm and head voice. Circe said I've always been able to access my magic, and if I look back, I'm sure I've used it in the past but didn't recognize it at the time. I think I've used it to win a few roles, and most importantly, heal my friend, Melissa."

I shook my head, still confused. "What does your diaphragm have to do with it?"

Robin slapped her forehead lightly. "Sorry, I forget you don't run in singing circles. Opera singers learn to project our voices through a combination of breathing techniques and using our diaphragms. It's the reason you can hear a diva from the back of the Paris Opera House."

I shook my head. "I had no idea. I just assumed they used microphones, like everyone else."

She tilted her head. "Well, nowadays they can. But we're still trained to project, which is handy in the right venues. Circe said I was a siren, and there's a lot more I can do with my voice than I realized."

Scáthach frowned suddenly. "Circe said you are a siren?"

Robin nodded. "Yes. She also mentioned that's exclusively a hereditary thing."

Scáthach's eyebrows gathered in a pinched fashion, and I got the impression she hadn't been expecting that when she spoke quietly. "You didn't inherit it from me."

Robin exhaled as if she'd had a theory confirmed.

I took her hand. "What does that mean? Is something wrong?"

She shook her head. "No, it just means I have more questions for my dad when we find him. Circe was suspicious my abilities came from his side, because she knows my mom doesn't have them."

Scáthach moved to the bench and sat, looking older and tired as she watched Robin with an inscrutable expression. "Magic can take many forms. It's not impossible you could have gotten the siren ability from my side, but I would be surprised. I would have known before."

Robin grimaced. "Circe said in order to have my gifts, I need at least one full-blood relative, someone in the not-too-distant family tree."

Scáthach's eyebrows shot up. "You don't mean–." When Robin nodded, Scáthach placed her palms against her cheeks. "I had no idea...I never...did she say whether you will have any of my abilities?"

Robin shrugged. "She said they would be different, although time and water are similar and she thinks I'll catch glimpses of the future at times; enough to know if things have shifted from how they were intended to be, so that I can fix them."

I considered her words in silence, allowing the implications to sink in. She was able to use her voice to influence others and could also tell what was supposed to happen in the future? The woman I'd been assigned to watch, who I had more than a small crush on, was actually a mermaid with superpowers?

It made my ability to find shit and have spooky dreams seem tame in comparison.

I realized she was watching me anxiously, so I took a deep breath. I looked at Scáthach, the book, and finally back at her. It was too much to process.

I started to laugh but stopped when Robin and her mom exchanged worried looks. Shaking my head, I smiled wryly. "I was nervous to tell you about my ability, because I thought you'd assume I was crazy. But that's small potatoes next to what you can do. Are you sure you need my help?"

Her mouth dropped open. "Don't say that! Of course I need you. I can't do this by myself, and... I don't want to." She paused, looking down.

I watched as a familiar rosy tint spread across her cheeks, and when she looked up through her lashes, I felt like she was promising me the world.

"I don't want to do any of this without you."

I couldn't stop myself. Completely forgetting her mom was standing right there, I leaned down and kissed her. It was the only way I could show her how I felt, because I didn't have the ability to find words at that instant. When Scáthach cleared her throat, I reluctantly pulled back and began to apologize.

Before I could speak, she held up her hand. "No need to explain. The moment you arrived here it was clear to me you are bonded to each other. All I ask is that you always treat each other with kindness and love, and you will have my blessing."

Heat crawled up my neck and across my face, prickling as it expanded until I felt on fire with embarrassment. "Um, thank you. I promise I'll—."

Robin's hand covered my mouth, cutting off the rest of what I was going to say. "You don't owe me promises. We haven't known each other long enough. I just want you to know that this—" she gestured to me, then back to herself. "...is real. But, right now, our focus is finding my dad. After that's, we can spend time figuring this—us—out."

Her words made my chest ache, but she was right. Exhaling, I did my best to clear my mind and focus on the mission. "I can agree to those terms." I managed to tear my gaze away from her and look at Scáthach. "Now that Robin knows something about her powers, what's next?"

Scáthach gaze was kind as she patted my arm. "You will get your answers when you are meant to know them. I'm sure you will learn more in the days and weeks to come, but I realize that is not what you wish to hear." A crooked smile crossed her face. "Now, it is time to see the books which began all of this. I still cannot decide if it was hubris or carelessness on my part. Perhaps none of what I saw was meant to be written down in any form. I am certain this would not be occurring now had I not."

I saw the conflict in her eyes, an uncomfortable combination of remorse and pride, but knew she wasn't apologizing for her actions. The love on her face as her gaze rested on Robin told me everything. If she hadn't written down her visions, she wouldn't have had Robin, either. One innocent action, such wide ripples.

What would I do for those I loved?

Even though someone was searching for the books with ill intentions, the act of creation itself hadn't been evil. Theoretically, if everything happened for a reason at the time it was supposed to, Scáthach had nothing to regret.

I'd never thought about life in terms of destiny, but after the last few weeks, it was impossible not to. In a way, there was a strange freedom in knowing if I tried my best, the outcome would turn out how it was meant to one way or another.

As these strangely transcendental thoughts were leaping around in my head, Scáthach took the two thin volumes from the table and laid them on top of the mermaid picture on the podium and stepped back.

At first, neither Robin or I moved.

After a few moments looking at the books with trepidation, Robin stepped forward. "Those are the books everyone wants? They're so... small."

Scáthach nodded. "Yes, these are the books. My journal, the one you call the Voynich manuscript, was written in my own particular shorthand, a combination of pictures and words of what I've seen in my visions." She smirked. "I hear it's caused a lot of frustration for scholars."

"Why did you make the codebook in the first place? I mean, if you'd meant to keep your visions secret?"

Scáthach sighed. Clearly, it was a question she'd wrestled before. "Why do any of us do the things we do? Shortly before I started writing it, I had been sick. I'd earned a small nick with a sword in training. In a time with antibiotics, it would have been no more than a simple cellulitis, but here it festered. It was the first time I'd felt my mortality, and I worried the knowledge my gift had shown me would be lost forever. That bothered me more than the idea of meeting death early, and once I recovered, fear galvanized me. I decided to make a codebook for those I trusted most. That was before I met your dad, of course."

Scáthach smiled at Robin, her face softening at the mention of the man.

"I tied it to both my blood and my love, hoping those two connections would keep the visions safe, and ensure only someone I cared for deeply would be able to use them." She looked down at the books and frowned. "It worked, but at a price. I had no idea my sister's jealousy ran so deep. She'd been gifted with her own magic, and it had never crossed my mind she'd covet mine as well."

I pressed my lips together at the heartbreak etched on the lines of her face. If my brother ever betrayed me, I'd be devastated too. "I'm sorry. It's because she's your blood she can access the books, right?"

Scáthach nodded. "Yes. The blood connection is crucial, but cannot distinguish the users' intentions. I guess it is the way of the universe. Good and evil maintain a narrow balance, and great generosity often comes at the cost of an equal greed. But it was in the depths of my disappointment with my sister that your father entered my life. Somehow, her betrayal no longer burned as much."

Robin stepped closer to her mom, lightly touching her arm. "How did he find you?"

Scáthach raised her hands then let them fall to her sides. "I have asked the universe that question hundreds of times. Was it because he *would* be my love? Perhaps he shares a distant branch of my family tree, or perhaps it was to make up for my sister's betrayal. It was a topic we discussed many times in the years we shared, but he knew no more than I."

Robin's expression became thoughtful. "I wonder if he has magic of his own."

"No," Scáthach replied, her voice certain. "We kept no secrets of such nature from each other. And, with the powers of a siren passing via the female line, it is possible he had no knowledge of their existence."

"Maybe it is meant to remain a mystery," I said.

Scáthach shot me a smile. "That is the answer I have resigned myself to. Even with my foresight, I am unable to answer the questions most important to me. Nevertheless, here we are. The codebook you see here should be able to take you to its twin in the future. As for finding your father..." She tilted her head, raising an eyebrow.

I nodded at her unspoken question. "That's where I come in. If I'm correct, the other book is in the nightstand at the hotel in Paris."

Robin's eyebrows lifted, but when she looked at her mom, her jaw was set with determination. "And all I have to do is focus on the book to take us to the present?"

"That is what I believe," Scáthach agreed.

Robin took a deep breath. "Will I see you again?"

Tears sprang to Scáthach's eyes. "I do not know. I am grateful I was graced with an opportunity to see what a beautiful, intelligent, and courageous woman you've become, but my vision will not extend to showing me my heart's fondest desire."

Robin nodded. Before Scáthach could react, she put her arms around her. For a moment, the two clung to each other, then slowly, Robin's grip lessened. When she pulled back, tears streamed down her face.

Her voice was thick with tears, but she smiled through them. "I'm happy I had the chance to see you. I want you to know I had a wonderful childhood and lacked for nothing except you. You couldn't have picked a better man to be my dad. He still loves you, you know."

Her voice broke at the end, and fresh tears flowed down her cheeks. Scáthach's eyes spilled over as well, and they shared one more hug before Robin reached her hand out to mine, pulling me over to the codebook with a watery smile.

"Ready?"

Chapter 28 Mark

"Here's where I placed the protection of my blood."

At first, I thought Scáthach meant it figuratively, with a spell of some sort, but on closer inspection, I saw a small, rust-brown on the bottom right corner of the page.

A fingerprint?

Scáthach smiled at my wide-eyed curiosity. "Interesting is it not? Sometimes, I wonder if magic and science are different entities, or if one is just an extension of the other. While modern science focuses on DNA, fingerprints, and other things we can see with our eyes, I believe it is all part of the same process. Like calls to like after all, whether we are able to explain it or not." She shook her head, a bemused look on her face. "You have no idea how fascinated I was to discover how far human knowledge has advanced since my time. Much of what ordinary people take for granted in the twenty-first century would be considered magic in this time."

I couldn't help agreeing. "I imagine so." Patting my pocket, where my cell phone was currently a useless hunk of glass and plastic, I smiled. "It's probably a good thing our phones don't work here."

Scáthach snorted. "Definitely. Technology was the most difficult thing for me to wrap my mind around—far harder to understand than magic, to be frank. Science has made so many things possible. I'd never dreamed of television, movies, or cellular phones prior to experiencing them first hand."

Robin cleared her throat. "As much as I want to stay and catch up with you, we have to get back. I know what you've said about the way time moves, but I won't feel better until I see my dad and know he's safe. How do we make the book work?"

"You need to read it. But given that Mark is not a blood relative to either of us, I recommend you maintain contact with him at all times. Holding hands should be sufficient, I think."

Robin tilted her head, suddenly frowning. "If it's that easy, why haven't you ever come back?"

I sucked in a breath, watching emotions move across their faces. Confusion and betrayal met with sorrow and regret, and for several uncomfortable moments, the room was deathly quiet.

Finally, Scáthach exhaled, dropping her head. "I was scared. I left to keep you safe, and I knew the threat was still out there. I couldn't have lived with myself if I'd led them directly to you by coming back." She shook her head, caressing one corner of the book with her finger. "I have missed you and your father every day, but I could not be the reason you experienced more pain than I had already caused." Her eyes shone with tears when she looked up again. "Not a day goes by when I do not consider using the book."

I saw Robin's face soften at her words.

"I can't imagine how difficult it would be. I just hope this isn't the last time I get to see you."

Tears spilled again cheeks as the women embraced.

"Me too," Scáthach said, stroking Robin's hair.

I focused on a point outside the window, feeling like an intruder on the private family moment once again. A moment later, Scáthach pulled back, briskly wiping her eyes, then gesturing at the book.

"I think you are ready. With Circe's help, you know something of your nature; enough to at least recognize when others present themselves as teachers, confidants, and allies. But don't forget—you will also find yourself faced with those who would rather fight for the side of darkness, and for the power that comes easily, disregarding the cost to their souls."

Robin clenched her jaw. She nodded at her mom's words, and her eyes blazed with determination as she looked at me. "I'm ready. Mark?"

I held out my hand and she gripped it, her hand firm and dry in mine. "Ready and raring. Ball's in your court."

Scáthach's lips curved in a smile as she regarded the daughter she'd lost so long ago. Her gaze shifted to rest on me, and I saw approval replace pride. "I thank the gods for the gift of seeing my daughter coming into herself, but it was nice to meet you as well, Mark Notting. Something tells me the future will be a better place with you in it. I pray I get a chance to see it again, someday."

I inclined my head, locking eyes with her for a moment. Out of the corner of my eye, I saw Robin gently turn a page. Her thumb had barely brushed the drop of blood when a shimmer exploded from the book, expanding outward rapidly. Her hand jerked in mine and her mouth fell open with a gasp. I wanted to grab her tight, but settled for squeezing her hand to make sure she didn't let go of me.

"It's time," Scáthach's soft voice sounded far away. "It was wonderful to meet you."

Robin nodded once then pulled me into the shimmering book as she disappeared.

I HELD ONTO HER HAND like the lifeline it was as we tumbled through space. Reality shifted around me and my stomach lurched as I swirled. Light, sky, and ground melted together for an eternity. When the kaleidoscope reality finally stopped, I breathed carefully through my nose for several moments, working hard to keep my breakfast down.

It took several moments of deep breathing, but I was finally able open my eyes. I looked down at my hand, relieved to find it clenched around Robin's smaller, paler hand. I relaxed the death grip on her hand and my knuckles creaked in protest.

Robin's eyes were still closed and her face was as white as death, but before I could begin to worry something was wrong, she opened her eyes and looked around.

Her face split into a smile. "You were right, Mark! We're back in the hotel."

I winked. "Well, what do you know? I guess I'm good for something."

Robin let go of my hand and smacked me on the shoulder with it. "Don't be silly. I couldn't have done any of this trip without you. But now that we're back; it's time to find my dad. Where should we start?"

Chapter 29 Mark

It had somehow escaped my mind we still had no idea where her dad was. With everything else we'd seen and experienced, I guess it had gone on the back burner. We stared at each other for a few seconds before Robin narrowed her eyes.

"If this entire thing is being orchestrated by a distant relative, what are the odds they kidnapped my dad because they thought he'd found the codebook?"

I thought about the odds, waiting to see if inspiration struck. Barely a flicker of interest from my finding ability, so not impossible, but also not specific enough to serve as a direction.

"Possible, but that doesn't tell us where to start looking. We have the book, which gives us leverage, but that's it. We don't have any information on who took him, or where. Without any way to trace him, we're still in the dark."

Robin seemed to crumple at the reminder, as gentle as I'd been giving it.

"I thought it would be easier when we got back. It doesn't feel easier."

I clasped my hands behind my back and began to pace across the thick carpet of the hotel room. I needed to use some of the restless energy that was growing inside me, but I couldn't exactly go for a run.

"At least we're in our own time, and we know the code-book can act as a passage between your mom's time and ours. Do you think your relatives know she made two?"

I stopped pacing and crossed my arms, letting the thought unravel in the silence. What difference did it make? If they only knew one book existed, it meant they were only after the secrets in the Voynich manuscript.

That gave me an idea. I spun around, startling Robin with the sudden movement. "If they abducted your dad and they didn't find it on him, they will need to find you next. It's the only move they can make."

Her eyes widened. "You're right."

I smiled, feeling smug. "All we have to do is wait for someone to contact you. And when they do, I say we give them what they want."

Robin's eyebrows furrowed. "I don't understand. If my mom was telling us the truth, we can't ever let them get the codebook."

I chuckled. "I didn't mean we'd give them the real book. We just have to make them *think* we're giving them the book. All we need is something approximately the same size and shape, then if *someone* added a little persuasion..."

Her face brightened until I opened the drawer of the bedside nightstand and pulled out the small, fake-leather bible that had been there when we arrived.

She pursed her lips, her voice dubious. "A bible? What makes you think they'll buy that's the right book?"

I smirked. "Your new abilities, of course."

She frowned. "You mean my voice?"

I nodded. "Exactly. If you can make people feel a specific emotion, why wouldn't you be able to convince them you're giving them what they want?"

She considered the idea then nodded, speaking slowly. "I could try. I *did* steer those sailors away from the rocks back to England."

"If it works, we can exchange the book for your dad and get away before they even realize we tricked them."

"Mark! You're a genius!"

Before I could say anything, she launched herself at me and squeezed her arms around me tightly for a moment before resting her head on my chest.

I hesitated only an instant, then allowed myself to smooth her hair down over her shoulders. Dimly I recognized the now familiar tingle of attraction swirling through my chest and stomach, before dropping lower, and forced myself to pull back. Now wasn't the right time to peruse it. I stroked one last wayward lock of gold off her cheek, and smiled. "As much as I enjoy having you in my arms, I can't promise I'll be able to stay on track if we keep this up much longer."

My cheeks felt hot, but it was nothing compared to the blush that spread over her face. She pulled back, wrinkling her nose as she smiled up at me.

"You're right. Thanks for reminding me. But...after we find him..." She cleared her throat, letting the promise hang in the air. "So, um, how do you propose we make this plan work?"

My mouth went dry at the images that popped into my head, and when I spoke, my voice sounded thick to my own ears. "I thought you could practice on me. Try to convince me the bible is the codebook. If you can make me believe, when I know the truth, you should be able to convince a distant relative who's never seen it."

"Distant. Let's not forget the distant part," Robin added. A hint of disgust flashed over her face. "Won't it seem suspicious if I randomly started singing during a high-stakes trade-off?"

She walked to the window, her face pensive as she stared out at the Paris skyline.

I followed, mostly because I wanted to remain close to her, but partly because my training made me nervous about windows in general. It was too easy to have a sniper get their sights on you. If that happens, you never get a chance to see it coming.

I placed my body so it partially shielded her from the best vantage point without blocking her view completely. "Er, good point. Where could you sing without it being too weird?"

I was temporarily blinded by the setting sun when she angled her body to face me. I blinked several times until the retinal after image faded, appreciating the view even while staying alert. It was like something out of a movie, even if it was partially obstructed by surrounding buildings.

"What if we met in a church? If the kidnapper knows anything about me, they'll know I'm a singer. I can say I'm singing to calm my nerves."

"That could work. What kind of song would make a person believe they'd found their heart's desire?"

She clapped her hands together, and a mischievous smile spread over her face. "I have just the thing."

She began to sing a haunting tune in a language I didn't understand. The melody wrapped around me, and in only a few seconds, it felt as if I was floating on a bubble of pure joy. I looked down at the book, certain the music was influencing me, but was disappointed when it appeared exactly the same. I looked up and was about to tell Robin it wasn't working but stopped at the image of her, a fiery angel as the sunset turned her hair to copper. Mesmerized by her beauty, I drank in the sight of her, unable to move or speak until she'd finished singing.

Seeing my expression, her shoulders slumped. "It didn't work, did it?"

I shoved my hands into my pockets, stalling. I'd said I needed her song to make someone see their heart's desire. "Maybe I'm not the best judge of this. We forgot to factor in one thing."

She looked crestfallen. If there had been a can handy to kick, I was pretty sure it would be halfway down the street already. "What?"

"My heart's desire has nothing to do with finding a codebook. When I looked at the book, it was still the bible. But I *did* feel different while you were singing."

She cocked her head to the side. "How different?"

Biting my lip, I hedged. "Um, well."

I was on the edge of one of those moments in life. Whatever I said next had the potential to change everything.

Death and danger were easy; the truth was terrifying in its simplicity. I had a choice to make, and even though it scared the shit out of me, I took a deep breath and told her how I felt.

"I saw you. Only you. The book was the same, but I could hardly focus on it. I was completely spellbound by how you looked singing. Maybe we should try it on someone else?"

The implication was there, even if I hadn't come right out and asked her to marry me. I wasn't ready to know she was my heart's desire, but it didn't appear I had much choice in the matter. Her song had revealed the depth of my feelings, and my own gift had confirmed it was the truth. But just because I knew didn't mean I had to scare her away, or make her feel she owed me anything in return.

When her disappointment at failing to make me see the codebook was replaced by a slight widening of her eyes and a faint blush, I was relieved.

Her eyes sparkled as she nodded. "Let's try again downstairs, in the store in the lobby. We can see what happens on someone there."

"Yeah, sure," I replied, wincing as my voice cracked.

Picking up the bible and holding it in front of me to hide my discomfort, I followed her out of the room.

Chapter 30 Mark

To our mutual relief, the next time Robin attempted the song the outcome was a roaring success. The young cashier behind the counter didn't see a codebook, but he had been overjoyed to see a first edition Marvel comic on the counter.

At least, until Robin stopped singing.

His excitement was immediately replaced by confusion. The moment her song finished, he picked up the bible, turning it over repeatedly in disbelief.

"Excuse-moi. I could have sworn...mais, no. I must be working too much." He shook his head, handing the bible back with the same look I'd once seen on my little brother's face when I'd accidentally popped his balloon.

I felt so guilty for disappointing him I bought a few extra snacks and quickly headed back to the room. We still had no idea how to find the kidnapper or kidnappers. When we'd checked our phones to see if anyone had attempt to contact us during our trip to the past, the batteries were dead. Apparently, even thought we'd returned close in our reality to when we'd left, the phones had continued to use energy in the past without the benefit of charging, thus making them into useless hunks of plastic.

By the time we'd finished running our experiment with the cashier, they'd powered up enough to turn back on. I sat on the couch with the snacks while Robin looked at her phone. I popped the tab on my soda at the same moment she gasped, and I turned.

Her hand was white-knuckled, and she was standing stock-still, clutching her phone to her chest. The look on her face told me everything.

"They called?"

"I think so. He.... they didn't leave a name; just said they had my dad."

Her voice was choked with emotion, and she blinked furiously to hold back tears. The pain in her eyes killed me so I stood, walked over to her, and gently pulled her into my arms.

I stroked her hair, wishing I had the power to remove her pain instead of just being a finder. "We'll get him back. It's going to work out, I promise."

"How do you know?" Her eyes brimmed, and she tilted her head back, searching my face.

I tried to sound confident. "I just do. Besides, the book is meant for you. If someone else tries to use the thing, the apple cart will get all unbalanced. If we can believe your mom knows what she's talking about, the universe wants balance. Ergo, we shall succeed."

She pulled back, her eyebrows drawing together as she tried to make sense of what I'd said. On the upside, confusion made her look less upset, so that was basically a win in my book.

She gave up, shaking her head. "I have no idea what you just said."

I chuckled. "That's okay, I'm not sure what I said either. I'm trying to say we've got this. We have each other, and we have a plan. Tell me about the message—actually, can you play it?"

She nodded, putting her phone on speaker before replaying the voicemail. The message was short; whoever it was simply stated they had her dad, and if she didn't bring the codebook at ten p.m. on April twentieth, they would make sure she never saw her father again. Then, they gave the address and hung up.

The message sounded professional, almost computerized, but even though the background noise made the gender difficult to determine, it wasn't completely without clues. The person was calling from a busy area, where car horns, pedestrian crosswalks, and the sound of what I thought was a jackhammer could be picked out in the background. I plugged in the address the caller had given and smiled.

"How convenient. Notre Dame Cathedral. An interesting and ideal choice for us. Our plan will work perfectly with the location they've picked."

Robin shook her head. "I'm not sure. With all the construction going on there right now, it's a hub of activity. How are we supposed to get in and out without being noticed? The last I read, most of the entrances were blocked off."

I inclined my head. "True, but there's less foot traffic without the tourists who would normally be there."

"What about security?" she frowned.

I winked. "Leave that to me. I need to check in with work anyway. Hopefully, I'm not in too much trouble for not checking in yesterday. I'll go to my room to call, just in case there's something confidential. If that's okay with you?"

"No problem." She held up one hand. "I don't want to have my memory erased for hearing something I'm not supposed to hear. But we need to move—today is the twentieth."

I dropped a light kiss on her lips, surprising us both. Allowing myself one extra, lingering moment of contact, I pulled back with a reluctance that floored me. I knew we didn't have time to get distracted, but I still couldn't believe how much I wished it was otherwise. "I'll be quick."

It turned out I wasn't as quick as I'd hoped. I'd missed quite a few phone calls myself, all from my boss, and each successive message had become more threatening in tone. As I played each in turn, I smiled ruefully at my phone. "Aww, I didn't know you cared."

By the time I'd finished listening to all nine messages, my amusement had faded. I had some serious 'splaining to do.

How much was I going to tell him? I couldn't give him all the details, particularly the bit about time travel and Scáthach. That was a sure way to lose sidearm privileges. So, before calling him back, I quickly rehearsed what I hoped was a believable story and took a deep breath.

The gruff voice of Agent Malcom Atkinson stabbed me through the connection. "Where the hell have you been, agent?"

I winced, holding the phone a little further away. "Sorry, boss. My phone died, and I wasn't in a location where I could charge it."

"Bullshit! I expect better than a rookie mistake like that from you of all people."

"I know, I'm sorry, sir. It won't happen again, sir."

I waited, knowing better than to give him an excuse, even though no cell service and electricity was a valid reason. If I went there, then the time travel bit would happen, and I'd be going down the very dangerous path of sounding crazy.

After a brief pause, he replied in a more measured tone. "I expect a full report. What's your current situation?"

One thing I'd always liked most about him was that he didn't waste time. He was clearly unhappy, but he was more interested in moving forward than berating me for what was past. At least, until after the case was wrapped up. I'd seen him make grown men collapse into puddles on the floor, so I didn't kid myself it wasn't still coming.

"Songbird was contacted by the kidnapper. Apparently the person who has her father may be one of her distant relatives, not the contact we thought was the culprit."

Another long pause. "Are you certain about this?"

I frowned at the phone. Something about his tone was off. "Sorry sir, I don't understand."

"Are you certain the kidnapper isn't tied to the man who hired the professor?"

I picked my words carefully. The way I'd gotten my lead was unorthodox, to say the least. "We have reason to believe the kidnapper is a distant cousin of Songbird, who would do anything to secure the book her dad was sent to retrieve.

They haven't succeeded in getting it though, which is why they are willing to make a trade."

"And how do you know that?"

"Because we found the book. As you instructed, I made contact with her in Paris, and she has taken me into her trust. We found the book while following the path her dad left and the kidnapper contacted her a few minutes ago. The exchange is tonight, at ten. At Notre Dame Cathedral."

This time, the pause was electric.

"A drop off tonight? Hmmm, interesting. How did the book come into your possession? And why is the first time I'm hearing of this?"

I hesitated. He hadn't pushed for why I hadn't checked in, even though I expected to explain later, but I had to give him something now if I wanted to let this situation play out.

"We found the book in the hotel room. Her father must have hidden it before he was abducted."

I thought of our meeting the bookkeeper and the video of the book disappearing. Magic as an explanation would never fly, but technically, we had found the book in the hotel. Suddenly, I remembered the rental car.

"Crap. Actually, I do need assistance. Are there any available agents nearby?"

"Spit it out. What did you do?"

I looked at the phone, wondering how much he knew. From his increasingly impatient tone, it was time to wrap this up. "We had to take a short trip to Scotland, and we came back via an alternative arrangement to shake a tail we'd picked up. I had to leave a rental vehicle on the Isle of Skye."

It wasn't the whole truth, but accurate enough. There was another long silence before he replied.

"Don't worry about the car. I'll send a guy. Tell me your plan. What do you need for tonight?"

I ran through it quickly, realizing how weak it sounded as I said it aloud. If I hadn't known about Robin's magic, there was no way it could work. But, to my surprise, he didn't interrupt until after I finished.

"I'll take care of the guards. You're heading to the cathedral now?"

At his easy acceptance of my shaky plan, I sat a little straighter. "Yes, sir. I figure approximately an hour to make the exchange. If you can place a few agents at the doors for backup, I think it's best if I go in alone with Songbird."

"Are you ready for that?"

I could have sworn I heard him smile. The idea was nearly more terrifying than having him scream at me. I took another deep breath. "Yes, sir."

"Good man. Call me as soon as you're finished. We'll make arrangements to fly the three of you back to Montréal."

Not wanting to push my luck, I agreed and hung up. I didn't need details of what he was arranging, just the all-clear to proceed. Besides, the details weren't important; getting the professor back without losing the book or getting anyone killed was.

Chapter 31 Robin

Mark returned to the living room with a funny look on his face.

"Everything okay?"

He shook his head, giving me a rueful smile. "Not really. I'll be getting my ass handed to me when I get home, but otherwise, things are fine."

I knew he was holding back, but I didn't get the sense he was hiding anything important. Ever since finding out he was an agent I'd expected there would be times when he couldn't tell me everything.

He looked at his watch, then looked at me and searched my face, his eyebrows furrowing with concern. "We should get moving. Are you ready?"

I put a hand on his arm, forcing a smile. "I'm fine. I'm excited and nervous, but okay. I'm trying to pretend everything will go smoothly. Is that crazy?"

He placed his hand on top of mine. "Nope, not crazy. One of the first rules of success in life is to be confident." He inclined his head. "Of course, preparation is helpful too. Confidence alone usually won't win you the prize."

Despite the situation, or perhaps because of it, a laugh bubbled out of me. "I'll work on being confident after this is over." Grabbing my phone and purse, I held up the room key and waited for Mark to follow.

WE ARRIVED AT THE CATHEDRAL with minutes to spare. I was sure I'd seem tense to anyone watching, but Mark was completely calm. He didn't even blink when he saw the security guards at the main entrance. The cabbie dropped us off on a side street, and from that angle, construction scaffolding took up most of the wall of the old church. The building had stood for nearly a thousand years, so I imagined many areas needed improvement.

A shot of panic shot through me. The bible! Searching my purse, I held my breath until my hand touched the cover of the book. With a shaky exhale, I closed my eyes and counted to five, hoping I could relax long enough to pull this off. Mark squeezed my shoulder, and I looked up.

He raised an eyebrow then leaned over to kiss my cheek. "Ready?"

I kept my hand on the bible and nodded, hoping I looked braver than I felt. He offered me his arm without a word as I exited the taxi, and after he paid, we linked arms. We strolled toward the church as if we were a normal couple out for an evening stroll along the Seine.

Once out of sight of the guards, Mark tugged me toward a small side door surrounded by shrubs and trees. He'd researched the floor plans of the old church before leaving, and the way he moved now told me he knew exactly what he was doing. His finding ability may not be needed right at this instant, but his human training had been invaluable so far. He was so self-assured and silent and hadn't batted an eye at the guards. I made a mental note to ask him later. Was he that good, or did he have backup?

I was pretty sure his boss would provide something, and the idea of back up made me a little more confident. Yet, if this situation had been orchestrated by a long-lost cousin of mine, whatever powers they had were more than a match for anything his agency could come up with. My mom hadn't been able to see who the kidnapper was, but knew that her sister's child had been obsessed with the manuscript and thought one of their descendants was after it. If I was able to time travel, perhaps one of them could as well, or they had another relative trying to fulfill the family obsession for them.

I remained one step behind Mark, waiting while he checked each corner, then waved me forward. We'd been told to meet by the confessional, which should be quiet this time of day. The whole church should be empty, but I'd never attended a Catholic church outside of singing at one, so I didn't know much about the normal workings.

Most of what I did know was from what I'd seen in TV and movies, and it had always seemed kind of peaceful, not to mention the idea of divulging all your worst secrets in confessional and being forgiven seemed like a kind of magic itself.

Mark found a bench across from the confessional and I place my bag out of sight from it before assuming my position. Once I was in place, Mark gave me a kiss and slid into the shadows without a word. I watched him go, more terrified than I wanted to admit. I knew his plan was to watch me from a safe, unseen place, but seeing him disappear into the darkness of the church wrenched my heart. What if I never saw him again?

But, the message had told me to come alone. Hopefully, if I couldn't see him, neither could my mysterious relative.

The moments stretched on while I waited, the only sounds I could hear was the blood rushing too fast in my ears and the far-off noise of traffic in the Parisian night until a faint scrabbling sound startled me. It came again, like a mouse scurrying somewhere along the wall. I spun around but saw nothing. The noise came again, louder, and to my left this time.

I jerked around and caught a glitter of eyes in a dark corner. The figure of a person appeared from the shadows, and all I could tell was that they were a few inches taller and wider than I was. They were dressed all in black with a hood hiding their face, and it was impossible to tell if it was a man or woman. But it wasn't until I saw they were alone that my heart lurched with dismay.

Where was my dad?

Chapter 32 Robin

The dark shadow moved and revealed a second person being dragged behind them.

My hand flew to my mouth. "Dad!"

While relieved to see him, I was shocked at his condition.

His face was dirty and his hair matted, almost spiked into place by the dried blood coating one side of his face, almost obscuring one ear. But, even as banged up as he appeared in his half-crouched, half-slumped position at the foot of his abductor, I could see his eyes glowing with a ferocity I'd never witnessed, and that gave me hope.

My usually mild mannered, absent-minded professor dad was furious. I tried to think of the last time I'd seen that look on his face, and I couldn't. He was more pissed than I'd ever seen him.

I narrowed my eyes as I turned to the stranger. "I'm here and brought the book as requested. Send him over. You'll have to forgive me if I don't trust you to follow through if I give you the book first."

I did my best to keep my voice steady, pulling out all the tricks I'd learned in acting class. I needed to be the best actress I could be to pull this off, pretending it was just another performance helped. Well, until a rumbling laugh turned my blood to ice, it did.

The figure stepped forward, and their hood fell back far enough for me to make out their features. I froze when a woman stepped toward me.

She raised an eyebrow in mocking as she gave me an unimpressed once-over. "So, you're the competition?"

I'd never seen her before, but that didn't stop a wave of recognition from flooding over me as I looked into a pair of indigo eyes so much like my own, set deep within a pale, ageless face. I hadn't expected a woman to be behind my dad's disappearance. Was she my aunt? I thought my mom had said she was dead, and that Edmund, her nephew, was the one after the book.

I sniffed, forcing bravado I didn't feel to cover my disequilibrium. "Competition? Hardly. I can't see what I could possibly have in common with a nut-job who kidnaps bookish English professors. The only thing I want is to leave here with my dad without any more trouble from you."

She laughed again, but the sound was brittle and sharp, cutting my eardrums unpleasantly. "Oh, to be young and stupid. This will be easier than I expected." She looked down at her nails, brushing one off before assuming a bored look. "Pass me the book. I'll send him over after I have it in my hand."

I planted my feet shoulder-width apart and crossed my arms. "No. You return my dad first then I'll give you the book. You know what they say. The proof is in the pudding."

Her brows drew together at the expression. Either she wasn't from my time, or I was channeling one of my dad's weird old sayings again. No one ever got them, which was irritating. In this case, it was useful because while she was confused, I began to sing quietly, gradually allowing the song to gather volume.

She took a step closer, shaking her head and ignoring my dad, who was still slumped over. His eyes glittered with such rage I wondered how much of his posture was for show. Most of it, I hoped.

"Don't think you can trick me. Maybe you aren't as dumb as you look, but I've been doing this far longer than you have. There's nothing you can try I haven't already seen."

I snorted, grateful she didn't seem to have mind-reading powers. "I hum or sing when I'm nervous. It's a bad habit I can't shake. Maybe my dad told you? I'm a singer by trade."

I winced inwardly, wondering why I'd said that. By trade? How old was I? Was it the roaring twenties?

She rolled her eyes, but I thought she'd bought it. She'd also continued to move toward me during the interchange, which meant my dad was nearly six feet away from her now. It was still too far for me to get to him before she could, but as I tried to figure out how to get between him and his kidnapper, something clattered in the shadows behind her.

She whirled toward the sound, giving me the chance to signal my dad. As if rehearsed, he inched closer to me, and widened the gap between them further.

She turned to glare at me. "Did you bring someone with you?"

My next move had to be perfect.

I controlled my breathing, trying hard not to betray any nervousness, and then raised an eyebrow.

She narrowed her eyes as she swept the room, but when nothing else happened, she scowled. "I hate old buildings," she said, nearly growling.

I gave her a measured look. "And yet *you* picked the meeting place. Let's cut the crap. Are you ready for the exchange?"

We locked eyes; eyes so much like my mom's, so much like mine. It was like a mirror where everything was upside down and I wondered what her powers were, and who she was in relation to me.

She didn't volunteer any information, but I didn't let that stop me. "Who are you? You look familiar. From what I know of the book, only someone special can use it for its true purpose."

Her eyes widened then a look of irritation flashed over her face. "My name is unimportant, but you could say we're related. Your mother is a great aunt of mine, a few times and centuries removed. My grandfather told me many stories about the book, and how it was rightfully his but your mother was so arrogant and selfish that she kept it from him. It is my birthright to have the book, and most importantly, to keep it away from *you*."

She spat the last word at me, treating me to a look I reserved only for liver and onions, my least favorite food. "Well, gee-whiz. I'm sorry to hear you feel that way. You know, if you'd been a little nicer and pretended to know my mom, my dad probably would've given it to you. He's all about sharing knowledge—basically part of his job description."

I was careful not to look directly at my dad while doing the obligatory drawing-things-out banter with the bad guy. During our talk, he'd continued to inch away from her and was now close to the wall, widening the gap significantly. Now, I noticed he was cradling one arm next to his body and felt sick to my stomach.

Had she broken it?

At her bark of angry laughter, my attention shifted back to her.

"As if he'd have shared the book with me. Imagine my delight when I found out he was searching for it. I'd been watching him, you see. I knew his success rate for finding old books was second to none, which was why I had a business associate offer him a contract. I knew once he was on the trail it was only a matter of time until it was in my hands."

I gave her a sympathetic look. "It must have been distressing to find out he didn't have it in that case. All that wasted effort!"

Her lips curled into a snarl. "It doesn't matter. I knew there was another who'd be able to find it if he was out of the picture."

I cocked my head to the side. "I'm sorry, do you mean me? Why? Can't you find it on your own?"

She scoffed. "Of course I can. What do you take me for?"

I was certain I was pushing it, but couldn't help myself. "That's just it – I don't know. You might be the smartest or the dumbest person I've ever encountered. You could have powers beyond anything I've dreamed of, or you could be just another grumpy, middle-aged woman with a van full of kids and pocket full of regrets about how their life turned out."

She took an involuntary step forward, lifting her hands into claws. I backed away. She looked like she was on the verge of trying to choke me, but she stopped, pulling back to breathe deeply.

Once she'd resumed control of her temper, she sneered. "To be so young and foolish. Who I am means nothing, and as true names contain power, I don't believe I'll share mine with you. But enough. I tire of this conversation. Give me the book. Now."

As if turning off a switch, her face went blank. She was done talking, so I had to time this perfectly. It was time to make my move if I wanted to get my dad away safely.

I made a point of looking around the small room before turning my gaze to her, trying to look as innocent as I could. "I hid the book a few pews away. I'm going to get it, okay? Don't get jumpy."

She answered with a sneer. "Fine. As long as you keep your hands where I can see them."

I nodded, holding them at waist height as I walked back to my bag. When I turned, I began to hum the song again. Hopefully, she wouldn't notice what I was doing until it was too late. I reached my bag without interference, slowly placing the strap over my neck and across my body.

Keeping my head down under the pretense of watching where I was stepping, I let my hair fall over my face to shield my mouth. I continued to obscure what I was doing until I was almost back to her, at which point I began to sing louder, and when I looked up, her eyes had the same glazed look I'd seen with both Mark and the cashier when I'd sang to them.

Hope leapt up at the small sign of success, and I kept singing as I pulled the bible out of my bag. Her eyes flashed with greed when she spotted it.

It was working!

"Hand it to me," she demanded, thrusting out her hands.

Now came the tricky part. I didn't know how long the magic would last after I stopped singing and I remembered how quickly the cashier's excitement had faded. I had to keep singing until my dad and I were safe. I glanced over to see him staring at the book with longing, and heard him whisper one word.

"Scáthach."

Shit. I hadn't thought about what he would see. That added a layer of difficulty I wasn't expecting, but at least he was looking at me.

I jerked my head toward the wall, and he blinked, moving toward me with stars in his eyes. Once I was certain I could get to him before she could, I held the book out toward her, doing my best to channel my inner Jedi.

"Here. It's all yours. We have nothing else you want, and you will let us leave. You do not want to follow us. We are not the people you want."

She held the book to her chest. "Yes, fine. Go away."

Squeezing the book tighter, she laughed. It was a creepy, maniacal sound, and I shuddered as I speed-walked to the back wall, holding my hand out for my dad to take. I still hadn't caught sight of Mark, but I hoped he was in position. With my dad star-struck at the song, I wasn't going to be able to get him out without help. On the plus side though, I knew the magic was holding as long as he was enthralled.

I met with no resistance as I gently tugged on my dad's good arm as I led us to the exit as we had planned. I prayed I wasn't hurting him as I pulled him forward, but didn't stop to check. We'd nearly reached the door of the chamber when he stumbled.

I looked back, catching a mixture of joy and confusion on his face as he blinked at me. "Robin? Is that you?"

At almost the same moment, a furious screech echoed throughout the chamber. We were out of time.

Looking into my dad's eyes, I shouted one terrified word. "Run!"

Chapter 33 Mark

Betrayal was a sour taste in my mouth as I watched our plan unfold from the shadows. When the kidnapper had dropped the professor on the floor and her hood fell back to reveal her identity, the cannonball that landed in my stomach made it a challenge not to abruptly lose my lunch.

How could I have missed it?

Now that the connection was staring me in the face, it was impossible to deny. The kidnapper had the same brilliant blue eyes as Robin and Scáthach. Eyes that I had idly thought were wasted on such an invisible woman. I recovered from my shock long enough to put in my earplugs before Robin began singing.

As much as I loved her voice, I couldn't take chances. The normal amount of desire I had when I was around her was distracting enough; I didn't think I'd be able to my job if I had my heart's desire supercharged by her magic. I waited until the dreamy look I remembered seeing on the store clerk's face settled onto Agent Elise Derny's, then I crept through the shadows to the door, reaching it just before Robin. I removed my earplugs when I saw she'd stopped singing, and was just in time to catch the angry howl of Derny as the spell wore off.

Beckoning to Robin, I dropped any attempt at stealth. "Quick, this way. There's another side entrance. Sir? Are you able to run?"

Brian Locksley was rumpled and bloody, but his jaw was firm as he looked at me. He nodded, and with effort was able to straighten slightly. He didn't look great, but I could see where Robin came by her perseverance. Glancing at her, I pushed her in front of me. "We need to move. Any idea if she has power?"

She shook her head. "No, but I'm not staying to find out."

I gritted my teeth, not happy about the unknown threat from such a well-trained operative, but there was nothing we could do about it now.

Robin moved quickly, but her dad was another matter. He was still upright, but limping heavily, and was relying on Robin to accomplish an awkward half-stumble, half-run in the direction I was herding them. I looked over my shoulder, and saw Agent Derny was close.

Too close.

I turned to face her. Maybe I could distract her long enough for Robin to get her dad outside. Letting my hands fall loosely to my side, palms up, I tried to appear relaxed as I blocked her view of them.

"So, Elise. I'm guessing you weren't sent here to help me catch the bad guy, hmm? Too bad. I could use a hand."

She gave me a withering look. Out of the corner of my eye, I saw Robin falter when I used the woman's name, but she recovered quickly. She was almost to the door when Derny curled her lips into a sneer that did all kinds of bad things to her face. The fury I saw there was unhinged, and it was hard to believe she was the same agent I'd worked with only a week earlier and thought resembled a tired soccer mom.

"Are you that stupid?"

I shrugged, keeping my voice deliberately light as I replied. "Nah, I know what you're up to, but I can't figure out why. Why go through all the work of training and working for years to protect others if the end goal was to steal this book and unlock the secrets of the universe? I mean, I'm assuming that's why you want the codebook. Cause otherwise, this is a super bad career move."

She laughed, and in that moment, I heard a depth of bitterness only a woman resentful of her entire life could hold. "My true mission has always been to find this book. It was my father's mission, and my grandfather's mission. You believe you're on the side of righteousness, but you are wrong. You, and your stupid songbird. Her mother was greedy and unwilling to share her words with those who were more deserving. It is *her* fault my father lost his life."

I wasn't pretending to stall now. I was truly fascinated by the new information. Maybe she could provide the answers we'd been looking for. "What do you mean?"

The anger darkening her face made her look barely human. "When he discovered Scáthach had traveled to his time, he thought his grandmother's legacy was about to be fulfilled. But she tricked him and escaped Montreal with the book. He died trying to stop her."

I frowned, recalling what Scáthach had told us about the car accident. "I think you've got that a little backwards."

"What would you know? You're a silly junior agent who made the fatal mistake of falling in love with the girl." When I raised my eyebrows, she chuckled, a cold sound that echoed in the empty cathedral. "Oh, yes. Didn't you realize? It's quite well documented that any agent who makes the mistake of falling in love on the job winds up dead."

I shook my head, stepping toward her but keeping my body loose, ready to react. "Oh, come on. This isn't a movie. That never happens. We both know that's a Hollywood plot device. Not to mention it's a lot harder to escape an internal investigation than movies make it look. You'd better have a solid getaway plan if you're planning to kill us, because otherwise, what you're about to do is plain stupid." I tilted my head from side to side, making a great show out of examining her top to bottom for a weapon, before I continued. "So, which is it? Are you stupid, or do you have magic? I mean, surely Scáthach's sister must've given her children gifts other than that quirky streak of insanity."

She snorted. "Wouldn't you like to know? But in your case, I was thinking a good old-fashioned bullet would do the trick."

I exhaled, shaking my head sadly. "Ah, geez, Elise. I'd like to accommodate you, but I've got to tell you, I'm not okay with that plan. You see, I kind of enjoy being alive. If it's all the same to you, I'm going to say goodbye before we get to that part of your diabolical scheme." I winked. "But don't worry; I won't leave you alone."

Her expression turned to one of confusion, giving me the edge I needed. I sprinted toward the exit, hoping my youth was in my favor as her footsteps picked up speed behind me.

Luckily, I'd planned for the possibility she'd try to keep us from leaving. Without slowing, I reached up, pulling a rope I'd tied around one of the large pillars earlier. Construction material fell behind me, and I raced to the next pillar to pull the second cord. A string of expletives split the silence as Derny was hit by a tarp. I bit back a laugh, but any smugness I may have felt died when a flash of gold lit the night.

I looked back, and my mouth dropped open. Somehow, she'd started a fire.

"Shit!" I ducked as heat whizzed by my ear.

Turned out, she did have special abilities, which apparently involved fireballs. Given the flammable construction materials we were running through, this was an awful discovery to make now. I ducked behind another pillar, moving in a zigzag pattern as I hid behind whatever I could find, but she was relentless.

There was only one pillar between me and the door. I couldn't see Robin or her dad any longer and I hoped they'd already made it out. Reaching up, I took a deep breath and yanked on the last cord as hard as I could just as another fireball came roaring at my face, followed closely behind by an enraged Agent Derny.

The fireball hit the canvas behind me, and the drop cloth that had been protecting furniture from the renovations burst into flames. I ducked instinctively, and it fell on top of her. I tried to grab it, but before I'd taken two steps, it flew up and into the eaves. Derny stood, her face purple with rage in the dim light as she made another fireball. I tore my eyes away from her hands and backed away, then dashed the last twenty feet to the door without looking back.

I burst into the fresh night air and would have collapsed on the grass, but two beefy guards yelling at Robin slowed my roll. One of them looked up and saw me, so I veered for them, fumbling for my ID as I held up my hands in front of me.

"You're not what I expected." The man raised an eyebrow. "Is anyone else coming?"

"Just the kidnapper, who was right behind me. Careful—turns out it was an agent, Elise Derny, who was behind everything." I gasped for air between words. "Oh, and she set the roof on fire."

"Sacrement!" He turned to the other. "Call the fire department."

The guard who'd been in Robin's face grumbled but pulled out his phone without delay. He spoke to someone in rapid French then followed the other guard back into the building, weapons drawn and ready.

I lingered at the door, placing myself between danger and the woman I was sworn to protect, but stumbled against her sudden weight when she threw herself into my arms.

"Mark! You're okay? She didn't hurt you? One minute you were with me, and the next..." She closed her eyes tightly, burying her face against my shirt instead of finishing her sentence.

I smiled, smoothing back her hair as I considered how lucky we were. "I wanted to give you time to get your dad out. It worked out well, considering." I winced, looking at the smoke curling out of the open doorway. "Sadly, I have a feeling Notre Dame isn't going to be the same after tonight."

She frowned. "I don't understand."

"Turns out ol' Elise had power after all."

"Elise? How do you know her?"

"She was one of the other agents assigned to watch you and your dad in Montréal. She always struck me as a bitter soccer mom. Guess she's got a few other reasons for bitterness."

Her face fell. "You mean there's been other agents watching me?"

I shrugged, looking at my feet. "Well, yeah. There're usually at least two agents, if not more, watching at any time. We do shifts. Normally, I would have been assigned somewhere else, but they were short staffed. They wanted someone to keep an eye on you as a secondary until your dad went missing."

She didn't look happy, but she didn't look mad either. It wasn't much, but I'd take it. I had no idea how I was going explain this turn of events to my superiors, and I didn't want to lose her after everything we'd been through because of work.

Robin nodded, looking at the smoke. "Now what?"

I frowned. The guards should have been back by now if Derny was behind me like I'd thought. The sound of sirens approaching grew louder.

"I think it's time to get the heck out of Dodge. I'm hoping the guards are okay, but either way, we need to leave before the local gendarme get here. I'll debrief with my people later. A good rule to follow for life in general— you can't get in trouble if they don't know you were there."

Without protesting, she turned to help her dad up and we slunk off into the night, one more shadow in the trees as a nightmarish orange glow filled the sky behind us.

Chapter 34 Robin

I held back my emotions as long as I could, and lasted until we were across the Seine, far from the sirens and flashing emergency lights, and paused to take stock. My dad was limping, and had been leaning on me for support since we'd left the church. I was exhausted, past any limit I'd even known I had, but he looked terrible.

I had no idea how he'd kept going as long as he had. The blood I'd seen earlier on his head was dry, and in the street-light, I could see it originated from a cut near his temple that was surrounded by heavy bruising. I hoped it looked worse than it was, but I wasn't a doctor. Could he have permanent damage from that kind of head injury?

I looked at Mark. "We need to get him to a hospital."

He narrowed his eyes then winced as he surveyed my dad's appearance. "He needs medical attention, but we need to get to the hotel first. I have to see what my supervisor wants us to do—we may need to avoid hospitals for now." Inclining his head toward the flames now shooting high up into the sky, his expression became grim. "Given a national monument is on fire, we don't want anything to tie us to what happened here tonight. Avoiding attention is wise, even if it wasn't our fault. If we showed up in any hospital looking like this, we'll end up behind bars."

I turned to watch the scene behind us and had to agree with his assessment. Even from here, it was obvious the church was going to have significant damage. Dealing with my dad's physical injuries would have to wait until after we'd gotten to safety.

"In that case, can you get a cab? He can't make it much further, and I can't carry him."

Mark nodded. Pulling out his phone, he made a quick series of texts then put it away. "Okay, ride should be here in the next two minutes."

Impressed, I looked at where his phone had disappeared, then back at him. "How did you manage that? Supervisor?"

He smirked. "No – rideshare app." When I blinked without commenting, he elaborated. "If we'd gone with a cab company, we'd be easier to track than Joe Blow off the street. Harder to find us if we pay cash to a local and delete the account after."

While I didn't much care how we got back to the hotel, when a small Mini Cooper arrived, I helped my dad in, grateful to be sitting.

The downside was the vehicle was approximately the same size as a clown car. I was cramped in the back with my dad, but Mark must have felt worse in the front, with his knees folded nearly up to his chest. After the terror we'd been through, or maybe because it was such a ludicrous contrast and I was nearing my breaking point, I had to hold back giggles most of the way back to the hotel.

It was after midnight when we finally arrived to a blessedly quiet lobby. The front desk clerk barely blinked at our disheveled state and only gave us a cursory nod as we headed to the central elevators. Mark had taken over the task of supporting my dad, and I was grateful because my arms were aching so bad I suspected I wouldn't be able to move them tomorrow.

The more I thought about what had almost happened, the closer to tears I came. It took me several attempts to use the key card with shaky hands before I succeeded in unlocking the door, then I stepped back, allowing Mark to carry my dad past me to the couch.

He arranged him gently, placing a pillow beneath his head and legs, and once he'd settled my dad to his satisfaction, he tilted his head and looked at me. "I have basic first-aid and can take a look, but I'm no doctor. Are you okay if I check him out?"

A humorless, borderline hysterical laugh escaped before I ruthlessly bit my lip. The sharpness of my teeth brought me back from the edge, and I nodded. "Be my guest." I said, crouching at the foot of the couch.

"Hey, Dad. Can you tell us what did she do to you?"

He moaned, reaching out his good hand to brush hair off my face. We were both filthy, but something about the gesture made me feel better, even so.

"I'm okay, sweetie. It's mostly my arm. I think I twisted my knee, back at the church." He moaned again, touching the side of his head, as if noticing it for the first time. "God, my head hurts."

"How did you get the cut?" Mark prompted.

My dad frowned, seeming to notice him for the first time. When he didn't reply right away, I was certain he was trying to decide if he could trust him or not.

"It's fine, Dad. Mark works for CSIS. He helped me find you. If it wasn't for him, neither of us would be alive now." When he only smiled faintly, I wondered if something else was stopping him from answering Mark's question. "What's wrong? Is it about the book? Don't worry; I doubt anything will sound crazy after tonight."

He sighed, opening his eyes. "It was the book. I saw it. The one I've been looking for. Your mother's book." He looked away.

I realized he thought I didn't know and gently took his good hand in mine. "Dad, you can stop protecting me. I know about Scáthach. She's the reason we found you."

His voice was choked as a look I'd never seen before passed over his face. "You saw her? How... How is she? I miss her..."

"She's fine. She showed us a few things and told us... other things. Dad, I understand why you made the decisions you did, and I'm not mad at you. With great power comes great responsibility, right?"

It was my turn to look away now. I got up, uncomfortable in the situation. How could we even discuss what had happened, especially now, while he was injured? There was too much ground to cover, and I wasn't strong enough to handle the answers yet, not after tonight. I walked over to the window and took a few deep breaths, turning at a familiar, light touch on my shoulder to find Mark looking down at me, a worried expression on his face.

"Are you okay? Tonight was a lot to handle. Heck, it's a lot for me to handle, and I was trained for hostage situations.

The magic bit... well, I don't think the bureau has classes on that."

I forced a smile. "Am I okay? Absolutely not. Will I be okay?" I looked at my dad, smiling at him. "Yeah, I think so. As lovely as Paris is, I won't be happy until we're back in Montreal. We've got a lot to discuss."

An answering smile spread over Mark's face. "I can agree with that plan. How about this; I'll call my supervisor, see if he can send a doctor over, then I'll work on tickets. How do you feel about business class?"

Chapter 35 Mark

I knew that the Lockleys were running on empty. So, after a cursory exam told me the professor wouldn't die imminently, I called my boss to explain the situation. As I'd hoped, they were able to send both a doctor and tech to the hotel to get portable X-rays. When they discovered nothing was broken, they patched him up suitably to fly back to Canada, and with a doctor's note in my pocket to allow early boarding and accommodations, they helped me move him to the bedroom I'd been using.

Robin had protested at first, but I stopped her. "I'd rather sleep on the couch. It's closer to the door, and I'm still on the job. As much as I hate to say it, she's still out there somewhere. I'll need to stay alert, and I doubt I'll get much sleep until we get back to Montreal."

The least welcome bit of news I'd received from my boss was that the guards at Notre Dame hadn't caught Agent Derny. No body was retrieved, and they'd found no one in the building for questioning. It was as if she'd never existed.

Normally, I'd have chalked her disappearance up to training and years of experience, but I knew that wasn't how she'd slunk away without detection. I had the same tingle I got when I was on the right track finding things, and it was telling me we'd have to face her again. I may have exaggerated the extent of my concern to keep Robin from making me take her room, but it wasn't impossible Derny would make another attempt tonight, while we were vulnerable.

Robin had fallen silent when I'd told her, and I felt a mixture of remorse and grim satisfaction. I didn't like seeing her suffer, but if she expected danger, I hoped she was less likely to be caught off-guard.

Next, I'd focused on Mr. Locksley. I offered to help him clean up further, but he deferred, shaking his head carefully before wincing.

"Thanks, Mark, but I'm too tired. I'll shower in the morning before we leave. Hopefully, I'll feel more up to it by then." He let out a deep sigh, arranging himself to protect his arm then closed his eyes.

I turned off the light and tiptoed out, entering the living room to find Robin standing by the window. Her arms were wrapped around herself like she was trying to hold it together, and the dark circles under her eyes looked like bruises. She was still covered in filth from the church, but I'd never seen anyone so beautiful.

"Hey." I moved slowly, not wanting to spook her. "Do you feel like company, or would you rather be alone?"

She turned at the sound of my voice. The faint ghost of a smile curled her lips. "I'm okay. Just thinking." Her voice was hardly a whisper at first, but as anger took over, it grew louder. "I don't understand why any of this happened. Clearly, that woman had no right to the codebook. Look what she was willing to do to get it!"

I stepped closer, holding an arm out. When she moved into my embrace, I wrapped my arms around her and stood breathing in her presence for a moment. She felt frail, like a beautiful ceramic doll, but the strength she'd shown in the face of danger told me she wasn't.

"You can't understand her actions because you'd never do anything like what she did. Maybe that's the point."

She tilted her head to look at me, confusion darkening her already tired blue eyes. "What do you mean?"

My lip quirked. "Good versus evil, remember? It's all about balance. You can't understand her actions because you're the good side of the coin."

She looked surprised before turning away, shaking her head. "How can you know that? *I'm* not even sure what I'm capable of. I still think about something that happened back in high school, and I know I'm capable of using my powers in horrible ways. It's a slippery slope between using my abilities to control someone today and using them to get my own way tomorrow. How do I know what's good or bad? How do I decide when it's okay to do what I did tonight?"

Brushing a lock of hair off her face, I answered her with a kiss. I may not have the answers, but I wanted her to know she had me.

I felt her tense muscles relax as I met her uncertainty with energy and hope, and when I pulled back, some of the shadows had left her face. I was tempted to kiss her again, and go further if she'd allow, but even if her dad hadn't been sleeping in the next room, now wasn't the time.

"The fact you're questioning your motivations means you won't use your power like that. People who worry about being corrupted are the least likely to have it happen to them."

"Thanks, Mark. Knowing you were assigned to protect me doesn't diminish what you've done for me. Because of your help, I have my dad back and met someone amazing."

"Oh? Anyone I know?" I teased.

She giggled, slapping my arm. I was happy to see her mood was better, even though underneath the laughter, her exhaustion was still evident. I kept my arm around her and steered her toward her room.

"We'll talk more in the morning. Right now, we all need rest. I'll make the arrangements for travel before I lay down, and do my best to find a plane that leaves in the afternoon. Sound alright?"

She nodded, giving a grateful sigh before raising her lips and leaning in. I dropped my head and obliged her with a lingering goodnight kiss then I watched her close the door behind her. Certain anyone watching would agree I looked like a ten-year-old mooning after his crush, I reluctantly got back to business.

"SO?"

The familiar gruff voice came through the line.

I debated what to say, finally settling on the minimum. "It's done. We retrieved the professor, and the codebook is safe. I still can't believe..."

I didn't finish, but the grunt I received in response told me all I needed to know.

"I wondered."

I blinked at the phone. He'd suspected? But he'd let her remain involved? That didn't sound like him.

There was a long pause before he continued. "When you get back, we're going to have that talk. You're ready to know more about this case."

This time, I almost choked. "I'm ready to know more, now that it's over?" I couldn't mask my sarcasm. "You mean, after I almost died and set a national monument on fire?"

He sighed. "Yes. Now you're ready. There's a lot you don't know. You weren't ready to know before this case. I've been keeping my eye on you. I know who you are, who your dad is. I needed to see how you coped in the field first. If you pay attention, you'll make an invaluable agent. I want to see you and the others in the office, as soon as you land."

I frowned, unable to read his tone. Was he angry? Resigned? It was difficult to tell over the phone. "I'm sorry sir. Are they in trouble? I mean, I understand if I am, but...."

There was a bark of laughter. "No, they aren't in trouble. But like I said, there are things which need to be dealt with in person. I'll email you the tickets. Don't miss your flight."

The line went dead, but I held the phone in my hand for several minutes before putting it down. Something told me my career was about to take a sidestep, and I hadn't seen the last of Agent Derny either. There was no way she'd give up on her destiny so easily. The familiar tingle sweeping over me was almost gleeful.

This was what I'd been waiting for.

Settling onto the couch, I folded my arms on my chest and looked up at the ceiling. Tomorrow was going to be a long day.

Chapter 36 Robin

I bit my lip as Mark helped my dad through customs, over-whelmed by emotion. Mark was giving him the perfect amount of assistance, but the stark contrast between his steadiness highlighted how frail my dad had become since I'd last seen him. He'd always been a rock, but the sling on his arm made him more off balance than usual, and the limp aged him at least a decade. I was pretty sure it was his face that made others stare at him, but as always, he didn't seem to notice or care. I'd love to not be bothered when people looked at me, but from what I could determine, only guys like my dad seemed to have the skill.

Aside from concern about my dad's appearance and health, I was a mess. Now that we were home, the magnitude of what we'd been through overshadowed the obvious phys-ical bruises. I had traveled to Paris for an audition, which seemed so long ago I barely remembered it, then we'd gone to Scotland on a wild-goose chase to track down my dad, dis-covered my mom hadn't died the way I'd thought, and in the process of that discovery, I'd found out I was a mermaid.

Cool, cool, cool.

If someone had asked how I'd cope with these kinds of life-changing events, I would have told them *not well*. At least I hadn't had time to think about it yet. Why? Oh, yeah,

277

because immediately after revelations that could give an older person a heart attack, I'd traveled back to the present to rescue my dad from a crazy kidnapper who was distantly related by using my new powers with the help of a man I'd met days earlier, who I may or may not have fallen in love with.

All in all, the fact I wasn't rocking in a corner somewhere with my head in my hands was a win, in my opinion.

I must have made a noise, because Mark's eyebrows drew together.

Giving me a concerned once-over, he asked, "Everything okay?"

Forcing a smile, I nodded. "Sure. Just tired. Ready to sleep in my own bed. This has been a *long* week."

Mark bobbed his head in agreement. "It's been a week, that's for sure. I'm sorry to keep you from home a little longer, but I have orders for us to check in with my boss first. He wanted to debrief you, er, all of us."

His face flamed, and he looked down and away, ostensibly helping my dad with his satchel, but I was pretty sure his sudden awkwardness was due to the word 'debrief.' That was the last straw.

I began to laugh, wrapping my arms around my middle as I bent over. Both Mark and my dad looked at me as if I'd lost my mind, but it felt so good to laugh. We'd made it home, we were all alive, and the book was safe in my purse.

BUT AN HOUR LATER, both my amusement and relief had faded.

We were waiting in a grey room with functional, yet somehow incredibly uncomfortable furniture. Mark's mysterious boss, Malcom Atkinson, was going to speak with us, but he'd been light on details. It was irritating, yet understandable. He didn't know how much trouble he was in himself, let alone what his supervisor would have to say about the events of the past week.

We'd gone over our stories on the plane to try to find a way to make what had happened sound a little less crazy, but it had meant leaving huge chunks of time out. I wiped my sweaty palms on my jeans, and as I did, the door opened. I stilled instantly, looking up to see a nondescript, middle-aged man enter the room.

At first blush, he looked like an accountant. He wore a dark blue suit, was average height and weight, but without the softness in the middle I was used to seeing on men around the same age as my dad. His grey hair was cut military short, but his eyes drew my attention.

They were a cold, winter blue that seemed to catalogue everything as he surveyed the room. Mark shot to his feet, but the man waved his hand.

"Sit down, Agent. No need to stand on ceremony. I understand the mission was a success, all things accounted for. Agent Derny?"

Mark shook his head once. "No sign of her, sir. She disappeared after the incident at the Cathedral as you know, and we haven't seen her since."

The man pursed his lips then let out a frustrated growl. "Well, what's done is done."

With a sigh, he moved around to stand behind the desk at the end of the room, then sat and steepled his fingers in front of him in a thoughtful manner.

"Mr. Locksley, Ms. Locksley, I am Agent Atkinson, but you can call me Malcolm. I trust you are well?"

I held back the laugh that bubbled up again. Something told me he wouldn't understand my humor was because I found the entire situation absurd, and I didn't want him examining me any more closely than he already was.

I cleared my throat. "Um, yes sir. I'll be glad to get home, but I'm happy that we were able to find my dad."

He nodded then turned, arching an eyebrow at my dad. "And you, professor? Now that I've seen you in person, I think a more thorough debriefing can wait until after you've rested. I'll have Agent Nottingham bring you back tomorrow, once you've had a chance to relax a little."

My spirits rose. After all we'd been through, part of me worried Mark would want to move on with his life and forget everything. I knew he wasn't the kind of guy who made false promises, but something about having his superior also guarantee I'd see him at least once more made me feel more secure.

"I'm happy to be home as well—I had no idea looking for an old book could be so dangerous." When Mark and his boss simply stared at him in disbelief, my dad chuckled, giving me a sly wink. "Alright, I may have had an inkling, given who funded my trip. At the time, it was impossible to pass up. I'd been searching so long, you see, that when I finally found the trail and miraculously found funding at the same time... ah, well. Hindsight is twenty-twenty, as they say."

He shook his head, losing some of the impact of the solemnity he was portraying due to the garish purple and green bruising that covered nearly half his face. Mark snorted, but covered it with a cough after a sharp look from his boss.

Agent Atkinson kept an eye on Mark as he redirected the conversation. "I've asked you to come in today so we could discuss the events of this week. I am fully aware details have been left out. That may be fine in the field, but I expect a thorough recap tomorrow."

He fixed his intent ice-blue eyes on mine again, and their wolfish nature made me gulp. The idea he could see my thoughts caused me to stop breathing for a moment, but just when I couldn't handle the scrutiny a second longer, he relaxed his gaze.

He leaned back in his chair, suddenly diffident. "Ms. Locksley, I have it under good authority your... abilities... allowed you to elude Agent Derny, thwarting her attempt to retrieve the book. Is that correct?"

Had Mark said something?

I shot Mark a glance, but his confused look told me he was as surprised as I was. I answered slowly, picking my words carefully. "Yes, sir. I was able to distract her, I guess."

I remembered my mom's words of caution before we'd left. She had been vague, but insistent. I knew I had to be cautious about what I told the government, but I'd seen enough movies to know that even without her warning. I mean, look at how many problems Superman had. Not to mention Cap. It was non-stop fighting all the time for them because people feared powers they didn't understand and couldn't control.

Atkinson nodded, narrowing his eyes, then looked at Mark. "We've had our eye on this situation for some time. Now that it has been resolved, we have a few other need-to-know cases in the works."

Mark frowned. "Cases, sir?"

Agent Atkinson raised an eyebrow then smirked.

He actually smirked!

"Yes, Agent Notting. I trained with your father and a certain Detective Avery nearly thirty years ago. At times throughout their careers, they are part of a special branch of handpicked agents that make up what you would consider a type of dark ops. No paper trail and all service records have been expunged."

I had no clue what he was speaking about, but I knew it was important by the way the color drained from Mark's face. I listened more closely, and nearly fell out of my chair at his next words.

"You've proven yourself capable of more responsibility, Notting, so it's time for you to assume a new role in the agency. So far as anyone knows, you are now IT. After we clear up the rest of the loose ends tomorrow, you'll report to McGill campus for further instructions."

"Sorry, sir. McGill? I don't understand."

A broad smile spread over Atkinson's face. "You'll be joining a small division affectionately nicknamed the Paranormal Police Patrol, or triple-P, by those who are aware of its existence. Of course, no one outside of the division is aware of its existence, but I think you'll find the work inter-esting enough to make up for the lack of public acclaim."

Mark opened and closed his mouth a few times before settling on a nod.

Why hadn't Atkinson waited until my dad and I were out of the room before telling Mark about his new job? If it was supposed to be a secret, it struck me as weird he'd talk about it in front of civilians.

That was when he swung his intense ice-blue gaze to me. "Ms. Locksley, how would you feel about joining the team?"

Chapter 37 Mark

I hadn't expected the meeting with Agent Atkinson to go well, but what had happened at the brief encounter hadn't even been on my radar. Not only had he transferred me to a unit that sounded incredible—triple-P? — it was clear he intended for Robin to join the team as well.

She'd sputtered a fair bit at the bombshell, but in the end, she'd nodded meekly. Atkinson promised to explain more once we'd had a good rest, but I wondered how much she'd sleep with that job offer hanging over her.

For me, it was a dream come true. From the moment I'd had my talk with Detective Avery in high school, I knew there'd been a secret division of some type with the agency, but hadn't been privy to the details. My dad and Detective Rob Avery, who'd I discovered was my godfather that same day, had shared only the bare bones of what they did when I'd come into my powers.

At the time, they'd warned me I had to prove myself before I'd get an invite to such an organization. Now, instead of screwing up my chances with the debacle at Notre Dame Cathedral as I'd thought I'd done when Derny escaped, it seemed I'd earned my invite at last.

I lingered as long as I could after escorting Robin and Mr. Locksley home, sweeping the house to make sure it was empty and undisturbed. Once the coast was clear I had no reason to stay, but I wasn't ready to leave yet.

Mr. Locksley clapped me on the shoulder. "Thanks for helping out, Mark. You seem like a strapping young lad. I'm glad you were assigned to watch my girl." His genial smile faded, and he abruptly narrowed his eyes. "Now, I may be injured and old, but if you hurt her...." he let the threat hang in the air.

"Dad!"

Robin's shocked exclamation made him chuckle.

I laughed as well, but my smile slipped as I glanced at him and saw the twinkle in his eyes tempered with warning. "Um, it's okay, Robin. Standard dad advice. It's not personal."

He bobbed his head in agreement. "Routine dad warning. Meant to frighten, rarely maim, and not personal; unless you actually do something offensive, that is."

I mimed wiping my forehead off, before accepting the hand he extended. "That's reassuring, sir. It was nice to meet you."

He nodded, shaking my hand firmly without trying to crush it. "Nice to meet you, too. Now, if you don't mind, I'd like to head to bed. You said eight, correct?" When I inclined my head, he groaned. "Too early."

Robin and I watched him disappear into the house. I couldn't tell what she was thinking because her face was half-hidden by shadows as she looked out into the night, but I waited a few beats after her dad left to ask. "Are you okay?"

She shrugged, giving me a faint half-smile. "I've been better. It'll take some time to wrap my mind around all that's happened." Her eyes widened. "Seriously, me, an agent? I've never considered being anything other than an opera singer. I don't know if I can do it. And yet..."

She spread her hands wide, letting them fall to her sides where I rescued them, squeezing them as if to transfer my happiness. She may have been floored, but if she joined me, I'd have everything I'd ever wanted.

"Give it a chance. Something tells me we were meant to work together." I smiled. "And I'm not just saying that because I want to spend more time with you. We've got to find Agent Derny, after all. Why not do it together?"

She looked up, the brighter-than-normal sparkle of her eyes betraying her inner conflict. "But what about *my* dreams?"

I brushed a solitary tear away before it could fall. "You can still follow them. What's a better cover than an international opera singer? You can go anywhere, be anyone. Remember what your mom said about balance? This could be a way for us to restore it. And best of all—we can be together. I mean, if you want."

Now, I was the one to look away. Had I overstepped, said too much? We hadn't known each other long, but I was certain she was it for me. I'd dreamed about her before meeting her and my finding talent had already told me the truth.

She was the one, for now, for always.

The soft touch of her hand on my face helped me chance seeing rejection, but what I saw in her eyes made my heart swell.

"That, I do want," she said, a smile lighting her face. "I'll come with you. I'm not sure I'm ready to accept, but who knows? Maybe you're right. Maybe this is a destiny we found without trying. I'm willing to take a chance on anything, as long as you're at my side."

As the spring evening settled around us, I answered her the only way I could. Pulling her into my arms as the distant sound of traffic faded behind us, I knew we'd be just fine. We may not know what the future held, but we could do anything, if we were facing it together.

Don't miss out!

Visit the website below and you can sign up to receive emails whenever H. M. Gooden publishes a new book. There's no charge and no obligation.

https://books2read.com/r/B-A-POWE-KJNKB

BOOKS 2 READ

Connecting independent readers to independent writers.

Did you love *A Destiny Found*? Then you should read *The Lost Soul*[1] by H. M. Gooden!

"*I could feel our chance slipping away. If we didn't find him soon, it would be too late for Paul, and I wouldn't be able to forgive myself.*"

When Mark wakes in the middle of the night knowing his best friend has been kidnapped before anyone else does.

Despite wondering if he's going crazy, he follows his intuition and discovers more than he bargained for.

Now, it's up to him to find his friend before he runs out of time.

---

1. https://books2read.com/u/3nv9AP

2. https://books2read.com/u/3nv9AP

If he suceeds, he'll have to come to terms with his entire life being a lie, but if he doesn't, his friend won't have a future. Read more at https://www.hmgoodenauthor.com/.

Also by H. M. Gooden

Born of Destiny
The Lost Soul
The Cursed Heart
A Destiny Found

The Dragons of the North
Mai's First Date

The Raven and the Witch Hunter
The Raven and the Witch Hunter: The Spirit of Big Bear
The Raven and the Witch Hunter: The Wedding
The Raven and The Witch Hunter: Honeymoon and Full
Moon Blues
Wendigo

The Rise of the Light

Fiona's Gift
Dream of Darkness
The Stone Dragon
The Phoenix and the Witch
Dragons are Forever
The Raven and the Witch Hunter
Zahara's Quest

Standalone
The Raven and the Witch Hunter Omnibus: Volumes 2-4
To Capture the Heart of Spring
Darkness on the Nile
I was a Teenage Vegetarian Zombie Detective

Watch for more at https://www.hmgoodenauthor.com/.

About the Author

H. M. Gooden has always loved the world of books, but over the last few years a new story has begged to be told, and as a result, this series was born.

In between dealing with children and work, the majority of the actual writing happens between four and six am and involves multiple cups of coffee for inspiration.

You can always find me on Twitter, Facebook, Instagram, Bookbub and Goodreads.

I always love to hear from readers!

Read more at https://www.hmgoodenauthor.com/.

www.ingramcontent.com/pod-product-compliance
Lightning Source LLC
Chambersburg PA
CBHW070654180626
46817CB00006B/2372